PRAISE FOR PAUL TREMBLAY

"How you gonna keep 'em down on the farm after they've read Paul Tremblay's hysterical comic dystopia, *Swallowing a Donkey's Eye*? Great characters, sharp dialogue, and a story crazy enough to tell the truth."

—Jeffrey Ford,
author of *The Shadow Year*

"Paul Tremblay's *Swallowing a Donkey's Eye* is a powerful statement, both a scathingly funny black comedy and an unflinching view of a very possible American future."

—Lucius Shepard,
author of *A Handbook for American Prayer*

"*Swallowing a Donkey's Eye* is fine, ribald work. There's a futuristic wackiness and bitterness that reminds me of the best of George Saunders's longer stories. It's brutal and hilarious, and Tremblay's narrator holds it all together with an ironic grimace."

—Stewart O'Nan,
author of *Emily, Alone* and *Last Night at the Lobster*

SWALLOWING A DONKEY'S EYE

PAUL TREMBLAY

ILLUSTRATIONS BY
SUSANNE APGAR

ChiZine Publications

FIRST EDITION

Distributed in Canada by
HarperCollins Canada Ltd.
1995 Markham Road
Scarborough, ON M1B 5M8
Toll Free: 1-800-387-0117
e-mail: hcorder@harpercollins.com

Distributed in the U.S. by
Diamond Book Distributors
1966 Greenspring Drive
Timonium, MD 21093
Phone: 1-410-560-7100 x826
e-mail: books@diamondbookdistributors.com

Library and Archives Canada Cataloguing in Publication

Tremblay, Paul
Swallowing a donkey's eye / Paul Tremblay.

Issued also in electronic formats.
ISBN 978-1-926851-69-3

I. Title.

PS3620.R45S93 2012   813'.6   C2012-902965-3

CHIZINE PUBLICATIONS
Toronto, Canada
www.chizinepub.com
info@chizinepub.com

Edited by Helen Marshall
Copyedited and proofread by Samantha Beiko

Canada Council   Conseil des Arts
for the Arts   du Canada

We acknowledge the support of the Canada Council for the Arts which last year invested
$20.1 million in writing and publishing throughout Canada.

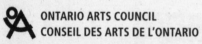
ONTARIO ARTS COUNCIL
CONSEIL DES ARTS DE L'ONTARIO

Published with the generous assistance of the Ontario Arts Council.

Printed in Canada

For Mom, Dad, Erin, and Dan

SWALLOWING A DONKEY'S EYE

"Underneath the bridge the tarp has sprung a leak and the animals I've trapped have all become my pets."
—Nirvana, "Something in the Way"

"When asked whether he was not happier now that Jones was gone, he would say only, 'Donkeys live a long time. None of you has ever seen a dead donkey,' and the others had to be content with this cryptic answer."
—George Orwell, *Animal Farm*

I

HERE Δ QVΔCK, THERE Δ QVΔCK, EVERYWHERE Δ QVΔCK, QVΔCK

Animal noises fill the air, and they make me tense up, like something is going to happen to me, even though nothing ever has happened to me, at least not in the sense I'm trying to get at. I've been trained, just like that Russian guy's dog. Funny how I remember the guy was Russian, but not his name, or even what kind of dog. No one ever remembers the dog.

The noises:

You've got your moos, whinnies, snorts, squeals, oinks, grunts, growls, ruts, barks, meows, mewls, bahs, brays, clucks, cock-a-doodle-dos, and quacks. The quacks are my favourite. This sector of Farm hasn't seen a duck in my three years, seven months, three weeks, two days, and roughly five hours of employment. I am counting.

Nothing is perfect, of course, and the tourists don't complain or even notice the ducklessness, the automated Muzak-quacks notwithstanding. Just like the dog, no one remembers the duck.

I say, "Oh goody, the hills are alive with the sound of music."

My co-worker and roommate Jonah bails hay next to me, and he grunts. His grunt fits right in. I lean on my pitchfork, wipe my brow, and watch him.

Here's what I see:

Two unblinking blue eyes and the harsh, dark lines of a cartoon face that drips a shaggy black mustache and beard. It's a face etched to give a think-ponderous-thoughts vibe, or maybe entrenched annoyance, depending upon the face viewer's mood. This mood-ring face perches above his muscular back. Not his chest, but his back. His legs and arms work in the wrong direction like he's a ruined insect.

But like the animal noises at Farm, this is also fake. Jonah's tattoo is a second face, a second skin on the back of his bald head made of blue and black ink, the curly black hair at the base of his skull fashioned into a mustache and foot-long beard. It's all sculpted to look exactly like Jonah's other face, his real face.

Jonah turns, ditching his tattoo face for his flesh one, and there's appallingly little difference between the two. He says, "For fuck's sake, another goddamn tour coming," and points his pitchfork at my chest. "That's it, I'm gonna poke out my eardrums, or yours."

We've been cleaning up cow stalls all morning and now we're in the corner of Barn 5 bailing and forking a mountain of hay. I say, "Please, be my guest."

Jonah is older than me, but not geezer old. That

said, I can't imagine him ever having been young. He had to have been born with that shaved-bald head, tattoo, and black beard.

He pulls a tattered blue baseball hat from his back pocket and slaps it on his head, covering up the tattoo. This is something he has to do whenever a tour comes by.

I say, "Isn't it ironic that when the fake animal sounds come on, you have to cover your fake face?"

"No."

"No?"

"What's so fake about my face, asshole?"

Jonah turns the pitchfork away from me and harpoons the hay. He means it harm. He mutters more swears and epithets, which are barely audible beneath the symphony of fraudulent animal voicing, and he bales, and he bales, and he bales. His arms are tan and taut, seemingly moving of their own accord, like they're his friends instead of his arms.

A quick electronic beep echoes in our stall. Only thirty seconds until a tour rolls by.

I say, "Get it all out of your system now, Jonah, and smiles, everyone, smiles!"

If we don't smile, if we don't follow the tour Protocol to the capital P, if we break any rules, if we're late for any shifts, if we swear at supervisors, if we swear at the animals, if we're caught having sex on the job with co-worker or animal, if we're caught stealing or eating or sabotaging the animals, we're contractually and severely punished.

Listen to those sounds. I still don't know how Farm does it, how they make it all sound so life-like. You'd think you'd be able to tell the difference between animal sounds pumped through speakers and sounds coming from real animals. But I can't, and apparently no one else can either. I've yet to see or find any speakers in the barns, stalls, pens, or peeking from beneath suspicious hay bales or manure piles, and not from a lack of looking. I can't describe it any better than to say the faux-animal sounds exist although I know they don't.

How do I know? Here are my first official five minutes at Farm:

The blood-red ink hadn't coagulated on the contract that gave Farm my next six years when the Barn Manager, the good ole BM, said, "All Farm animals are engineered."

I said, "Really? Don't you, or we, have an advertisement campaign built around our 'natural stock'?"

BM held up a stop hand, smoothed his waxy handlebar mustache, tossed me an unreadable facial tick, and said, "All animals are engineered for silence. No vocal cords, kid. When civilian tours come by, we pump in computer-generated sounds. Keeps the folks happy, reassured, consumer-esque if you will."

Reeling from the engineered-animal revelation, and ever the bright-eyed, fresh-from-City-newbie, I said, "Why not leave the vocal cords in?"

He said, rapid fire, "Because we don't want to."

I was getting a little cranky with this conversation. Cranky because he called me 'kid,' which is a micro-step above calling me 'boy,' and cranky because I was already having second-third-fourth-fifth thoughts about the Farm gig. Thoughts like: Should I have left City and my mother behind for six years of labour at Farm? Would Mom be okay? Would she ever speak to me again because of how I left her?

So, suitably cranky, I kept at it with BM. "Sorry to be a pain, but that doesn't make sense. If you left the animals' voices alone you wouldn't have to waste money on the fake animal sounds."

BM, with his hair like a comb and a neck-wattle to rival a cock-of-the-walk rooster, looked at me like I told him his son and/or daughter was a good fuck. He said, "Kid, I like the cut of your jib. And I think we're going to be work pals. I can just feel it. But a little advice: if you have any more helpful comments or suggestions, bright ideas, solutions to life's little problems, keep them to yourself unless you want me to stuff a silo up your tight little ass."

Ah, the country life. I often marvel at my own stupidity for ditching City and signing my tight little ass to Farm. And I just as often try not to think about it.

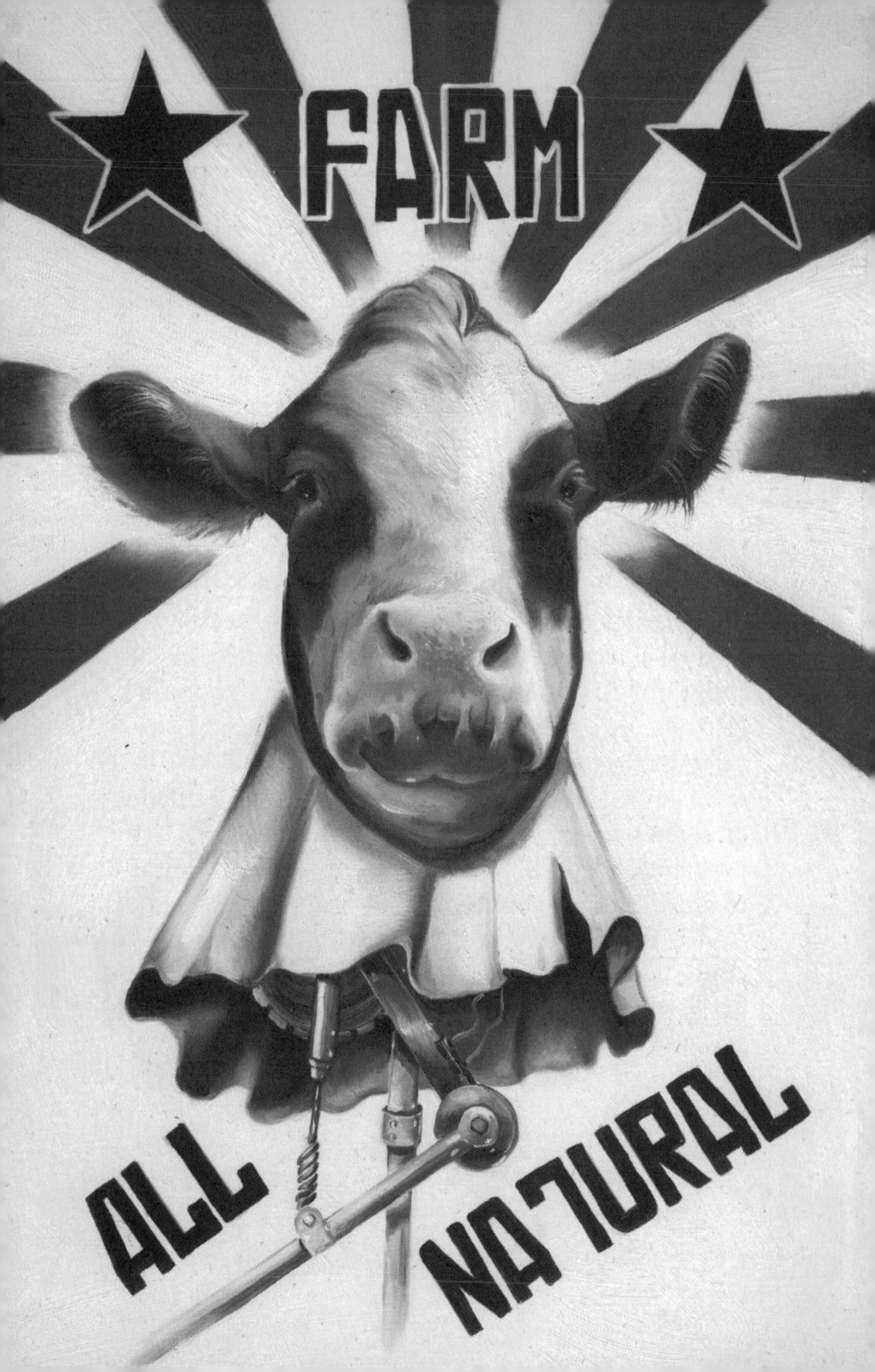
FARM
ALL
NATURAL

2

YOV'RE NO CHICKEN

Sometimes, when I watch the animals closely, they all seem to lip-synch to their fake noises, like the fuckers are trained, like they know how they're supposed to sound and they play along. I'm probably just projecting. Sometimes I think Farm does the animal-noise thing just to mess with us, the workers, and sometimes I believe BM: they do it simply because they want to and they can.

Maybe it all sounds so real because this lifelong City dweller has never heard a real barn animal. I've only heard those animals on TV, the 'net, in movies (usually animated movies), and now through Farm's speakers. For all I know, a real chicken and duck could be capable of singing barbershop quartet tunes. All of which gets me to thinking about how much I think I know is fake and fantasy. How am I supposed to know what's real or not?

A tram full of clueless gawkers from City rolls on by. Tourists. I used to worry that I'd see my mother or somebody I knew on the tours. But I haven't seen anybody from back home and I doubt anyone has seen me. Speaking of which:

Jonah talks through the side of a fraudulent smile. "Sorry I didn't wake you for your Calling Time last night, man. Really. My fuck up."

Missing Calling Time means I can't call Mom for another month and she'll be pissed or worried, likely both. I'm not mad at two-face Jonah, though. I knew he'd forget to wake me. It's why I asked him to be my alarm instead of actually setting one. I used Jonah as a built-in excuse to miss my Calling Time session. The last half-dozen or so phone conversations with Mom have been awkward. It's not all her fault. Mom puts on a solid everything-is-fine phone act and doesn't blame me for anything. The problem is, after talking with her and after I hang up, I feel guilty for leaving her alone in that shit-neighbourhood of ours and for not being able to send enough money home to help her out. You see, yesterday was a another shit-day in a years-long string of shit-days, and I didn't want to deal with the guilt. I couldn't face that monthly reminder of how dumb and damaging my decision to come to Farm turned out to be. So I slept through Calling Time. Son of the year, I'm not.

I say through my own sunny-side-up smile, "Don't sweat it, Jonah. No big deal."

Today, the Duck is the tour leader. Duckie's suit is brown, but with a green head, which makes it a mallard and male. Don't know why I've bothered remembering what kind of duck it is, since it doesn't exist, at least not here, and if it's not at Farm it might as well not exist for me anywhere. What matters is that I hate the fucking Duck. Somehow that duck fucker hasn't been caught yet, but when his tour isn't looking, he grabs his duck-crotch or wipes his duck-ass with a wing pointed in our general direction, or he shoots us a feathered middle finger. We've tried to find this guy in the dorms, but no one admits to knowing who the Duck is.

The Duck points and quack-speaks into a mini-mic clipped to some chest feathers. I have no idea what Duckie says, and I don't really care.

Jonah says through gritted teeth, "I hope you moult, motherfucker. I'll stick that mic up your cloaca."

Jonah said the same thing about the Chicken tour leader last week, but the Chicken is okay. He's a little weird—spends most evenings in the dorm cleaning his feathers and comb and practicing his clucks—but okay. I think Jonah hates the Chicken because he tries to bring a little professionalism to his job. I don't know, I admire his effort, but clucking and preening away his nights smacks of the ultimate in uselessness, of why-bother, and it depresses the shit out of me.

There he goes again. That Duck prick just shot us the finger. Goddamn bastard will get away with it too, and there's nothing we can do to retaliate.

I have the strange urge to yell, "You're no Chicken,

duck-ass!" like it would be some cool insult Duckie would never live down.

Duckie flaps that fuck-you-finger-waving wing at us again, this time trying to get his tour to look in our direction. Most of them ignore us. A few kids giggle and wave. The kids wear expensive designer Farm gear: overalls, flannels, and shit-kickin' boots made to look inexpensive but authentic, like they've worked six years of their lives in those little boots, and the crazy part of it is their boots look more worn, more authentic than mine. More fantasy versus reality, reality versus fantasy, and maybe by the time I'm done with my indenturetude at this place I won't care about which is which because no one else seems to.

The kids shout to me and Jonah, telling us we're so cool, telling us they want to be big strong Farmers when they grow up. Their parents pat their heads and laugh at such silliness, while throwing us the look.

The look:

Our little cherubs, the ample fruit of our ample loins, the family egg-mixed-with-ejaculate will never ever ever ever be Farmers, they'll never be fuckups like you, and if you look and smile and wave back at the kids too long we're going to report you to the supervisor and insist that you are gelded.

In accordance with official Farm Tour Protocol, we do our best to ignore the parents. So Jonah and I stand there, a couple of animatronic scarecrows, holding our pitchforks in one hand, waving back at the kids with the other, and we spread our lips and cheeks into the biggest smiles you've ever seen, all like we're supposed to.

Jonah talks through that smile again. "I'm really sorry for not waking you up last night, man. I feel terrible about it."

I don't say anything, and I try to convince myself that I know my smile is fake.

3

LET'S-GET-DRVNK-AND-INSEMINATE-NIGHT

I've come to a radical conclusion to the question of why Farm has us all wear the same overalls, besides the obvious cost benefits, uniformity, and all that happy horseshit. I'm talking about some outside the Skinner-box thinking, and here's what I got: it's to help ease the consciences of the tourists. If they see all us lower-than-low wage schlubs wearing the same nice, clean overalls, it'll be easier for them to forget we're not just part of the Farm scenery and machinery, easier to forget we denim-clad humans are dirt poor and miserable. Our overalls makes us a *them*, a collection, not individuals, certainly no one who needs pity, compassion, or, Farm gods forbid, love. *Them* are unworthy. *Them* are faceless, feckless, forgettable, flawed. . . .

But good goddamn this woman standing in front of me is smoking hot in her white, dress-overalls.

She flips her long brown hair like it's a luxurious burden and says, "Hi."

I say, "Hello. Are you new?"

"I've always been new."

I laugh, although I don't know what that means.

She asks, "What do you think of this?"

I have no idea what she's talking about. Doesn't matter. I'll tell her *this* is great. This is the most magnificent this in the history of this, and whatever this is, I'll kiss it, touch it, and fuck fuck fuck it. Yes, it has been that long. In my hornier-than-Hugh-Heffner condition, I blurt out, "What do I think of what?"

"Let me finish. Jesus. At least pretend you want to listen to me before trying to get into my pants."

I'm not dumb enough to mention that she, technically, isn't wearing pants. Instead, I just say, "Sorry." It's a word I regurgitate far too much in this place. "The music is too loud, and I wasn't sure what you'd said. Go on." The music is a mechanical, industrial: fast, electronic, processed.

Everyone complains about this night. They complain about the music, the feel-nothing condoms, the cheap Farm-produced hors d'oeuvres (finger hot-dogs tonight, too orange, like miniature pylons), the equally cheap hard cider, mulled wine, vodka, and beer, and mostly they complain about having to wear their Farm-issued white, dress-overalls while trying to get laid. But they're all here. Even the Chicken put down his feathers for one night. He's actually hanging out with Jonah. They're talking to the two women Jonah and I talked to six months ago. Those six-month-ago women are still laughing at, staring, and touching Jonah's tattoo. Six months ago just happens to be the last time I did any *talking to*.

The woman standing in front of me smiles lopsided, like a rip in a shirt. Her arms fold across her ample chest. The metal buttons and clips jingle on her overalls straps. To my libido it's the dinner bell. Me as that Russian guy's dog again. I'm ready to be social.

She says, "Okay. So even though you were right and I am new, I came up with a nickname for tonight. Wanna hear it?"

One lousy night a month we're corralled into this dance hall for our beloved Farm Social Night. Or, you could choose one of the many nicknames us Farm servants have dubbed this most unspontaneous of whimsical events: The Meat Grinder, The Cattle Call, Stud Night.

I say, "Let's hear it."

"Let's-Get-Drunk-And-Inseminate Night."

"Not bad, but I don't think it'll catch on."

"Ah, what do you know?"

I stuff my hands into my pockets and wrap a paw around the Farm-issued-and-required condom. Despite the car-wreck music around us, I hear the cellophane-wrapped condom crinkle in my pocket, and I think about the small stack of unused Social Night party favours sitting on my dresser. I say, "Very little, actually."

She looks around the room and I know she's looking for someone better, someone who doesn't look fifteen years older than my twenty-two. Everyone in the room seems otherwise engaged and the night is getting old, old, old.

At this point I don't fucking care. Sure, she's attractive, but what's another month without insemination? I say, "Looks like you're stuck with me."

She says, "Tell me your name. I know everybody."

I play along. I tell her.

She doesn't hesitate with her response. "Really? Is your mother's name Mary by any chance?"

"Yes," I say, too shocked by her response to do anything other than tell the truth. I should've lied. I suddenly don't want this person or anyone else in this place knowing anything about me.

She moves in and her mouth is open wide enough to swallow me. She's all teeth, and says, "I hear poor Mary isn't doing too well these days." She grabs my hand and pulls me away from the crowds and toward the exit.

"Wait? What did you say?"

"Shut up, you're spoiling my mood."

What could she possibly know about my mother? Besides her name.

4

PISS-GIRL AND MOMMA'S BOY

When Mom took me grocery shopping, she wouldn't let me out of the kiddie-seat in the shopping cart. A paranoid practice she insisted upon well past my he's-too-big-to-be-riding-in-the-cart phase. The metal squeezed and pinched my thighs and left raised welts on my brown skin, especially if we had one of those carts with a bum wheel that spasmed in every direction at once. I'd fight tears, squirm in my seat, then would adjust the plastic bags of produce on my lap to make sure I wasn't squashing the blueberries, but there wasn't much wiggle room in the cart. I'd complain, and loudly, and she'd just tell me that being uncomfortable for a short time was better than being kidnapped by some psycho.

Those old shopping trips strangely occur to me as I let the woman I just met lead me out of the dance hall and into the hallway.

I say, "My mother. What's wrong?"

"Oh, a momma's boy. On most nights that'd be

cute. But not tonight. You're coming to my room right fucking now." She flips her brown hair again, reloading.

Other couples with locked hands or lips or even hips spill out of the exit and flow around us like we're a broken dam in a river. I say, "I'm not moving until you tell me about Mary."

She stomps her foot on the floor, squeezes my hand, and swears under her breath, but regains composure quick, too quick, like someone hit a reset button. She pushes me against a white wall and clamps her legs around my right thigh, grinding her crotch into my leg. I feel her warmth through our layers of overalls and my rooster is instantly at attention. Mommy or no Mommy.

That shark smile of hers is back and just inches from my face. She says. "Word around Cronin Street was that she was days away from being evicted."

Cronin Street. That's where Mom lives. That's where I used to live. Missing last night's Calling Time was worst-idea-number-one.

"You're lying."

"Don't you want to know what I'm going to do to you when we get to my room?" There's more grinding on my leg. She undoes two side-buttons on my overalls, and I think I'm going to pass out.

"No," I say. I think. I think I say *no*.

"You're going to sit on my bathroom floor and I'm going to piss all over you, mamma's boy."

For a moment, I see myself doing this. Going to her

room, squatting on the floor, or probably squatting in the tub so the clean-up is easier, her with overalls off and panties (if she's wearing any, which I'm guessing is doubtful) around her ankles, her hovering above me in a lover's squat, and then she pisses on me and I'm getting pissed on, and it really doesn't sound so bad. Then I think about how I'll stink afterward and my dress-overalls might get all messed up in the heat of passion, and I know I'm as crazy and damaged as anyone else is.

"Um . . ."

She stuffs her hand into my overalls and grabs a handful of me. She talks and growls real low, I'm talking subterranean low, an earthquake just starting its shakes and shimmies. She says, "And then, maybe, we'll see. Maybe I'll fuck you senseless. Absolutely senseless. You'll feel it in your toes. Maybe I'll fuck your toes and your elbows and anything else you got. I'll fuck your ears. I'll fuck your chin. Fuck, I'll even fuck those love handles you have hidden in those overalls. You'll be a puddle of goo. You'll be a pissed-on little bitch whimpering for mercy. You'll be a helpless baby sucking at my tits. You'll be calling *me* Mommy. . . ." She's still talking about all the nasty things she'll do to me and she works me inside the overalls, but the Mommy shit gets to me.

"Stop. I can't go anywhere until you tell me what you know about Mary. It's important. Please." I pry her hand out of my crotch. I do all I can to convince myself she's bullshitting me about Mom. That it's all part of some fetish game. She found out Mom's name and addy from somebody at Farm, maybe Jonah, and she knows I missed my Calling Time last night and she is just fucking with me.

"I told you, evicted. Soon to be homeless. She'd been living with a junkie anyway, so it's her own damn fault." She tries to stab her hand back inside my overalls but I block her and then wiggle my thigh out from between her legs. She grabs my hair and says, "Enough, let's go."

I try to be strong. Like I don't need her your-Mom-is-homeless shit tonight. Like I don't need *her*. My voice is full of helium and lust, and I say, "I think I'll pass on the piss bath. I get enough of the submission thing in my day-to-day life, thanks."

"Too late. I've marked you, and I'll piss on you, you fucking sissy, eventually." She licks the side of my head, from chin to ear, and says in a mock lilt, "Bye bye, mamma's boy."

5

A GOOD BM IS EVERYONE'S FRIEND

Last night, me and my painful erection walked back to my dorm. Alone. I decided piss-chick was lying; she had to be. I was going to forget about my mother and piss-chick and go back to my dorm room and take care of myself. It was going to be that easy.

Instead, the sounds of fucking filled my floor's hallway. Groans, slapping skin, squeaking bedsprings, breathless oh-my-gods and some real cheesy sounding stuff like *oh yeah, oh yeah, baby*, all of it muffled behind closed wooden doors and it all sounded fake, like it was coming out of old, scratchy speakers. And when I made it to our quaint corner dorm room, there was a white sock on the knob. The Jonah-is-inside-and-occupied signal. Maybe I should have just gone home with piss-chick.

So I didn't sleep at all last night. I could blame the insomnia on Jonah and his fuck-fest forcing me to try and sleep on a mouldy couch in our dorm's game room, but I spent the night thinking about Mom.

I shouldn't have skipped out on calling her and I shouldn't have skipped out on her just like my father had. I spent the night thinking about how I was no different from anyone else because I didn't learn anything from my history.

Now it's fifteen minutes before my shift starts. I press the little red button, calling for the elevator. No dice. It's shut off. Of course it is. So I walk up the tight spiral staircase to the BM's office, which is in the rafters of Barn 5. The wrought iron is rusty and shakier than a bad excuse. The staircase yo-yos me up and down, side to side, walks the dog. Flecks of black paint break off under my hand as I grab the railing. I'm a good thirty feet above the ground. Jonah, down below somewhere, says something snarky about a violent death plummet and processed Farm beef.

I stumble and fall into BM's office, his all-windows office. I see the whole Barn operation from up here: cow stalls, milking units, slaughter pen with its conveyor belt and sluicing floor, chicken pens and hen houses, everything.

BM is bent over a golf ball. He putts. The white ball rolls evenly across the office's real-grass floor (took Jonah and me two weeks to rig the sprinkler and drainage system) and drops in the middle of a hole between my feet.

BM says, "I am the man!" Then he scurries and squats behind his desk.

"Nice shot."

BM wears a tomato-red bowtie. All he ever wears are bowties, and they piss me off. Like that touch of character somehow makes him more of an interesting person than the rest of us non-bowtie-clad plebs. Like wearing that isn't-he-eccentric nonsense doesn't mean he's an uncaring asshole just like the rest of us. Maybe I'm reading too much into a bowtie, placing value on a symbol that doesn't symbolize anything.

Hey says, "Hey, buddy, how you doing this morning?"

Told you he's a bowtie-wearin' asshole. His jocularity is an act. It's as bogus as the animal sounds. I'd respect him more if he was the same belligerent BM I met on my orientation interview more than three years ago. I'd respect him more if he'd still say fuck you to my face.

I'm still breathing hard and heavy from the stair-climb. I spill into a chair in front of his desk. The plush chair wobbles on its chopped legs. I sit a good two feet lower than BM and his desk. His chicken-head hovers above that bowtie, which looks clown-sized from this supplicant view. I want to spin the tie, see if it doesn't start rotating like a propeller and lift BM's ass off his chair and send him flying around the room like an oversized mosquito.

I say, "I have a quick question about my salary disbursement."

He gives me his wire-thin stare, his mouth a rumour beneath that ludicrous handlebar mustache.

"Okay, kid, let's hear it. What can I do for you?"

"If it's possible, I wanted to see if my mother is still receiving the payments I have directly sent home."

"Two days a week I'm allotted fifteen-minute periods to devote to employees' financial files. I'll look up your disbursement figures then and get back to you. All right, buddy?" His stare relaxes, his wrinkled and loose skin softening into a smile. Fucking guy is warped. He's giving me a look he'd give a friend. Guy doesn't even know my name, just my employee code, but I bet he's imagining that I'm his friend right now, the friend with a problem for whom he's bending over backwards. He wants to get up and pat me on the back, talk about baseball, tell me a tasteless joke about women or his favourite ethnic group. He wants me to retort with good-natured ribbing about his tie or his mustache, that dead caterpillar under his nose. Goddamn it, he's smiling and happy, genuinely happy that he has a codified and documented answer to his buddy's question, a solution to the little problem in his office.

I'd give my left nut to wipe that *There's no problem here, pal* look off his face.

I say, "But . . ."

"Hey, did I show you this? This is us on our little beach trip last weekend." He slides me a framed picture of him and his three grandkids. I am not part of his *us*. I pretend to give it a good look. BM and his progeny are doing something really expensive and supervisor-salary-like. This is BM being BM. This is

BM keeping that overlord-underling bond and order friendly but stronger than his denture adhesive.

I say something like, "Very nice, they're growing like weeds, they look just like you, you must be proud . . ."

"Thanks. I knew you'd get a kick out of that, kid. There's nothing more important than your family, right?"

"Right. And that's sort of why I'm here. So my disbursement issue: this really can't wait. Please, I know it's probably just a couple of clicks away on your computer and there's still a good ten minutes before the shift starts."

BM holds up that chicken-foot stop hand. Facial reading now reporting: disappointment. I'm still his buddy, but now I'm his numbnuts, dumb-fuck pal. The one who can't fix a flat tire, the one who'll never get married and never get anywhere, but he'll take care of me, like a mascot. He says, "Your shift starts in ten minutes, but mine started an hour ago. I am working here, kid. I don't come here for my health. Ha!"

If I was indeed his friend, not an imaginary one, I'd say this: *Thanks for reminding me you can leave Farm, you pasty, clock-watching, dehumanizing, condescending, bowtie-wearing, syphilitic retarded hunk of engineered cow dung.* Because I'd say something like that to a friend who could leave Farm on a whim, afford to take his family to some resort, and who wasn't willing to spend thirty seconds looking up my financial records. But I'm not his friend, and I need this information, so

I say, "I didn't mean to imply you weren't working."

"Don't worry, I won't hold it against you. I can't stay mad at you, pal. You're too cute. Ha!" He's enjoying this now, that bag of rabies and all that's vile and dirty.

"My mother may be in trouble. I heard that she's on the verge of becoming homeless."

"You 'heard?' Speak plainly, son. How exactly did you get this information?"

Fucker has called me pal, buddy, kid, and now son. "A newbie co-worker told me Mom was about to be evicted."

"How does this co-worker know?" There's something in his mustache right below his left nostril. Some yellowish brown thing, like a piece of bruised apple, or partially chewed doughnut cud. It's trapped, intertwined into those thick, pepper-gray hairs. It's disgusting but I have the urge to pluck the unidentified-fly-hair-object from the mustache and hold it inches from his face and tell him how this putrid crumb, not the bowtie, is the symbol of his character, his unyielding, unrelenting ridiculousness as a person. Then I'd tell him to shave his mustache, because it's what friends do.

"I don't know how she knows. She just knows. Look, I only need to find out if my mother has been receiving and cashing the portion of my salary I have sent home each week."

BM leans back in his chair. The chair squeals like a torture victim. He folds his arms over his thin chest and says, "When was the last time you heard from your mother?"

"Over a month ago."

He leans forward, tortured chair screaming again. His look of surprise is over-acting hammy.

I say, "I know, I know. I usually talk to her once a month, but I slept through my Calling Time the other night."

"Tsk, tsk, tsk. Well I suggest you call your mother during your next Calling Time. My God, you have to take care of your family, kid."

I stand up. Arms held out, hands open, and I'm begging, pleading. I say, "I know and I'm trying. But I can't wait another month to call her. In the meantime . . ."

"There is no meantime. As I'm sure you know, my schedule has been honed and regimented for optimum efficiency. I don't run the best Barn by accident, son. So, in two days I have my scheduled time with employee records. But I'll tell you what I'll do because this is about family. For you and only for you, pal, I promise to make your disbursement inquiry tops on my list. Does that sound good?" He doesn't wait for an answer. He gets up, walks around the desk, slaps me on the back, punches me in the shoulder, and pats my fanny while shoving me toward the door. Then he walks back behind his desk, turns on the elevator, and two wooden panels slide open behind him.

"So I guess this means you probably aren't going to

grant me a few days leave of Farm so I can go check on my mother."

He steps into his elevator and presses a button. The sprinklers come on. Water assaults my feet and ankles. BM says, "Time to get to work, son. Another day and all that," and he winks, which is all somehow worse than him laughing or making a lame wisecrack about the chances of leaving Farm being Jack and shit, somehow worse than him just saying no.

There's no fanny-pat invite to join him in the elevator and the doors close. I walk back to the staircase, the decaying and descending spiral: *my* symbol.

6

THE ΔPPLE OF HIS EYE

So now I'm thinking about piss-girl and everything she said. *Dwelling on* would be a more apt description, or obsessing. My mother with a junkie, my mother homeless, my already-once-abandoned mother who I then re-abandoned, left alone in City. . . .

The idea was that me being a gainfully kept, penned-in employee at Farm would make us enough money for our lives to be at least tolerable if not totally dreamy. Everything hasn't exactly worked according to plan. Maybe it's time for a new plan.

Jonah and I pull pitchforks and shovels out of the shed, preparing for another stall-filled workday.

I say, "I'm so sick of the smell of this place."

Jonah says, "The smell of this place doesn't bother me. I'm used to it."

"Bullshit."

"No pun intended, right?"

I mock scream. "It's physiologically impossible to get used to a smell. You smell because microscopic particles, physical matter belonging to whatever it is you smell, land on receptor cells, waiting to be processed by the brain."

"Yummy."

We walk to a stall. Jonah works the password on the antiquated, tour-friendly lock. The Chicken calls out our names from across the Barn. He heads our way, driving a four-seat ATV. He and his chicken suit take up the two front seats.

I say, "This place stinks."

"Smells authentic, right?"

"Why not genetically alter the animals not to smell, right? It's always there. Every morning, lunch break, quittin' time. Every night when I go to bed. Doesn't matter how many showers I take. I smell it and there's no getting used to it. Because it, the smell, is an *it*. It exists."

"Nope. I'm used to it," Jonah says. He ignores the approaching Chicken and opens the stall door, loosening a chewy waft of animal and wet hay mixed with manure.

"No, you're not. You're just ignoring your nose. Your nose tells you this place is wrong, and you ignore it, just like everyone else. Why should their noses be any different than their eyes and ears?"

"What's got you all wound up?"

"Long story. So what do you think the Chicken wants?"

"Who cares? I hope that motherfucker moults." Despite their Social Night double date, Jonah is back to hating the Chicken. He gets like this whenever he punches in, whenever he's on Farm time. He immerses himself into his pissed-off Farm-hand role.

The Chicken pulls up next to us and says, "Gentleman, you may put away your pitchforks. You have been temporarily assigned to Orchard today."

I ask, "Picking or ground duty?" Picking is better than ground duty. Both are better than the stalls. I wonder if BM is trying to throw me an I-won't-look-up-your-records-right-now bone. If he is, I'll accept it like a greedy, half-starved mutt. Look who's the dog again.

"I don't know, but I'm to escort you there. Please join me, gentleman," he says and points a wing at the back seats. "Oh, and Jonah. Would you please cover your tattoo for the ride over? We may pass tours en route."

Jonah puts on his hat, mumbles something about an egg-laying errand boy, and climbs in the back. Chicken and I ignore him.

We ride through the length of the Barn 5 enclosure and emerge into bright sunlight. No one talks. I lean back (Chicken's feathers tickle me if I don't), close my eyes, and aim my face at the sun. It feels so good on my skin, so right, even though I know there's nothing innately good or moral about that giant ball of gas. I inhale, trying to smell the sun, trying to get it inside me, and on this most unexpected and welcome trip outdoors, there are new, even joyous smells: cut grass and flowers (we must be passing the Greenery now but I'm not opening my eyes to see) and fresh manure-less soil, and Orchard and its blossoming trees and fruit. But underneath it all, a virus infecting the system, is the smell of our Farm, the real Farm. The shit and piss and slaughtered carcasses and giant compost heaps and machinery exhaust and hours upon hours of human sweat. It's on Jonah and on me and it'll never leave us.

Our moment in the sun is heartbreakingly brief. The ATV jerks to a stop at our new work area. Jonah sneezes, wipes his hand on the back of my overalls, and says, "This hay fever is gonna kill me."

Orchard is immense. Sixteen square miles of apple, pear, orange, palm, maple, rubber, and eucalyptus trees planted and grown in grids. Farm engineers its trees to withstand the climate and to be able to grow in such proximity. The canopy blots out the sun and sky if you're on the ground and not on one of the grid-roads.

The Chicken leads us to our new gear and brusquely gives us our assignment. Jonah waits until the Chicken and his ATV disappear, then says, "Of course we get fucking ground duty. No sun for us dirty pigs." He sneezes again.

Ground duty: gathering up all the fallen fruit by hand. Apples today, as Chicken dropped us in the apple-grid. I say, "It's better than the stalls."

We wait at the grid-road to let pass a Harvester (a heavy duty ATV hitched to a flatbed loaded with white scaffolding almost forty feet tall). The pickers nested in their carefully assigned areas of the scaffolding, wave and laugh at us. Apparently, us ground-duty folk are low on the Orchard food chain.

Jonah says, "That's the only cool job in the place. They're in the sun all day, climbing up and down the scaffolding like kids on a jungle gym. And we're stuck at the bottom like moss. We're fucking mobile moss, man."

We lead our sputtering hand-cart across the road. The sun warms our backs for the brief road traverse, and then it's back under the canopy. We park the cart just off the side of the grid-road. It can't crawl between the crowded trees or over the gnarled and exposed roots, which sucks. We have to gather fallen apples in our satchels and lug them all the way back to the cart and the grid-road. Farm has the technology to harvest fruit and pick up fallen apples with more efficient machines, but since Orchard has been the most popular Farm area to tour, the higher ups, the mucky-mucks, have focus group data that supports workers gathering apples by hand as more quaint, more tour-friendly.

"So tell me about your long story." Jonah says.

We walk into the dark heart of the apple-grid. The thinnest of rays breaks through some leaves, but it fades out when the wind blows through the canopy. The light ducks and hides from us.

"What long story?"

"When you came out of BM's office, I asked you why you were so wound up. You said 'long story.'"

I don't feel like talking about it. So I attempt to distract Jonah, the self-appointed expert on Farm operation procedures, with this: "I can't believe there aren't more leaves and apples on the ground." Tree roots snake over each other, blanketing the ground. A short grass covers what little space the roots don't claim. There are only a few still-green leaves and a handful of apples beneath each tree.

"You serious? Farm engineers its trees to grow apples with stronger stems, so the apples hardly fall." Jonah pounds the trunk of a tree with his righteous fist. "They could make it so the apples never fall, if they wanted. But tours seeing no apples on the ground wouldn't seem right. So they've perfected trees with a pick to fall ratio of 28.5:1."

"Now I know you're making shit up."

"Nope. No shit. Don't ever forget, this place is all about the show. And the leaves don't really fall either, unless they're accidentally knocked down by careless pickers. Well, there is one autumn-grid in the northwest corner. Raking those leaves is such a colossal pain in the ass. You wouldn't believe it."

"I believe it." I bend down at the base of a tree and pick up three apples.

Jonah walks to the tree across from mine, and says, "So back to the long story. And why did you meet with BM before the shift? Is this day-trip the result? You and BM are chummy-chums now? I didn't think you were an ass kisser."

I say, "No, nothing like that. I wanted to make sure my salary disbursement was working right. Just checking to see if my money was going where, you know, it was supposed to. Doesn't matter, he wouldn't look up my info."

"So we get rewarded with a day in Orchard?"

I pick up more apples, my satchel almost full. "I guess so."

There is no follow-up question. That's because like most of the rest of us Farmhands, he doesn't pry or ask about anyone's past. Asking about the past, about pre-Farm life only reminds us that we're stuck at Farm.

I've been Jonah's roommate for two years and I know nothing about the why of Jonah's tattoo or his family or anything else that was him before Farm. He knows nothing about the pre-Farm me. That's just how it is.

We work in silence, filling our satchels and walking back to the road to dump them in the cart. Tours go by. We wave and smile. Jonah with his hat on, that hat covering his past. I think about my mother the whole time.

I say, "I was checking to see if my mother is getting the money I send home, Jonah." I think about what it means if in a few days BM tells me Mom hasn't been cashing the checks. I think about what it would mean if she doesn't answer the phone when I try to call her next month.

"What?"

"Today. My chat with BM. It was all about trying to make sure money is still going home to my mother."

Jonah takes off his hat and shakes his head, beard and fake-beard fly around. Then he puts it back on.

I keep talking. "Remember that crazy chick I told you about?"

"Piss-girl?"

"Yeah. She knew my mother's name."

"You gotta promise to point her out to me next time."

"I will. She told me my mother was on the verge of being homeless."

"Me and her need to meet and greet."

"Enough with the piss-girl."

"Sorry, mate."

"What am I going to do if piss-girl was telling the truth?"

Jonah doesn't ask *what happened to your father?* or *why would your mother be homeless?* or *where did she live?* or *where is she now?* or *how much money do you send home?* He doesn't ask *why did you leave your mother to come here?* Jonah follows all of Farm's rules, including the unwritten ones: thou shall not ask why or how somebody came to Farm because no one is willing to answer thine questions about the biggest mistake of their lives.

Jonah shrugs. "Don't know, guy. But that sucks." He walks to another tree, one farther away from me, and picks more apples, real fast, like he has to catch up on work because of our little chat.

Jonah puts on big airs about hating this place, but he is this place. That two-faced phony is Farm. He wants nothing to do with this problem, my problem, and now I'm just a rusty cog in the Farm machine to him. The kicker is I actually feel ashamed, like I should apologize for my apple-picking inefficiency.

But I'm also pissed, pissed at him, at BM, at Farm, at my mother, at myself for allowing all this to happen.

And just like that, I'm ready to do something, ready to break rules. I form a new plan: I drop my satchel and claw at the trunk of the nearest tree, scrabble for a grip or foothold.

As a kid, I used to climb on my apartment building's fire escapes and shimmy up lampposts. There was this one time, late afternoon, close to dinner, and I remember the sky was the same colour as our brick apartment building. The sky was made of those same crumbly bricks. I climbed up my usual post, the one with the burnt-out bulb. Green paint flaked off under my fingers. I got to the top and made the hero's leap to the fire escape, which had its own flaking black paint. I was only eleven. My parents' bedroom window was two floors above me. They'd gone in a half-hour previously and locked their bedroom door. I spider-crawled up the fire escape, and the metal shook under my weight. I was afraid the thing might fall down with me on it, a broken elevator car. But I thought it would be cool, too. I could ride it down like it was a skateboard. I made it to my parents' window and hovered outside. I was a vampire bat, testing the hole-filled screen. The lights were off and it was dark inside, but there was my father's naked pale skin pressed up against my mother's brown skin. I knocked on the frame and yelled, "Lovebirds." I'd planned only to yell boo or something similarly jokey-scary, something to teach them to not lock the door on me. My father was outside and waiting on the sidewalk before I slid back down the lamppost. He was shirtless and wearing baggy gray sweatpants with paint and coffee stains, those skinny legs of his lost somewhere inside. I said, "Dad, put a shirt on, you're embarrassing me," then tried to laugh it all off. He didn't laugh. He was embarrassed and pissed, so he grabbed me, and said, "I knew you'd climb up there." My father had always claimed he was psychic, but only after something had already happened. He dragged me inside the apartment and threw me into my room. He didn't hit me, but he squeezed and yanked on my arm awful hard. I cried and pretended he broke my arm. Mom stayed in the bedroom. Dad joked about the whole thing the next day, but for a week, Mom couldn't look me in the eye. The still sore-armed part of me enjoyed her embarrassment.

I wonder what Jonah or Chicken or BM or anyone else here would say or do if I told them that story. I wonder what they'd say if I told them that the post-Dad-desertion Mom was no longer embarrassed so easily.

I slide down the trunk, scraping up my arms and hands. Damn thing is too wide and thick for a shimmy. Would Jonah care that I've never climbed a tree?

Jonah says, "What are you doing?" but then he turns around, shows me his back.

"I'm climbing this tree. If I make it up, I'm going to pick an apple and eat it."

"Are you fucking nuts?" He still hasn't turned around and he still picks up fallen apples.

"Nope. Just going home."

"You do whatever it is you're doing, guy. Leave me the fuck out of this. But you'll never get out of here if you climb that tree and eat a new apple. Trust me," he says and adjusts his hat to make sure none of that face is showing. He shakes his head at me then disappears into the trees. I wish he'd at least take off the hat.

As angry as I still am, much of me is hurt and shocked that Jonah isn't physically stopping me from climbing the tree, that Jonah really doesn't seem to care what I do. Shit, I'm losing steam. I let go of the tree and wipe my hands on my pants. I can't climb the thing anyway. I pick up my satchel and put it back on my shoulder. It's heavy.

I weave through the trees looking for Jonah. No sign yet. I pull an apple out of the satchel. It isn't any good; it has bruises and is flat on one side. The apple must've fallen from up high.

There he is, and I run up behind him and knock off his hat. He doesn't turn to face me. All he gives me is that tattoo face, that fake face.

As loud as I can, I yell, "Boo!" If there are birds in the canopy above, I imagine they're scattering. Then I bite the apple. And it's bitter.

7

LAW AND ORDER

Within an hour of apple-consumption Farm Security (them with their double-barrel shotguns, straw hats with shot-glass-sized blue sirens flashing on the top, and their blue overalls) cuffs me, removes me from Orchard, transports me to the cavernous main offices, and dumps me in a darkened conference room. After another hour or so of waiting, a fleet, a veritable army of lawyers enters the big dark room, and they keep it dark. Spotlights appear from the ceiling only when necessary. Throughout the meeting, a general rumble of lawyer-speak is always present. They accuse, they argue, they pick through my Farm contract, and they argue some more. They yell at me. They call me names. They try to get a rise out of me. I give them nothing. They read eyewitness reports. They read character descriptions from BM, Jonah, Chicken, and others. They read a list (a small list) of people I'd slept with while at Farm. They constantly remind me how many millions my case and the lawyers' fees are costing Farm. This goes on and on and on. I only ever leave my seat to go to the bathroom. I eat small meals and sleep while sitting at the conference table. The lawyers don't leave. When lawyers tire, new ones take their place. This goes on and on and on. After two days of interviews, of badgering, of case studies and histories, of going over the surveillance vids, of reciting and memorizing contractual codes of conduct, of insisting to them that I acted alone and that Jonah was not on the grassy knoll, they convene to make an official recommendation. I sleep while they deliberate in an adjacent room. After only two hours, the lawyers reappear and make their recommendation: death.

Now, I am no lawyer, but I reject their thoughtful recommendation as is within my rights stipulated by line-item 15.15.23.4 in the basic Farm contract, and request my case be heard by the Arbitrator. The Arbitrator will hear my case in two-to-four weeks. They blindfold me and transport me to the Hole.

8

A LITTLE CITY IN THE HOLE

I'm in the Hole now. I've been in the Hole for two weeks. I'm told I'll be here for another week, maybe more. It is dank, soil-infested with bugs and mice, a six-by-eight-by-six of living space with my bathroom bucket in one corner. They give me a new bucket once a day. There's a porous tarp covering as a ceiling. Rain and sunlight drip through it. They feed me three meals of tepid water, stale bread, a hunk of something that once belonged to an animal, and some fruit but not the good fruit. They give me rejects that show obvious signs of falling out of trees, and yeah, the fuckers are mocking me. My bed is a mat of damp straw and hay. My blanket is scratchy wool pocked with moth holes and cigarette burns. They give me two packs of cigarettes every morning, but I don't smoke them. I've stuck a bunch in the ground, buried up to the filter so only the rolled-tobacco sticks poke up, like little columns and posts. They give me a pack of gum every morning, and I chew, but after chewing I use the gum as adhesive joints and attach cigarettes horizontally to the columns, to the posts. I've made struts and support beams. It looks chaotic, but I know it works. I use the paper plates to cover it, making a ceiling, or a floor depending on your point of view. I stick paper cups on top of the plates, making buildings and houses and stores.

I'm making a scale model of City and its Pier below. Can't explain why I'm building it. Just like we don't know who-why-when the real City and Pier were built. There are many origin legends and theories, and there's even a religion that worships the Pier. All of it is quaint, folksy, entertaining, and about as useful as an abacus in my everyday life. It doesn't matter. City Pier's existence wouldn't change any if I knew the why.

So why am I building the model? It's something to do, I suppose. The cigarettes as the Pier, as all that wood, as all those stripped-but-still-standing sequoia trees with trunks as thick as skyscrapers, branches molded into the intricate lattice of support beams, struts, joints, and elbows, the cigarettes as stand-ins for the practically infinite network of wood stretching for miles and miles along the coastline, the cigarettes as the giant wooden shoulders of City, sprawling two hundred feet above the ocean, a manmade forest pushing City to the clouds. Bugs crawl on my City and on my Pier. There's a fat cockroach walking the wrong way down a one-way street between two cups, two buildings. That one is where I grew up. My home was an eight-story tenement building, four apartments on each floor. Me and Peter (he lived on the fourth floor) used to catch cockroaches, some as big as the one crawling on my City, and put them in a ring box and scare the neighbourhood girls, or we used them as bait to catch rats. We never caught any. Now, this cockroach on my model is fat enough to be a cab, or even a truck going down my street. Peter's dad drove a cab, and then a truck before he and his family left. I don't know where they went and my parents never told me.

Flies land and eat some unseen morsel off the plate-floor, or plate-ceiling if you're below City. They wash themselves and then take off and then land and then repeat ad infinitum. There're more flies underneath the plates, hanging out in the Pier. Spiders and other bugs join the flies, climbing the Pier cigarettes. I hear them crawling. I hear a few bump into the ceiling above them. The ceiling that's a floor. After Peter and his family left I asked my mother the hard questions. She told me that they moved. Dad-the-psychic then told me that he could sense and see Peter and his family living happy in a more affluent section of City. My parents told me they weren't homeless. They told me even if they were homeless, City's homeless policy went into effect the year before I was born, so Peter and his family would be exempt by the grandfather clause. I don't know if what they told me was a lie, exactly, and I never bothered to check up on it. Maybe I'll ask Jonah if I ever see that two-faced prick again.

That said, my parents' story about the homeless policy being a recent innovation has all the feel of a parental lie, one that's supposed to be good for you as a kid. You know, hide the ugly truth from the innocent because it's so ugly. I'm sure City has always deported its homeless below City and to the Pier. I'm sure there has always been street sweeps and the deportees have been forever crawling Pier's lattice. My City-Pier-*why* theory is that people wanted to build a place where they could literally sweep it all under the rug, a magical rug that would never get pulled from under their feet. The fuckers, all of them. I'm under that rug right now. Or at least a tarp.

My model City and Pier is done. I won't need any more cigarettes. Now I just sit and watch it under the weak, green light that makes it though the tarp. I'm watching the residents of my City scurry around.

I wonder which of the bugs crawling on my model represents my deserting father, or my mother. I wonder if those plates are a floor or a ceiling for her. I wonder if she's a spider or a fly.

9

NO VS IN HER ME

This happened three years after Dad moved out:

I crawled back to the apartment after another night of running the alleys behind the strip joints and sex clubs in the Zone, trying to sneak a peek. As usual, no dice. Instead, we did what we usually did: drank cheap wine and beer, tipped dumpsters, and threw stuff at windows. I was fifteen.

My mother was waiting up for me. She sat at the kitchen table smoking a cigarette. Her legs were crossed with a free arm wrapped around her chest. She was wound tight, coiled.

Old grocery bags dripped off the table. The faux-chandelier fixture above had two working bulbs out of six. Mascara-filled tears ran down her cheeks and onto her lips. She didn't wipe any of it away.

I swayed on unmoored feet and wanted to leak out of the kitchen, pretend I didn't see her, but it wouldn't have worked. So I said, "Get a haircut today?"

"Yes."

Her hair was real short, tight to her skull. Everything was tight.

"I like it."

My mother was only eighteen years older than me. She looked my age, and she looked fifty years older than me.

"That bastard dumped me today."

"I'm sorry." I wasn't, really. Whoever this new boyfriend was, I didn't care. She'd told me all about him but I made it my business to forget. He might've been a cop, a banker, a cabby, a classmate from night-class, anybody. I didn't remember. I used to work at not remembering.

"The worst part was that he fucked me before telling me it was over."

The room got fuzzy, her words made me more drunk, if that was possible. Her words crossed my wires and killed the engine of my brain, so I leaned on the wall. It didn't help.

She said, "He made so many promises. He was going to take me away from here. He was going to make my life better."

The fifteen-year-old me noticed there was no *us* in her *me*.

And right *there* is the obvious: the fifteen-year-old me still blamed her for everything. I was such a painfully predictable teen. Angry at the person I needed the most, but it was mutual. She was angry at me too, and might still be.

More black tears fell out of her eyes, but she wasn't

crying, at least not in her voice. Her legs and arm squeezed tighter and she chomped on the cigarette. "I knew I was just a fuck to him, but I couldn't admit it to myself."

Almost numb from embarrassment, I managed another, "I'm sorry." Then I hugged her, knowing I smelled of garbage and alley and booze, hoping she'd say something to scold me, hoping she'd say anything else.

10

YOV GOT MAIL

The tarp above the Hole rustles. I sit up, wanting food. A security dweeb pokes his head inside.

"You got mail," he says.

I didn't realize the Hole received postal service. An unexpected perk, one I'd gladly trade for a piece of barbequed clone-meat.

Security dweeb tosses me an envelope. It's too light to be a care package from someone who cares.

I open it. It looks like this:

*You really screwed up this time, kid.
I'll do what I can to put in a good word
for you. But as promised, your salary info.
from the last six weeks.*

Employee Number: 42-9-33LB-A

CO. FILE DEPT. CLOCK VCHR.NO 010
C5R 010034 53400 0000120042 1

Pay period ending:

04-02-33: **Gross pay** 336.49
             -88.29(FITax) -23.67 (SSTax) -12.28 (Mtax)
         Net pay 212.25:
          100 transit 42-9-33LB-A 112.25 transit 232898547

04-09-33: **Gross pay** 336.49
             -88.29 (FITax) -23.67 (SSTax) -12.28 (Mtax)
         Net pay 212.25:
          100 transit 42-9-33LB-A 112.25 transit 232898547

04-16-33: **Gross pay** 336.49
             -88.29 (FITax) -23.67 (SSTax) -12.28 (Mtax)
         Net pay 212.25:
          100 transit 42-9-33LB-A 112.25 transit 232898547

04-23-33: **Gross pay** 336.49
             -88.29 (FITax) -23.67 (SSTax) -12.28 (Mtax)
         Net pay 212.25:
          100 transit 42-9-33LB-A 112.25 transit 232898547

04-30-33: **Gross pay** 336.49
             -88.29 (FITax) -23.67 (SSTax) -12.28 (Mtax)
         Net pay 212.25:
                  100 transit 42-9-33LB-A 112.25 transit
              account terminated, returned to 42-9-33LB-A

05-07-33: **Gross pay** 336.49
             -88.29 (FITax) -23.67 (SSTax) -12.28 (Mtax)
         Net pay 212.25:
                  100 transit 42-9-33LB-A 112.25 transit
              account terminated, returned to 42-9-33LB-A

Account terminated.

I'm not daydreaming anymore. The now-me, the shouldn't-be-here me, the sitting-in-a-fucking-pit-waiting-on-my-death-sentence me notices the choice of word. Her bank account wasn't cancelled or closed or moved or reassigned or discontinued. It was terminated.

TOUR FARM TODAY!
SEE OUR ANIMALS!
SEE THE ORCHARD!
FARM, ONLY THE BEST
FOR YOUR FAMILY

II

ARBITRATOR, APPLES, AND EVE OH MY!

Security pulls me out of the Hole and blindfolds me again. We take a ride. Then we stop. They force me to walk with my hands behind my back. Then an elevator, and a long hallway. Their shoes clack and crack on the linoleum. We enter a room. I sit. They uncuff me. I'm told to put my hands on the table. They take off the blindfold. It's still dark and I still can't see, but I know I'm back in the same conference room.

The last of the security leaves and light fills the room. I'm blind again, but it's a new blind. It takes more than a few minutes of squinting and blinking to adjust. Across from me is one large mirror covering the entire wall.

Eventually there's a voice. It fills the room.

"Am I speaking with employee number 42-9-33LB-A?" The voice is modulated: deep, digital, metallic pitched. They're protecting the identity of the Arbitrator, if there really is one. Could be a computer or Zombo the Clown for all I know.

"Yes." I stare at my reflection in the mirror. An older, beat-up man stares back.

"Why have you requested an Arbitrator?"

I have to pull it together quick. I want out of here, but I don't want to be, you know, dead. I cough and rub my face. "I wholeheartedly disagree with the lawyers' recommendation of death. I don't deserve to die."

"Everyone dies."

"I don't deserve to die now, then."

"I've been reviewing your case for the past three weeks and I'd like to ask you some questions."

"Please, ask away." I'm suddenly homesick for my Hole, my bugs, and my little City Pier. I can live in the daydreams, too.

"Do you feel remorse for your act?"

Best to keep it simple. Don't want any sarcasm slipping out. I've tried not to dwell on how angry I am that they're willing to terminate me over a fallen apple. But I manage a "Yes" to that question, and I drop my head like I'm so broken up about my transgression that I can't stand to look at my mirror self.

"Are you sorry you were caught?"

"Yes, I mean, no. No, I . . ." Wasn't expecting that question. I should've been. I certainly had enough time to prepare for this interview. I'm about to float out some *glad I got caught because I learned an important lesson, yes sir!* lie, but the Arbitrator jumps right in.

"Thank you. Do you know what Farm does with its fallen apples?"

"No."

"Farm is developing thrashers and plows that run on the fallen and rotting apples. Nothing here goes to waste, as you should know."

Sounds like a so-full-of-shit Jonah-story to me. I say, "Wow. I did not know that."

"Would my telling you that I am a woman strike you as ironic?"

Talk about out of the blue. I say, "No, I don't think so." I'm telling the truth.

"Do you know anything about Christianity?"

I stop myself from asking what does any of this have to do with me? "No. Not much. My father used to say 'Jesus Christ' a lot." This is a half-truth. That's all she gets.

"Do you know about Eve and the apple?"

"No, I'm sorry. Like most, I never learned much about religion." Yes, I'm pretending I know less than shit because you seem so much less threatening when you're stupid, so much less likely to be able to make your own decisions. Goddamn it, I'm following the same legal advice Jonah gave me a long time ago. Like he hasn't done enough to me already.

She says, "My time and talents are being wasted on you."

I have no answer to that. Anything I say will sound smart-ass or unappreciative of the Arbitrator's efforts. Pissed off or not, I do not want to piss off the person deciding whether or not I die because of an apple. And believe me, none of this strikes me as ironic.

She says, "I was hoping for a deeper conversation today."

"I'm sorry, but I'm nervous." That's the wrong thing to say and I know it as soon as it falls out of my mouth.

"Are you implying that if you weren't nervous you'd be able to discuss Eve and the apple, and irony?"

"No. I just meant . . ."

"Are you implying your nerves are compromising the integrity of our meeting today?"

"No."

"What did the apple taste like?"

This is worse than the lawyers. I've lost any semblance of control so quickly. "It tasted old, bitter, I guess."

"You're guessing?"

"No, I'm answering to the best of my ability."

"On the morning of the incident, why did you make an inquiry to your financial records?"

"I wanted to see if my mother was still getting the money I send home."

"Is she?"

"I don't think so. According to my financial records, her bank account has been terminated."

"What are you going to do with this information?"

The questions are coming fast. I answer quickly and stare at the mirror. It's like I'm talking to myself in two different voices. My mouth opens and closes and my voice and her computer-modulated one come out. "Try and contact my mother. See if she's okay."

"Will you follow proper protocol while attempting contact?"

"Yes."

"What happens if you can't find her?"

"I'll keep trying."

"You do know your contact options are limited. What happens when those options are exhausted?"

"I'll just keep trying."

"Why did you eat the apple?"

"I was hungry."

"You knew you weren't supposed to, correct?"

"Yes."

"Do you hate Farm?"

"No."

"Do you hate your Barn Manager?"

"No."

"What about your roommate and co-worker, Jonah?"

"He's fine."

"Can you still work and live with him?"

"Yes."

"Is your mother's name Eve?"

"No."

"Do you hate me?"

"No."

"If a starving man was next to you in Orchard would you willingly break the rules, consequences be damned, and feed him an apple?"

"I . . . I don't know."

"Yes or no."

"Probably, yes. Maybe."

"If your mother has fallen out of contact, what do you fear has happened to her?"

"That she's homeless. That she'll be shipped below City to the Pier."

"Do you hate your mother?"

"No, of course not. I love her. She's the reason I came here."

"Do you see your mother as Eve being banished from the garden?"

"No. City is no Eden."

There's a silence.

Then:

"Did you say Eden?"

I said *Eden*, didn't I?

She says, "You must be less nervous now since you suddenly seem to know more about Christianity than you previously claimed."

I shrug my shoulders and can't look at myself in the mirror. Caught and caught so easily. I'm screwed. So fucking screwed. Why the hell did I listen to Jonah's long-ago legal advice anyway? I should've just told her anything and everything she wants instead of playing goddamn games.

She says, "You must do one thing for me before I render my decision. I want you to fully explain your, and not your mother's, current situation in terms of irony and the Eve-and-apple parable."

What do I do? I hesitate, rub my beard stubble. Look at the mirror for an answer, there is none.

"This is very important for you," she says.

"I'm Eve. I ate the forbidden apple. Ironic because I did it purposefully to be tossed out of Farm, banned from our little Eden. Ironic because those fucked up gender roles are reversed: me as Eve, you as God, or the Christian God, anyway. Ironic because God didn't make these Farm-engineered apples, unless you want to get metaphysical about this whole mess, or unless you're still God, then I guess it's possible that you made the apples, though unlikely since your Arbitrator duties likely don't leave you time for engineering and growing. Ironic because . . ."

"Thank you."

"Should I compare myself to Snow White next?"

"No. Please wait patiently for my decision." I hear a door shut behind the mirror.

I wait. I beat myself up for everything I said, especially that Snow White crack at the end. I wait. I think about my mother and her terminated bank account and my stomach is a mess. I wait. I think about how I screwed up, and I think about how Jonah said it was always a gamble to go to the Arbitrator as her decision is final and legally binding, but applying even my most base and admittedly lacking logic training, I figure my sentence can't get any worse via the Arbitrator. It just can't get worse than death.

12

HATE BEING WRONG

Hours pass. Then without pomp or circumstance, a print-out emerges from a slot in the mahogany table at which I'm sitting. First forty-three pages are a line-by-line description of the case, then a detailing of the legal fees that goes on for forty-three more soul-numbing pages, then seventy-six pages of legal mumbo-jumbo in a font so small I can only make out a few words per page, and finally, on the last page and in large block letters, her Solomon-like decision (to keep the Christianity-vibe going):

—FARM IS TO GARNISHEE YOUR LIVING-WAGE FOR THE PRICE OF THE APPLE.

—FARM IS TO GARNISHEE YOUR LIVING-WAGE FOR THE WASTED CIGARETTES IN THE HOLE.

—FARM IS TO GARNISHEE YOUR LIVING-

WAGE FOR THE COST OF THE PSYCHIATRIC APPOINTMENTS NECESSARY FOR YOUR CO-WORKER AND ROOMMATE, EMPLOYEE NUMBER 34-4RT44-G.

—FARM PLACES YOU UNDER PROBATION FOR THE DURATION OF YOUR EMPLOYMENT.

—FARM ADDS ANOTHER FIVE YEARS TO THE DURATION OF YOUR EMPLOYMENT CONTRACT IN LIEU OF LEGAL FEES.

Can't be worse than death?
I hate being wrong.

13

SPITTING IN THE SHAFT

Just like that I'm back in my room, lying on my bed, my eyes open; position assumed. Might as well be back in the Hole.

I wait for Jonah to come back from wherever he is. Dinner isn't for an hour, so he might be with his goddamn paid-for-by-me therapist. I'm putting a quick end to that party. But I have no idea what I'll say to him, or do to him, other than blame him. I blame him for all of this. I need to blame somebody for my mistakes.

My father used to say, "Don't dwell on past mistakes, go on to make bigger and more expensive ones." What an asshole he was. Mistakes aren't trifling little things to be patted on the head. Mistakes need to be isolated and corrected before they become infinite in number and effect. Example: me coming to Farm. *Muy mal* mistake, right? We already know my life sucks and my mother is likely homeless, hiding from the street sweeps, or worse. But let's think bigger picture. If I hadn't come to

Farm and instead got a job in City that helped people—some environmental gig or social service, not that I was ever afforded the opportunity to training for such careers, but let's pretend for a moment that anything is possible—then I could be out there pushing for reform and helping and inspiring others to do the same. I could've made the world a better place in a million-million possible ways. Instead I'm here, inspiring no one, and ruining people's lives. I'm a contributing cog to the dehumanizing, environmentally toxic mega-conglomerate. My complicit choice to smile and wave during tours will no doubt result in future success in Farm employee recruitment. I ruin all those lives just by being here and playing along. There's also the subtle effect of my recent insubordination: BM's future judgments concerning employees will likely be more strict and unbending, ditto with the Arbitrator and lawyers, because you know those lawyers don't like their recommendations overturned. Future employees will be that much more miserable because of me, and it'll perpetuate itself: a perpetual motion misery machine.

So okay, blame it all on me. I can take it.

When I think about all my stupid decisions, all my little embarrassments, all my idle cruelties that might've changed someone's path, I attempt to place the scenes in order of severity of regret. It's crazy, but there's this one little scene I keep replaying, the mouth sore I keep poking with my tongue. And it's not what you think.

There's a jangle of keys then some clicks and clacks. The door opens. Jonah is home.

He says, "Hey, welcome back."

I hop off my bed and walk across the room. He closes the door and walks a wide path around to his desk like there's some force-field pushing him away from me. We're the opposite ends of a magnet.

I say, "There was a glorious three-month stretch when the elevator in my old apartment building worked. We lived on the third floor and there wasn't much to the walk up the stairs, but I loved that elevator. The adults hardly ever used it. I'd ask why and they'd tell me that they didn't trust it, or they didn't want to break it, or they wanted to keep it nice, it was so hard to keep things nice in our building and neighbourhood. There was old Mr. Lopez—he was all hunched, and kind of looked like peanut shell—he told me he would only use the elevator when he absolutely needed it. 'Best not to waste it, boy,' he'd say. He always called me 'boy,' but that's what he called all the kids in the building, so it never bothered me. He used to tell us bad puns if we saw him on the sidewalk or in the hallway. He'd leave a bag of Tootsie Rolls at our apartment door for my birthday. Nice guy that Mr. Lopez."

Jonah sits at his desk. He doesn't look at me. All I get is tattoo-face. He asks, "Why are you telling me this?"

"Now, I used the elevator. I used the shit out of it. Before school I woke up extra early so I'd be the only one awake, the only one riding the elevator. I'd ride it to the top, tenth floor, then back down, savouring the dropped stomach feeling and that instant of jellied legs. When the sliding doors opened on another floor I'd step off and pretend I was walking into another city. One better than mine.

"Then I started doing this: I waited for the elevator to rumble up to my floor, clanging its pots and pans ride through the guts of our building. I crouched low onto my hands and knees in front of the doors and when they opened I watched the elevator rise that last spastic hitch up to be level with my floor. I stared into that empty space, maybe half an inch wide where the elevator and my floor didn't meet; kinda like a slice of elevator shaft. Still on my hands and knees, I hovered my head carefully above the thin line between floor and elevator, then bombed away with spit. I spit into the shaft and listened, hoping to hear it hit bottom, but I never did.

"One morning, there I was in full crouch, my ritual pose, and the doors opened, and I did my spitting routine. When I looked up, there was someone already in the elevator. It was Mr. Lopez. I quickly stood up like I was caught with my pants around my ankles. His face was all folded up and he said, 'What are you fucking retarded, boy?'

"I froze. He shook his head, laughed a little bit, and breathed real heavy, like breathing was a chore. Then the doors shut just inches from my face, and the elevator took Mr. Lopez away.

"That was the last day I used the elevator. It broke a month later anyhow. After getting caught spitting,

I avoided Mr. Lopez whenever I could. I was so embarrassed to be caught doing my harmless, weird, little thing. My next birthday there was still a bag of Tootsie Rolls at my doorstep, but I didn't eat them. I gave them all away.

"That whole elevator scene seems kind of funny now. And I can't tell you why I was spitting. Just seemed like the thing to do, you know? But I was so goddamn horrified at the retarded crack and at myself. And whenever I think about that morning, all the old embarrassment and shame returns, full force. Crazy, huh? Of all the stupid things I've ever done— and that list is quite long and getting longer—I wish I could take that one morning back."

Jonah swivels on his desk-chair, giving me a side-long glance with both faces. That fucker squirmed throughout my whole little spiel, and I loved it.

Jonah says, "You're not helping me by telling me these things."

I say, "Just thought I'd share. Since you just came from your shrink, I thought the sharing would make you feel more comfortable."

"Shrink? I was working out."

He's twice my size and could kick my ass from here to the infirmary but I don't care. Besides, he's already wilting like an over-watered flower. "I know about it, Jonah. I know because Farm is making me pay for it."

He melts deeper into his chair. "Oh, I didn't know that, man, I'm sorry."

"Of course you knew."

"No, really I didn't. They told me it was covered under our medical insurance."

"Fine. But know this: you've just gone to your last appointment," I say and stick a finger in his face.

He sighs, then says, "You yelling at me isn't helping me cope."

Has he always been like this and I just didn't notice? "I just spent five weeks in the Hole, my mother might be homeless, they sentenced me to another five years at this fucking place and you're the one who needs to cope. So what does shrinky tell you to do? I'd like to know. Give me some free coping advice, Jonah. You're always so easy with all the other Farm advice. You're lousy with it. Now let me benefit further from your wisdom. Lay it on me, brother. I'm ready and waiting."

"This is exactly the kind of stuff Dr. Dale wants me to avoid."

"Dr. Dale? That's cute. I bet that's the shrink's first name."

"Look, I just want to keep my head down, do my thing, and let everything else happen around me. I just want to be. I resent you trying to push your mother or spitting problems onto me. Why do I need to know your or anyone else's miseries? I've got my own."

I leave him at his desk, and I pretend to inspect our white walls with our three Farm-approved paintings, each landscapes of the outskirts of Farm, places I've never actually seen during my time here.

I say, "My mother's bank account has been terminated."

Jonah nods, and says, "I've been here for twenty-two years. I'll probably be here for another twenty-two. And it's all been my choice." His voice sounds far, far away.

"Why?"

Jonah gets up and shrugs. And that's it. A shrug. A shit-happens gesture to give reason to why and how he's spending his life. Maybe it's an honest response. Maybe he really can't explain it to me, or to himself. Maybe he's just spitting down the elevator shaft. Maybe if I just accept his shrug as the end-all-be-all answer to everything, I'll be happier too.

He unbuckles his overalls and changes his shirt. I still marvel at his size and physique given his age and that eroded face.

He says, "Let's go to dinner. I'm hungry. I bet you're ready for some good food, right?"

"Damn it, actually, I am."

He slaps me on the back and says, "Just make sure we don't sit with the Chicken, that feathered-fuck has been stalking me while you were gone. He even asked me to be his roommate if you didn't come back. Do you believe that? We should pluck his ass."

And just like that he's the old Jonah. The pre-Orchard Jonah. The Duck-Chicken-Farm-tour-hating-and-tough-talking Jonah. Like all things and beings related to Farm, he's depressing the shit out of me.

14

A CVCKOO IN THE CLOCK

Back at the stalls. I've never left, really. Here comes the Chicken again. This time he's with BM and they're driving an ATV with a trailer. They pull up next to our stall.

BM says, "Hey, guys. Working hard or hardly working? Ha!"

His joke is almost as funny as the note he left me last night. This is what it looked like:

> I'm sorry to report that you missed your telephone-night while in Farm's custody. I tried like heck to get a co-worker or dorm-mate to switch a turn with you, but no one would budge. Sorry, kiddo. The call home will have to wait until your turn comes around again. Which is in three plus weeks.
>
> B. M.

P. S. Welcome back to the fold.

P.P.S. You're still my guy, buddy.

P.P.P.S. Don't be late tomorrow.

Remember, you are on probation.

The jerk actually signed the note with "B. M."

The killer is that if I think about all the previous phone calls and visits I've had with Mom, there's really nothing there, nothing of any consequence. I get only a blurry collection of fragmentary chit chat: *how are you?* and *you look good* and *I'm fine* and *oh, about the same.* Everything very safe and very forgettable. On the first visit she brought a care package of cookies, meatballs, underwear, and other motherly kind of stuff, stuff that she didn't really do when I was a kid. I do remember she seemed a little embarrassed by her gesture, even put off that she felt like she had to do such a thing. I told her she didn't need to go to the trouble. She didn't on her next two visits, which was fine because her cookies were hard, meatballs fell apart, and underwear wasn't Farm-approved. And that's just it. All those phone calls and the three visits: they were fine. I'm not trying to put this all on her. I was just as reserved and distant as she was. When the calls or visits happened, I'd get real quiet, say a bunch of nothing, and hurry myself out of the visitors' tent or off the phone as quickly as I could, like I hadn't been sitting in my room looking at family pictures and counting the days, hours, minutes.

"Good morning, gentleman," Chicken says and climbs out of the ATV.

Jonah and I mumble greetings back at him.

Chicken nods and walks to the Barn entrance. He bobs his head, clucks and bucks, and he perches on the motionless slaughterhouse delivery conveyor belt. Jonah and I stand at ease with our pitchforks. Animal sounds kick in. A tour is only minutes away. Jonah puts on his hat.

BM says, "BM needs you guys for a special job." He refers to himself in third person, now. "Security has some vid of an animal carcass up against the perimeter fence in the Free Range Field. The Free Range workers are busy with the quarterly inventory and we need you guys to go get it, clean up the fence if necessary, and whatever else you can think of while you're out there. BM appreciates it. But let this tour go by first."

Chicken hops onto the tram and becomes the tour leader. The kids wear straw hats and carry plastic pitchforks. The adults wear oversized Farm tee shirts, baseball hats, and sunglasses. Jonah, BM, and I stand, smile, and wave. Chicken asks the kids for a chicken-salute to us workers. His tinny voice crackles with microphone feedback. The tourists all cluck and wave. As the tram passes, two boys pretend their pitchforks are guns and shoot us. BM puts a hand over his heart and feigns death. We've all done this before. Even those kids. This isn't their first tour, and it won't be their last. The kids keep shooting and BM wraps an arm around my shoulder and laughs like I'm his long lost son. Only, I know I've never left. I've always been here. Just like Jonah, I'll always be here. I'll always do the same thing like the cuckoo in a clock who shrieks the same shriek at the beginning of every hour.

BM, still smiling, says, "So what do you guys say? You up to this special job?"

We nod.

"Great. BM knew he could trust you guys to help out." He tosses Jonah the ATV keys. "Jonah, you're in charge." BM rolls his eyes and nods his head in my direction. He's as subtle as a kick in the shins.

Jonah's shoulders sag. I'm his burden. Being in charge of me is the last thing in the world he wants. Can't say I blame him.

BM ambles away. I hop into the ATV passenger seat. Jonah crawls slowly into the driver's side. His head is on a swivel, looking all around, looking for help, maybe. He's not going to get it.

He starts the engine and I say, "Are we there yet, Daddy? Huh? Are we there yet?"

Jonah says, "You're not going to do anything crazy or stupid while we're out here, are you?"

Crazy and stupid are both good ideas. We're going to the perimeter fence and I'm going to look for a me-sized hole and dive through it. It's my new, simple plan.

I say, "Nope. I'm done with crazy and stupid. You can probably take off your hat now."

He does, resting the hat on the gearshift. We start on the long trip out to the Free Range Field and perimeter fence. Outside the Barn it's overcast, sky the colour of a wasp's nest. Shovels and other tools clank and clink in the trailer behind us. We drive out past the row of Barns, then into the Free Range field, driving past cows, llamas, turkeys, pheasants, horses, donkeys, cattle, goats, and sheep. All those animals open their mouths at me, but nothing comes out. I wonder if they want to say something, if they feel like they should have noises coming out of their hairy faces, or if just opening their mouths is enough for them.

As we drive, the animal population thins out, and eventually we're by ourselves in the field, but still with miles to go before we hit the perimeter fence. I take Jonah's hat off the gearshift and pull it over my eyes, looking for a quick nap, and perchance to dream of my vainglorious escape.

I say, "Remember, you're in charge."

15

SWALLOW THE DONKEY'S EYE

"We're at the fence," Jonah says and whacks my shoulder.

This is my first time out here. I wake, unslouch in my seat, and put Jonah's hat back on the gearshift. To our left is the perimeter fence; twenty-foot tall picket-fence, whitewash and all, supposedly tour-friendly in its gargantuan but quaint appearance. It's just another engineered mutant, or freak.

City and my mother are somewhere behind that fence. I say, "See anything yet?"

"Nope. But we should be getting close." He downshifts, and we slow to a roll.

"I think I see it." There's a brown lump against the giant white fence, just past the next swale, maybe one hundred yards away. As we get closer, there's a terrible smell, like a burnt rug. "Oh man, what's that?" I cover my nose and mouth.

"Toasted animal, I'm guessing."

"Toasted from what?"

"The fence is electrified. You can't really see it, but thin filaments cover the fence and weave between the pickets and posts. The animal must've touched the fence and *zap*."

"They must lose a shitload of animals this way." I want to tell Jonah he's full of shit with his invisible filaments story, but the zapped-animal aroma is compelling. We pull up next to a steaming carcass. The smell of burnt hair and shit is overwhelming and I put my arm across my face. Jonah seems unaffected.

"The fence isn't electrified for the animals," Jonah says and shuts off the ATV. He lets that one hang for the obvious implications. I nod and inwardly lament the loss of my dive-through-a-hole-in-the-fence ambitions.

Jonah says, "The animals have their own invisible fence and a chip in their backs that delivers a small shock if they get too close to the perimeter fence. This one must've bolted through the shock, or maybe his chip stopped working, or something." Jonah drones on with more theories of our fried animal.

I'm too beaten and tired to argue with him and the oversized and electrified picket fence. In fact, I'm making it official. Farm has broken me. I'm done, fried, zapped. For the tenure of my now extended work contract, I'll open my mouth and say nothing, like the rest of the animals, and wait until I'm upgraded, cancelled, terminated, replaced.

He says, "I think this thing was a donkey."

Too small to be a horse, its mouth is open but silent, tongue halfway out, caught trying to escape: a swollen, pink slug, bleeding. Its lips are burnt, rolled back and over its yellow teeth. Smoke blows through the chimney nostrils. One fleshy eye-socket is empty. I step toward the beast, extend a foot out, ready to nudge it with my boot.

"Whoa, stop. Don't touch. This ass's ass is still touching the fence. You wanna get fried?"

He's right. The donkey's backside is still on the fence.

Jonah goes back to the ATV and calls in on the two-way cell. He says, "We need the juice cut on the fence between posts 3658 and 3659." I have no idea how he knows the post numbers, but my dive-through-the-fence plan is alive again.

"The idiots are shutting off this part of the fence. They'll beep us when they're ready.

I notice angry-proletariat-guy Jonah is back. But I don't say anything, I just nod, and stare at the fence. Wonder how far I can run before security nabs me; *nabs* being a more pleasant word than the phrase *summarily executed*. Let's pretend I'm able to make it past the initial hurdle of the fence and Farm security, how would I make it through the checkpoints and into City?

Jonah says, "What a fucking mess, huh? We'll have to wash the blood and shit off the fence, and look, his belly split. We'll have to shovel all that fucking goo up, too. Goddamn donkey. My mother used to call a shit-job, 'swallowing a donkey's eye.' Anything that you had to do but was the last thing you or anyone else wanted to be doing, she'd say, 'I guess you just gotta swallow the donkey's eye.'"

Then he winks. Jonah actually winks at me. I hear the first piece of any real information about the guy who I've shared more hours with than anyone this side of my mother, and then he gives me a smart-ass wink. I want to punch him, render him unconscious, then maybe hug him before I jump through the fence.

"No shit. What did your mother do?"

Would Jonah try to stop me from running through the de-electrified fence, or will I have to knock him in the head with my shovel?

"She was my first BM," Jonah says, and then breaks up laughing; bends over, slaps knees, and eyes shut.

I have no idea if he's making this up, or if it's real. But it doesn't matter because I laugh too. And hard. We slap each other and the ATV. Jonah tries to say something, but the words break up and tear apart. We laugh and laugh and laugh.

The cell beeps. The fence is clear. I stagger past the ATV and to the back of the trailer to grab anything that might help me once I'm outside the fence. I'm still laughing. Laughter brings more oxygen into the body, and laughter gooses the release of adrenaline and other feel-good chemicals only the body can produce, and I'm feeling better. I feel like this can work and even Jonah will understand my defection. I'll get to City and find my mother. It'll all be okay.

Then there's this sound.

16

L IS THE LONELIEST NVMBER

Back when I returned to my dorm room, I didn't tell Jonah the whole story about the elevator. I don't feel guilty about it, because people never give the whole story. I didn't tell him about the elevator breaking.

After it broke, Dad-the-psychic told me he knew it was going to break, which was why he didn't use it. Mom, she told me later that the elevator had never been inspected and that the lift lines, supports, and breaks were rusted and rotted due to mould, due to too much moisture in the shaft. I knew they weren't telling me the whole story and that my spitting into the shaft had nothing to do with the excess moisture and the elevator breaking. I still believed it was my fault, though.

Mrs. Lopez was going to leave her apartment by herself for the first time in a decade. I'd only ever seen her when I went upstairs to visit them. She'd had her hip replaced years ago and needed a walker to get around. The stairs were impossible. Mr. Lopez convinced her that the elevator worked just fine, he'd been using it himself, a nice smooth ride, and she was plenty safe walking to the corner market to play her numbers if she wanted to. Mrs. Lopez loved her numbers, and Mr. Lopez had bought tickets for her every Tuesday and Saturday. He wrote her numbers in blue ink on the back of his hand, a temporary tattoo that was always there. But on that Saturday morning, Mrs. Lopez was going to pick her very own numbers, buy her own tickets, try her own luck. She had planned for a week. She picked a new, special set of numbers just for the occasion, telling me each one and what significance they had. I can't remember what they were anymore. Like her husband, she wrote them on her hand. It was practical; she wouldn't have to fumble through her pocketbook for them. She wore her nicest blue dress, nicest orthopedic shoes, and nicest hat, although, I was told she'd tried on at least five other hats before deciding on the blue one that looked like a curled up scarf on top of her head. Mrs. Lopez filled her pocketbook with change and she kissed Mr. Lopez on the lips. At the funeral, he told my mother after that the smile she gave him before leaving was a horizon, or maybe it was a sunset. Maybe it's something my mother made up to make me feel better.

Mr. Lopez watched her work her way down the hall, that walker's rickety and squeaky wheels barking and chirping the whole way like an excited dog going for a walk. He watched her horizon-sunset disappear.

Mrs. Lopez crept onto the elevator on the eighth floor, and then everything broke. The elevator was in free-fall for most of its trip. It crashed in the lobby.

Mr. Lopez used to tell a story about his youngest son, one I never met and who had long since moved out. His son thought that "L" for lobby was the real number one because **2** always came after **L** on elevators. I don't know if Mr. Lopez was full of shit, but it didn't matter. All the kids in the building loved to hear that story. We never failed to oblige with laughter at the end and someone would mock sing *L is the loneliest number*, and there'd be more laughter, comfortable laughter as if the L-to-2 story would always be there for us, would always be funny, warm, and safe.

I saw Mrs. Lopez's body. I was in the lobby. There was a ding after the crash, and the doors simply opened like they were supposed to, like nothing was wrong. Her crumpled blue hat rolled out onto the linoleum, along with other debris and some blood. Before I turned away and ran outside, I saw her legs. Her nicest dress was hiked up a bit. Her orthopedic shoes were still on her feet and somehow her legs were propped up, resting on the lower of the two bars on her mangled and squashed walker.

I had been playing in the lobby, rolling quarters up against a wall with my friend Jimmy and three other kids. The closest to the wall won the quarters. I was up three dollars. I was playing, but I was also waiting for Mrs. Lopez. I was supposed to keep an eye on her for Mr. Lopez, and help her out if there was any trouble. Not that I would've been able to stop trouble from happening.

On that day, there I was, with a fistful of quarters. The elevator was behind me. Then there was this sound. Not a crash really, but a roar. An animal roar: a giant, angry, confused, violent, dying animal, roaring its last and loudest. It leaped on and through me, and forced me to the floor.

Now, on this day, Jonah and I, we're laughing and I'm standing behind the ATV and at the back of the trailer, reaching for the shovels, and when there's this sound. I hear that animal. It's a new one, but the same. It lifts me off my feet and forces me to fly.

17

MARKING TERRITORY

My face is in the grass. I hope it isn't there all by itself.

I try and push myself up, but I fall back down. Things are hazy with smoke. My ears ring, but the whoosh and crackle of fire is somewhere behind me, and close. The skin on my forearms burns. My neck is sore. I roll over and sit up.

I'm at least ten feet away from the overturned, bent, smoking trailer and ATV. The perimeter white picket fence has a large, jagged hole. The wood around the hole burns. White paint turns black, wood turns to ash, and entire panels of the fence collapse. Translucent threads of filament hang and curl around the hole and the fire.

There's blood, hair, and skin on my body and on top of my clothes. Not *my* blood and skin and hair, at least, I don't think. I stand up, wobble, then throw up. But I can walk. And I do.

There's a body on the ground, on his back. His head is all twisted around, face pointed up at that gray sky, looking behind him for something, not at the ground. His eyes are open and not blinking, even with ash landing on his face.

I remember there was a donkey here. There was a donkey and it didn't have an eye. Someone must've swallowed it. That makes sense to me. Only, there's no donkey here anymore, just a charred, black spot on the ground in the shape of something, an outline, a disappearance. I fall on my ass.

Voices, shouts, and engine revs come from outside the fence and from behind me. A Jeep explodes through the fence hole, knocking out some of the white teeth, pushing through the ruined electrical circuit. The Jeep has no cover. Its passengers wear animal suits, but some of these look homemade, not the professional stuff we have here at Farm.

I think a dog is driving. Its eyes are offset, and cartoonish, and a goose or a swan is next to the dog, and behind them, two cows. The cows stand, gripping the rollover bar. Their udders are saggy, impotent. All those animals have guns. Big ones. A second and third Jeep follow the first.

The animals shout and make noise. The animals point their guns at me and then there are a couple of real loud growls and buzzing flies around my head but the flies don't stop to land on me. The third Jeep runs over Jonah's legs. He doesn't move. He doesn't mind. The Jeeps circle and I scoot over by our ruined ATV and sit, leaning my back against its dead body.

I try to shake the cobwebs out of my concussed

head. What am I going to do next? Screams and gunshots echo in the not-too-far-away distance. I feel a warm liquid on my head, and it runs down my neck and onto my back. It's very warm. Am I bleeding? How injured and messed up am I? If it is blood it seems I've suddenly sprung a catastrophic leak because it runs everywhere, soaking my front and back and arms. I focus on my pounding head, the source, and now it feels more like blood is landing on my head instead of pouring out, and underneath all the smoke and ash, there's this new stink, a pungent Barn kind of stink, a familiar-everyday-disgusting stink. And then a splash on my face, and a taste.

"Fuck!" I scramble away from the ATV into the open, the sudden movement making my head hurt worse.

There's that tour-leading, middle-finger-waving Duck standing on the ATV. And there's the back of his mallard head. That Duck straddles and hovers above where I was sitting, with its duck-leggings around her ankles. *Her* ankles. Those are definitely a woman's ankles, legs, and heart-shaped ass.

I put a hand on my soaked head and it comes back clear and wet and stinking. The Duck just pissed on me.

"You should've come back to my room that night. I told you I was going to piss on you," Piss-girl says. Lower Duck-half pulled back up, she shakes her tail feathers at me, flips me the finger, then shoots the ATV grille and console with double-barreled shotgun.

She jumps to the ground and points the gun at me. "I must say that was *sooo* good." She squeals. It's a sound that shouldn't come from a Duck. "I think I just came. We have to do this again. Looks like I might have to come back for you when this is over. Keep you as my darling pet. Oh, I'm getting tremors just thinking about it, momma's boy."

She grips her shotgun like a baseball bat, swings, and connects behind my knees, buckling my legs. I go crashing to the ground again. Maybe I should stay there. The Duck runs and jumps into the lone remaining Jeep, idling behind me, and zooms off. I watch her and then other Jeeps in the distance, the drivers wearing the bulky animal uniforms, waving their guns and driving in a migratory formation, going south for the winter.

18

BEING A CHICKEN IS NO WALK IN THE PARK

Jonah isn't breathing. Not that I expected him to be exchanging any oxygen for CO_2 at this point. I stare at his tattoo-face. Those ink-eyes open and expressive. There're no lids to pull down. Maybe I should roll him over onto his back, but I really don't want to see the damage. I can convince myself that he'd prefer to have his fake face up like this. It's only fair, that's how he lived. No, that's not a nice thing to say of the dead, especially since the dead is someone who I lived with for more than three years. But I'm done with nice. Looking at the hole in the fence and Jonah's body and smelling like someone else's piss, I'm so done with nice. I want real. I want true. Nice has nothing to do with real or true.

Another Jeep approaches. I hear it before I see it. It's too close and I'm too hurt for a quick dive and dash through the fence hole. I pick one of our shovels off the ground, then crouch and hide beneath the flipped ATV trailer. I just hope that whoever is in the

Jeep didn't see me. They'll probably be able to smell me, though.

The Jeep pulls up and stops next to Jonah's body. Everything is quiet. It's the Chicken driving, and he's alone. He hops out of the driver's seat and surveys the scene, muttering to himself.

He walks slowly around Jonah's body, and I wait until he stands with his back turned to me. Then I attack. I scrabble out of my hidey-hole brandishing my shovel. The Chicken turns to face me, but he's too slow. I whack him in the arm, maybe breaking a wing, then hit him like the Duck hit me, behind the knees, sweep out those chicken legs. He cradles his bum wing, screams, and goes down hard. An effective technique, but I'm not going to piss on him.

I grab a fistful of feathers, pull him close enough that my spit will land on his beak. "Did you come back to make sure I was dead?"

"Yes. I mean no, no, I came to help you. Jesus!"

I want to hit him with the shovel again. He looks like a piñata. "What the hell is going on here, Chicken?"

"Look, man, I didn't want any part of this, I swear. I didn't help them, but I had to keep quiet. Just about all of the tour leaders were in on the attack. They spent months trying to get me onboard. I don't agree with Farm's policies, but I wasn't willing to kill over it. I told them no way."

"Who's them?"

"Farm Animal Revolution Today. But I left the

group before the attack, I swear."

"This didn't all happen from within, did it? I saw Jeeps coming from outside the fence."

Chicken says, "There's a camp out there, in the woods. They've probably shut off the Farm access road by now. Dammit, you broke my arm!"

We're running out of time. Sirens sound and blue lights flash on the perimeter fence. That hole won't stay open forever. "All right, get up and let's go." I pull the Chicken up by his beak and push him up against the back of his Jeep. "You're driving."

"Where are we going?"

"City."

"What? There's no way. Even if we get past Farm security, how are we going to get by the revolutionary's roadblock and camp?"

The Chicken blabbers on more and I'm having trouble focusing because I see a Duck suit stashed in the back of the Jeep. Same as piss-girl's. A mallard duck.

I say, "Somehow I think getting through the camp is the least of our worries, Chicken." I wiggle out of my wet overalls, take the duck suit, and quickly put it on. "Just so you know, I fucking hate ducks. If I ever see a real one, I'm going to crush its skull." I hold up the shovel to show that I mean what I say.

"Hey, being a Chicken is no walk in the park, either."

We climb into the Jeep, roll away from Jonah's body, the ATV wreckage, toward the hole in the fence. Once we're through that ring of fire and onto the access road and grassy field beyond Farm, the Chicken says, "So why do you smell like piss?"

19

A GOOD COMPANY MAN

It's eerily quiet on the access road. Not much out here between Farm and City. Open fields give way to granite and rock quarries along with other industrial-excavation type monstrosities. Everything looks abandoned, but the mechanized and automated diggers and trucks do their thing on their own access roads that run parallel to the Farm road.

I expected security and SWAT vehicles to swarm, or helicopters to buzz us. But there's been nothing. Maybe the attackers have taken over Farm without anyone else knowing. We've been driving for a while now, with the bumps and potholes rocking me toward sleep despite my headache.

After I land a few more swipes on that bad wing of his with my shovel, the Chicken volunteers the following information. "I thought they were going to kill me today, because I was a tour leader that wouldn't help them. But they left me alone, completely ignored me as they overran Farm. It was kind of weird. My ex-girlfriend probably saved me. She's one of the biggies in the group."

"That's so sweet. Who is she?"

When he doesn't answer, I give him two more whacks on his arm with the shovel.

"Ow! Stop it! Okay, she's the Duck."

Fuck a duck. I hit him again. "So let me get this straight. You knew about their planned attack, which means you knew about the donkey bomb waiting for me and Jonah, didn't you? You son of a bitch! You let us drive out there. Jonah's dead because of you."

"No. No, I had no idea how they were getting in. I swear." Chicken's voice goes castrati-high. He begs and pleads, and feigns ignorance to the donkey bomb and the coup in the coop. After the attack started, he says he heard about the perimeter fence explosion, and he drove out to check on me and Jonah.

I don't really care if he's telling me the truth at this point as long as I can use him to get me back into City. I hit him one more time with the shovel. He cries out, but there isn't much force behind the blow. My movement is limited in the duck suit.

I say, "So your group calls themselves Farm Animals Revolution Today. You really call yourselves FART?"

"The founder was an ex-Barn Manager who liked the idea of media broadcasting terror reports using the acronym FART. He insisted it would help recruitment and viewer ratings with such a jokey name. I even heard he focus grouped the thing."

Chicken rolls down his window and spits sunflower seeds out of his beak.

"Where'd the hell you get those?"

"What? The seeds? I had them on me. Brought them with me, inside the suit."

"You always carry seeds with you?"

"Most of the time. Why? Is there a problem?"

We drive for another mile or two. He spits more seeds. I sit and stew.

Then, up ahead there's a truck and two automatic rifle toting Cows blocking the access road. Chicken slows and I say, "Let me do the talking," even though I have no idea what I'll say.

"No. I can get us through this. I know the password."

I really don't have any other choice than to trust him. We stop, the Chicken waves and says, "Baby beluga in the deep blue sea." The Cows lower their weapons and look at me. I wave and quack. It's all good enough for the Cows. They funnel us onto a dirt road to our left, one that disappears into a thicket of trees.

"Nice password. I thought you said you didn't know anything, weren't a part of the group."

"I only know a few things because of Sheryl."

"Sheryl?"

"The Duck."

"Right. I really don't like her."

"I surmised. So what's your plan?"

I blow a lot of air through my duck beak. "I'm working on it."

The Jeep's wheels bounce around in deep ruts. The Chicken says, "We'll be at the camp in three or four miles, I think."

"How do you know? Have you ever been there?"

The Chicken hems and haws his way through a yes. Then he says, "I know it looks bad, but I'm telling you, I didn't know anything about the specifics of today's attack, didn't know anything about the donkey bomb, all right?"

"Jonah was right about you, Chicken."

He shakes his head, and I know I'm imagining an expression (must be my concussion) on his chicken head, but he slumps and looks hurt. "Look, let me make it up to you. Maybe I can help scrape you up a new vehicle and some IDs, something to help you get back into City."

"No thanks."

"Or I can give you directions to Dump. You could hitch a ride on one of the automated trucks. It's easy."

I like that second idea, but I'm not telling him that. I say, "Stop here. Now. Or I start swinging the shovel again."

All the fight has gone out of this rooster. He pulls over, stops, and doesn't say anything. To his credit, he knows enough not to say he's sorry, to not lie to me again. I tell him to wrap his arms around his chest, and he does. I take the tips of the Chicken's arms/ wings, stretch them as far as they go, and tie them together. Voila, a makeshift straight jacket. I do the same to his chicken feet, and then I rolled him off the road, into the base of a thick bush. Should occupy him for at least an hour, maybe more.

I jump in the Jeep and start back down the double-secret dirt road, presumably toward the FART camp. I think about how easy that was with the Chicken. How he wordlessly complied with everything I did to him. He's back to being a good company man.

20

DON'T CALL ME JONAH

I curse myself for dumping the Chicken before asking how his ex-girlfriend—the revolutionary piss-girl Duck—knows my mother. How does she know that Mom is living with a junkie and on the verge of being homeless? Maybe the Duck was completely bluffing. Maybe Mom's terminated bank account is a coincidence, though that strikes me as highly unlikely.

It's too late to turn around and try to pry out some Chicken answers to those questions, because I'm here. I lay on the baby beluga password to a couple of coyote-looking guards, pass the checkpoint, and hit the camp.

Hidden among the trees, there are ten to fifteen large olive green tents forming a central compound, and dozens of smaller, individual sized tents dotting the area along with parked Jeeps and fifty or so people milling around. Some wear full animal suits, some wear the body with no head, and a few wear camo fatigues. It's kind of nice seeing someone, anyone, not wearing overalls.

FART members dressed in their campy mascot suits wave at me and the Jeep with their hands, and with their guns, some give me thumbs up, at least, the ones who have thumbs. I imagine Farm and then City under siege, attacked by these oversized stuffed animals. Teddy and Pooh Bears with machine guns, Pound Puppies with grenades and donkey bombs, and they dip their foam tongues in our blood during this, the first of the last wars, fighting plush-tooth and plush-nail, fighting like humans.

I continue my slow roll through the camp. I'm nervous about passing through the checkpoint at the other end, as I don't know if a simple password is going to allow me to simply drive toward City. My feathered-belly full of nerves is well founded as I find the checkpoint on the other side of the camp, and it's more heavily fortified: six machine gun toting guards and an iron barred barricade. I'm not driving through that. Baby beluga or not.

I turn around and park the Jeep next to three others in what looks to be an empty car pool. I'm hot and I smell, and ducking into one of the bigger tents to hunt for water and a change of clothes is something I consider. I decide not to press my luck. Instead, I take my trusty shovel and, with everyone else too busy to watch this duck, disappear into the woods.

The sun peeks through the clouds long enough to show me where it's setting, which is good, because it gives me a bearing on my position. I need to head south, across the Farm access road and hopefully, if I can trust the Chicken, to Dump and their automated trucks.

It's completely dark out by the time I emerge from the woods and hit the empty Farm-access road. There's a fog smelling of salt air and exhaust. There are no stars and no moon visible in the sky, not that I expected to see anything this close to City and its omnipresent smog and cloud cover. But I am close enough to see City's neon aura to the East. I cross the road, keeping City's glow to my left, and wade into a field of duck-bill-high tall grass, hopefully toward a different access road.

I stumble up gravel embankments and into mouldy troughs, through weedy patches, and crash through the muck and mire of a stagnant swamp, raising armies of mosquitoes and gnats that are able to find the cracks and breathe holes of my suit.

Hours pass. The swampy land finally gives way to a field of dried brush, then a flat and arid stretch that fills my lung with dirt and sand, the used minerals of a dead land. The bugs are still with me, though, and still getting bigger somehow. The good news is that there's a truly appalling smell filling my nostrils, one that I'm not used to. Dump can't be too far away.

One more mile of walking, my feet hit the jackpot. Pavement. I've found another access road.

Sticking my hitcher's thumb out isn't going to work. Quickly, I gather rocks and dried branches and lay them across the road. Hopefully it's enough to slow down and temporarily stop an automatic truck, but not enough to close the road. We'll find out. I sit in the bushes on an elevated embankment, and wait. It's here where I take stock: I still don't know for sure if I'm in the right spot. I don't have any ID on me. And even if I do get into City, don't get picked up in a street sweep or at the border, and by some miracle I find my mother, how am I going to help her? I'll likely be deported to the Pier with her.

I try not to sweat the details, and just hope that if Farm is truly in the midst of a revolution, me escaping will slip through the cracks, and I might be able to access my bank account somehow once in City. That, and I'm still wearing a duck suit, white feathers covered in muck and dirt, and it's all I've got.

My wait at the side of the road is surprisingly brief. An automated garbage truck rumbles down the access road. I think it's a garbage truck, anyway. It's too dark to glean a positive ID and the thing motors along without its headlights on, which is good news because it means the truck is in fact automated. It rolls to a stop before hitting my little road block, the pile of sticks and stones that couldn't break any bones. Once stopped, all manner of lights flash on: headlights, taillights, floodlights. The silver beast is a rear loading garbage truck, small front cab, and all metal and engine.

I jump out of my hiding spot and creep to the back of the truck. Up front there are electronic blips and bleeps. It must be scanning the road, determining if it can safely pass over the road block, which hopefully it can. I grope the rear side panels and find a button. I press it and the pneumatic compacting door opens. The garbage smell almost knocks me off my feet, but I climb inside the trailer.

The compacting door closes behind me. I figured that would happen, but it's still hard not to panic in the utter darkness of the closed trailer and give into visions of the door pressing me into flesh cubes. My duck feet slip and slide on the coating of leftover slime and gunk from its most recent Dump deposit.

The compacting door doesn't press me flat and the truck moves under my feet. We're off again and going up an incline. I slide up against the door, mashing my beak pretty good. I sit and hug my knees to my chest, to try to limit how much I slide, but I move with the slightest pitch in the road, falling left, right, front, back, as if direction has any meaning in the total darkness. And I laugh at myself, out loud, the manic sounds echoing off the tin can walls. I laugh because I'm still in a duck suit. I laugh because I'm stuck in the belly of the mechanical whale with no idea of how I'm going to get out.

Don't call me Jonah.

21

GETTING ΛTTENTION

There's this:

I was in sixth grade. I'd run home, again. Skipped out on the City bus, the unused tokens adding up in my backpack. I had no one to protect me. Jimmy wasn't out of school yet and no one else from my neighbourhood went to the private catholic school downtown. St. Sebastian's School, named after the saint who was plugged full of arrows. At that time Dad was a fill-in math teacher even though he never liked math. He usually stayed late to give the older kids extra help, or at least, that's what he told me. Can't say I ever saw him giving extra help, and Dad-the-psychic was always lousy ESPing that I needed him or his help. He sent me home by myself usually.

I skipped the bus and ran home because I was ducking those Coomer Project boys from two blocks north. They had a rep for taking kids off the bus and knocking the snot out of them, or making them eat stuff in Dumpsters, or making them give hand jobs or all of the above. I'd never been caught by the Coomer Project boys or seen them in action, but the stories of their exploits were good enough for me.

No bus. I opted for duck, cover, and run.

Mom knew what I was doing. She must've heard the jingle of metal when I ran into my bedroom and dumped the tokens into the not-so-secret stash I kept in my underwear drawer. But she never said anything to me.

I emerged from my bedroom, breath and galloping heart rate slowing down to a mere panic. Mom was in the kitchen and she leaned into the hallway. She said, "Everything okay?"

"Yeah."

"Come here."

I walked down the hall. I tried to hide my shaking legs and sweaty forehead but there were no hiding spots. I said, "What?"

"I want to give you some attention."

Attention was something she'd learned from her mother, so she'd told me. Mom hadn't given me her version of attention in years. I'd long grown out of it. We never said as much. It was a silent agreement, one that made sense and had permanent age boundaries in place. I was almost a teenager. Clearly too old for attention. I was embarrassed she was even bringing it up.

She put a hand on my shoulder and led me into the living room, then said, "Lay down."

I cocked my head, and couldn't speak without a rush of tears falling out.

She dropped to her knees and patted the rug. "If you don't want any attention, that's fine. I understand."

I lay down on the rug, on my back. The ceiling above me had cracks in the plaster. Mom tied her straightened hair up so it wouldn't fall into my face, then swung a leg over my stomach so that she kneeled above me. She smiled and hovered for a second. "We haven't done this in a while," she said and leaned forward. Our noses were only a few inches apart. She cupped my head under her hands. "Oof! Your head is much heavier than it used to be. My little baby is so grown up now."

"Mom."

"Okay, here's your attention."

She twitched her hands up and down. My head bobbed in a gentle and soothing *yes* motion. My face pushed up toward her round, still-young face and fell away and back up and away again. Our noses touched every so often and we giggled when they did.

This is part of why I'm going to look for Mom in City even if it means my own Pier deportation, arrest, or death.

22

LOOK WHO CAME TO DINNER

The truck has stopped moving. I hear voices outside, and some banging on the truck, but I'm strangely unconcerned that I'll be found or caught. Though I am a little frightened of what that means about me.

The truck starts again, going up another incline. Over the grumble of engine and wheels, I hear faint traffic noises. And with that, I know I'm in and riding the City streets in style.

The truck stops again, abruptly. This time the pneumatic pistons groan and I brace for an onslaught of light that doesn't come. It's still night, or early morning. There's some light, and it's artificial, engineered, of course; street lamps and neon signs and headlights, but nothing too bright. Not even bright enough to make me squint. The City light is dark and dirty. I don't know what I was hoping for or expecting. Maybe a baptism, a cleansing by golden light to welcome the prodigal son back to City. Nothing ever works out the way you want.

Two garbage bags fly in through the half open door. I fend them off with a wing and crawl toward the open door, and get there, swinging my legs out first, and kind of just spill onto the street. There are two garbage-collectors on either side of the truck. One has his hand on the compacting door button. They look at me, then at each other, shrug, and hop on the back of the truck and continue on their route. They didn't throw the escapee dressed like a duck more than a glance. They couldn't be more ho-hum if they tried. So much for City's famed no-one-gets-in-without-Us-knowing-about-it security system. That said, my head is on a swivel looking for any sign of City Eye, the surveillance vid that supposedly covers every inch of City.

I'm in the Industrial Center with factories and plants and smoke stacks towering above and around me. This is good. This means I'm in the south side of City. My old neighbourhood is only a handful of blocks northeast from here.

It takes a minute to lose my sea legs, and then I break into a jog, past the occasional diner and convenience store, past crumbling warehouses that lean on newer ones, past rows of smoke stacks, their mouths stained to ash, spitting their guts into the sky like they're doing everyone the favour of spewing their toxins a hundred feet above us instead of right in our faces.

Quickly enough I make it out of the Industrial Center and into the South End tenements. Here are the high rising apartment buildings and poverty-track housing mixed with decaying antique brownstones. Here's my old neighbourhood.

It's 4:30 AM. I spied the time from an ATM. There's a hard wind and needling drizzle dampening my feathers. I'm freezing, but maybe it'll knock some of the garbage-truck smell out of me. Sirens wail, but they're far away and don't seem to be coming closer. I pass a few shop owners. They sweep their sidewalks and prepare to open for the morning rush, but I don't pass anyone else on the street. The occasional cab drives by, the on-duty lamps dark.

I have no money or ID and I'm dressed like a duck. I have no friends or acquaintances here. No contacts. Nowhere to hide. Nowhere to go. Except my mother's apartment. I'm on autopilot, walking through memories to my childhood home. There's no thought as to what happens if Mom is there or if she is not there. There's no *if* anymore. Just my walking. And I'm walking the plank, but I'm ready, calm, accepting of whatever lies ahead.

There's my building. It looks an age older than I remember. The lamppost out front is down to one working bulb, and it flickers. No lights are on in the building. I stop myself from shouting to old friends who were probably never really my friends, who surely no longer live there. The sidewalk is cracked and displays its soupy papier-mâché of old newspaper strips, market bags, and cardboard food-containers. I find hints of drug paraphernalia too; nothing as overt as needles or vials or clips, but dead lighters (although I fish around and find a lighter that works), browned strips of filter paper and shards of bottle glass with caramelized spots.

I shimmy up the lamppost, then onto the rusty fire escape. My mother's bedroom window is open. I crawl inside, take off my duck head, and put it and my shovel on the floor. Even in the dark, I know the room is empty. No bed, no furniture, no pictures on the walls. I feel around for a light switch, find one, but it doesn't work. I don't need the light on to know that I'm in the right apartment. There's no way Mom would've moved without contacting me. Empty apartment and terminated bank account can mean only one thing. She's gone. More than gone, Mom is homeless. It's only a matter of if she's been shipped below City to the Pier or not.

I flick on the lighter and walk into the hallway, and I'll admit that faced with her homelessness and the *what am I going to do now?* circling through my head like a vulture, I wish I'd stayed at Farm where I was safe, where I was kept.

A flashlight joins my weak lighter flame in the hallway. There's a man holding the flashlight. He wears all black with a white collar. He's a priest. A father. My father.

Dad says, "Hey, kid! How the fuck are you?"

23

HERE ARE THE FOND AND QVAINT MEMORIES

Here are the fond and quaint memories of my father:

PAUL TREMBLAY

24

ALL THAT ANYONE NEEDS TO KNOW

Did you blink? Did you miss all those warm and fuzzy Daddy memories? If I could regress my memory to the moment of conception, daddy-sperm poking into mommy-egg, then that might be the sole fond memory of dear, old Dad.

Is that fair? Probably not. But I don't really care.

Honestly, I no longer harbour any active resentment toward the man. I understand he was a young adult when he made the decision to leave me and Mom. Was the decision right or wrong? Depends on who you ask. Probably for him, it was the right decision. For Mom and me? Didn't work out so good.

He's a father in name, and of course by vocation, but I really don't think of him as the person who filled the role of 'my father.' The thing of it is, shortly after he left I simply chose to remember very little about the man.

So here's all that anyone needs to know:

He's a Catholic priest and amateur psychic who left his wife and twelve-year-old child so he could be more priestly.

25

CONSCRIPTION CONNIPTIONS

My father says, "Nice suit. I'm so proud."

I still have my shovel with me. I should whack him once or twice with it, for old time's sake. I walk toward him and say, "Where's Mom?"

"Don't really know to be completely honest with you." He looks the same. Tall, thin but solid, anglo, short hair, close shave, big blue eyes hovering above an I'm-smarter-than-you smirk. He's the guy who'll always be older than he looks.

"I don't believe you."

"Believe what you want. Faith, some say it's a beautiful thing. Saps, mostly. But I'm just telling you that I found her apartment empty two weeks ago." He stops, then adds, "It's paid up for another two weeks," like it matters.

"She's homeless."

"Eh, I don't know about that. Not getting any of those vibes." He waves his fingers in the air like he's tossing around pixie dust.

I flash to some broken down church half-full of people attending his sermon, listening to gospels and his psychic vibrations, and I wonder which is more appealing. I wonder which gets more Amens and Hallelujahs.

I say, "Her bank account is terminated."

"So is mine, I think. Who am I kidding? I keep my dough inside a mattress. Interest rate blows, but it keeps the tax man and those pesky where's-this-money-coming-from questions away, you know what I'm sayin'?"

Oh, I know all about his mattress bank account and how because of his religious status he wasn't required to pay any child support. "I don't really fucking care about your situation," I say.

"Such disdain for your fellow man."

"I'd say I learned it from the best, but that wouldn't be accurate, would it? You didn't stay around long enough to teach me anything, *father*."

"Have you considered she could have a different, new account? You gotta consider all the possibilities before you jump to conclusions, man. And don't forget about my vibes now, I'm never wrong."

"I've considered the possibilities and of course I know it's possible she won the lottery or she ran away to Never Never Land. It's possible she hopped the back of a cow and jumped over the moon, too, right? Yeah, it's all possible."

"No need to get snippy with me, kid. I'm just saying she might not be where you think she is."

"Look, I try to deal in reality. She would've told me if she switched accounts and moved."

"Maybe."

There's a silence, and now it's time to ask the obvious. "What are you doing here?"

"I came to see you, my man."

"Wow, you really must be psychic then." I say it with all the sarcasm I can muster, hopefully so loaded on to make the sentence heavy enough to inflict bodily damage.

He takes the flashlight off himself and shines it in my face. The battery-powered yellow blinds me and throws him into deep shadow. There could be other people behind him, I have no idea.

"There's that. And City was watching you ever since you left Farm. Nice touch dumping that guy in the Chicken suit, by the way. He looked like a square and he's already been picked up, and dealt with, if you catch my drift. Sorry, but there was nothing I could do to save him."

There's no bluff calling here. I knew it was too easy getting in to City. My father must work for City now and wants something from me, wants to make some sort of deal. No way. It's time to make a mad dash out of this apartment. But after that, where to?

He says, "Ease off the paranoid thoughts, kid. I don't work for anyone but myself."

I say, "Not that I care, but I find it painfully fitting that the psychic priest who left his family presumably to save more people is telling me he couldn't save someone."

He shrugs. At least, I think the movement was a shrug. It's hard to see with the flashlight in my face. "Hey, I do what I can. Can't save them all. I'm just a working stiff, and all that jazz. But you, my fine feathered friend, I can save. Or at least, I can save you from the other dude's fate, or worse."

I stop myself from questioning worse. I already learned that lesson.

He says, "You're in deep dung, me boyo. This ain't gonna make you click your ruby-red shoes together, but there is a way out. That way out is me."

"You as my guardian angel." I can't stand it. My well-being, whatever that means, depends on this guy? No, he doesn't really care about me, he wants me for something, and whatever it is I don't want to do it. Instead of telling him to fuck off, I'm trying to be rational, weigh those proverbial options. I'll only get out of this mess and find Mom if I stop to think on my feet. Fighting the urge to run away screaming, I lean against the wall. "I'm listening."

He laughs. The fucker laughs at me. Now I think maybe I was too harsh on my old BM. His fraudulent camaraderie, his pretending that I was actually a human being was in fact preferable to honest, bald-faced hostility. My father's open and unfettered mockery is worse.

He says, "I'm not gonna lie to ya. What I have to tell you is nuts."

"I'm sure it is."

"No really, it's off-the-wall, looney-tunes, pass the ketchup, around-the-bend nuts."

Like I said. I'm sure it is. I'm sure it's as ga-ga as animals living secret lives as ventriloquist dummies, as gonzo as Farm and City poisoning the environment with behemoth gas and oil consuming machines because those machines and fuel sources boost the economy or at least boost the economy of some, as crazy as City's bureaucratized version of a higher moral power deciding to ship its homeless below City and into the Pier without any means of survival is somehow right and just and for the greater good.

I say, "Get on with it."

"I'm here to recruit you."

My turn to laugh. He wants to turn me into a priest or a monk or Igor or something, which of course, would mean forgetting about Mom. "What? Into the Church? So how is Catholicism treating you, anyway? Those no-meat Fridays must be tough."

"Jesus. Please. Don't be an asshole. I know you aren't white collar material. Trust me on that. You wouldn't last a day. It's City who wants you." Father Deadbeat-Psychic-Fraud-Dad dances a jig and points a finger at me, posing like one of those old Army recruiting posters.

"City wants me for what?"

"City wants and needs you to run for Mayor."

I don't say anything. I can't say anything. What he tells me isn't making any sense.

"I told you this was nuts. But it's gonna work out, trust me, kid."

Okay, listen to this:

A few hours after the elevator had crashed and Mrs. Lopez had spilled out, my mother and I were in my room. I was crying and she tried to soothe me with attention again. It wasn't working. Then Dad came flying into the room, all hustle and huff, and said, "What a shame. Sorry you had to see that, kiddo. Shit, I knew it was going to happen too. I tried talking to Mr. Lopez about it the other day. Wouldn't believe a word I said. I guess I probably should've told you yesterday about the crash. You know, you could've prepared, or the very least, made sure that you weren't in the lobby to see the damn thing happen." My mother wouldn't look at him and didn't stop the attention. My head kept bobbing, my father's form shaking in and out of my vision. I thought about Mr. Lopez and how he must've felt knowing Dad was right. I thought about what I would've done if Dad-the-psychic had told me. Then I wasn't sure if I believed him, if I believe he had tried to warn Mr. Lopez, or even if he'd had a vision of the elevator crashing. I wondered if all of everything he said was a lie, or if just part of everything was a lie, which would be worse because I didn't know what parts were lies. Did the truth matter if it was unrecognizable? Dad left us a week later. Neither Mom nor I saw it coming.

And right now, I feel like I did then.

He points the flashlight to the floor and says, "Yo, talk to me. You're starting to freak me out."

"Mayor?"

"So you did hear me. There's an election in two weeks."

"I don't understand."

"Neither do I to be totally honest. I'm not one for politics. Fucking crooks and liars the lot of them, but we're supposed to meet with your campaign managers and they'll connect the dots for us."

"Campaign managers? Wait, wait, wait. You're telling me you don't know the whole story?"

"Right now I'm just a messenger boy. Now you know as much as I do, almost. Congratulations."

"What about Mom?"

"If you're elected Mayor you can find anybody you want, shithead. We gotta get you out of this mess first, then you can worry about finding Mom. Christ, I wish you'd believe me when I say that I sense she's fine. She's okay. She's Jim and Dandy."

I look around the obviously abandoned apartment. She's gone and my father is here speaking nonsense about becoming Mayor. Do I think about this? Do I really think about all of *this*? Or do I just play along. I know what's the easier of the two options. It's always the easier of the two options.

I say, "What if I tell you and City to go screw?"

"Then you and your duck suit will be picked up and dealt with within twenty minutes. Sorry, kid, this running for Mayor gig is the only thing I could work out, and it will work out. I'm getting those kinda vibes."

"I don't believe a goddamn word of it."

He shrugs then rubs his hands together like a craps shooter looking for his seventh seven in a row. He walks toward me and says, "I can't remember the last time we were in this apartment together."

"I do. It was the same day you left."

"That's the spirit. Now put this stuff on." He tosses a small pile of clothes onto the floor. On top is a baseball hat with shoulder-length hair sewn into the brim. Inside the hat there's two balls of fur that look like dead mice. "Your clever, inscrutable disguise. Mustache and beard. I'm jealous. Could never grow a real one myself, kept falling off."

"Humour me. If I'm running for Mayor, why do I need a disguise?"

"A little slow, aren't you? Your mug is all over City TV and on the 'net. You're not a Mayoral candidate yet. You're still a dangerous FART terrorist; a bona fide villain who killed his way out of Farm and somehow managed to break into City. I've seen a preview vid of your escape, thrilling Bond-type stuff, man. If you weren't so goddamn ugly, you might make a good action hero. Regardless, when the rest of the public sees the vid, we'll be lucky if you aren't gunned down in the street." He bends down and picks up a long coat off the floor.

I can only imagine what the vid shows. I hope it doesn't show the Duck pissing on my head. I'd like to think the censors wouldn't allow something like that, but you never know.

He pats my back and says, "All right, let's go to church, kid. Then we gotta meet those people in the Zone. Heh. I know you're thinking that order is kinda screwy, right? Should probably hit the Zone first then church, you know what I'm saying?"

I want to say something cool, mean even. I've only spent ten minutes with my father-the-father and I want to hurt him, but goddamn me, I want to impress him too. It's all so fucked up. This is what I come up with: "You have no idea what I'm thinking." My timing is terrible. He's already walking down the hall, toward the front door of the apartment. I didn't say it too loud either, so I don't know if he even heard me.

He says, "Take your thumb out of your ass and let's go. We gotta get to the church on time."

26

TO NOT BE SEEN IS A SKILL

We stop in the dark and empty lobby of Mom's apartment building. I can't see much, but like the sidewalk out front, there's debris and used drug paraphernalia.

I say, "Before we leave, can't we ask people in the building if they know what happened to Mom?"

"There's no one here. Can't you tell this building has been cleared?"

Lovely. The building has been cleared and he'll still tell me he has a good vibe about Mom.

He says, "She's fine, kid. I'm not going to say it again. We'll get through this, too, but only if you do what I tell you." He talks low and fast. "A nice side-benefit from years in my cozy confessional booth is a lesson in how to evade City's Eye. As far as them law abidin' citizens know, there's vid cameras everywhere in City, in streets, alleys, public buildings, and even the cabs and buses, and they're constantly monitored. But I know where the hidden cameras are positioned and even where some don't work right. I know how to walk along the facades of certain buildings or along the left hand or right hand side of curbs and sidewalks and along the gutters of certain streets. I know when to cross to another sidewalk, when to merge with a crowd, when to walk under the shadow of a lamp. To not be seen is a skill. One that I have. So you just stay close behind me, so close we could be playing grab-ass."

I want to try and make a cool and smart-ass comment again. But we're out the door, and there'll be no talking now. It's brighter out than it was earlier, but most of City is still asleep. There's very little traffic, and the streetlights, lampposts, and the holo-boards wink on and off in cycles; City employs dead-of-night rolling blackouts to try and take the pressure off their energy grid. We walk underneath one holo-board that changes its ad with each flash. A tough guy smoking cigarettes with mostly-naked women draped on him, then a tough guy (might be the same actor, he looks the same) drinking beer with mostly naked women (and yeah, the women look the same too) draped on him, then a tough guy in jeans with clothed women draped on him, the women showing off tight asses in tight jeans, then a recruitment ad for Farm with those women somehow mostly naked in their Farm overalls, then a public service announcement decrying domestic violence and it features one of the previously almost-naked ad-women as a battered and bruised heap, then back to the cigarettes and booze and jeans and Farm and domestic violence.

There's a breeze and it moves my fake hair around. I wonder what Jonah would've thought about my disguise. I'm on El Priesto's tail and he leads us on a route that isn't very populated. He walks fast, and with purpose, doing as he said he would, crossing streets at seemingly random points, then cutting through some industrial parks and then ducking into dank alleys and garbage-strewn side streets I didn't know existed, which strikes me as damn odd. I thought I knew City, but I'm lost already.

Overflowing Dumpsters and orange City trashcans are everywhere. Blackened windows and a sooty film on so many of the buildings and parked or abandoned cars we've passed, and there's this smoke and chemical combo smell that I imagine will only get worse when the work-day kicks in.

We walk like this for an hour, then two. There's more light, but not much. Still dark out, and I get the sense today might be one of those dark City days. Clouds, ocean fog, and exhaust act like sun-block for City. Buildings that line the street disappear into the inkblot sky. We walk down more alleys and past buildings I don't remember. More and more lefts and rights and rights and lefts and City must be growing. I'm exhausted and hungry and lost. Now, we're passing people as we walk, but no one pays attention to us.

We're through another garbage-lined alley behind some broken-down tenements and liquor stores and emerge onto a cobblestone street. We're in Annotte, the government-sanctioned historical section of City. Holo-boards and vid screen advertisements aren't allowed here. The buildings in Annotte are the oldest on record in City. Some have claimed its Longesian Library even pre-dates Pier. The buildings here, even the tenements, are tall, brick and mortar, and cylindrical shaped, like posts; it's all very Pier-like. I know his church borders Annotte and it gives me hope we're getting close.

He says, "I know what you're thinking, kiddo, but we're on the other side of Annotte."

Goddamn ESP bastard. I think his ESP only works to make me miserable.

At least we're out of the alleys and walking on some main roads now. We walk past the Thomas Square market place. City workers erect a giant, circular tent and venders and shoppe keepers are all scurrying about. There's a grill and a deep-fry set up and I hear something sizzling and I smell doughnuts and cooked meat and my stomach folds into itself I'm so hungry, so hungry that I have to ask.

"Can we stop and get something to eat here?"

"Aw, asking Daddy if he can have little snack . . . no. We're on a tight schedule."

"I'm going to die if I don't eat," I say like a whiney little kid.

"A little suffering never killed anyone."

We don't stop for food. We walk through and then away from Thomas Square, and through more winds and curves and everything is maddeningly circular in Annotte. Pedestrians pack the cobblestone streets. Another two hours of walking passes into three, then four. It has to be past noon now. My limbs shake. My head hurts. I alternate watching my feet plant on the grimy cobblestone with boring a hole into my father's back and then gazing at the sky to see Annotte's pillars and assorted cylindrical buildings disappear into murk. But I still follow him. A walking machine, my thinking circuits turned off and needing a reboot, there's only left foot, right foot, left foot.

Annotte's cobblestones finally and abruptly give way to cracked and pot-holed pavement. Finally, we leave Annotte and hit Downtown. And there, right after that line in the sand, is the church.

There's only one Catholic Church in City compared to countless Temples of the Pier and the assortment of one-room back-alley joints catering to other religions and cults. It's only one church, but it is a big sucker. A magnificent wood, brick, and marble cathedral, five stories tall, replete with stained glass and spires sharp enough to make the sky bleed. I follow him up the marble front stairs that taper off and drop us at gargantuan, wooden front doors. He parts the great doors, my Moses of cured and stained wood, and their creak echoes inside the dark and cavernous church, and to me it sounds like the Pier is falling.

Faux-candles alternated with real ones line the walls and there's more walking. More lefts and rights and then a room-for-one-person stairwell and our footsteps echo like old, unanswered prayers. At some point we cross into the rectory section of the church as we pass empty living quarters, then up more stairs and into another lonely hallway, we stop halfway down and my father unlocks a solitary door and then into the lonely no-window room. There's one bed, and I go to it.

27

GROWING LIKE A MELANOMA

He enters the room like an explosion, and I wake up.

He says, "Like my dwelling? Fit for a humble servant of the Lord."

"How long have I been asleep?"

He doesn't answer. I think he wants to keep me confused, hungry, exhausted, compliant. But the joke is on him because I'm used to it.

He says, "I don't stay here as much as I used to." There's a bed, a closet, a desk with nothing on it, not even a Bible, a crucifix, and that's it other than the hardwood floors and plaster walls. He walks into his closet and defrocks.

I guess I'm supposed to care why he doesn't stay here as much as he used to, or care about where and what he's doing now. I don't. And I won't pretend I do. I sit up on his bed. The springs clang and groan. My head is a cloud and I get the sense I managed an impressive Rip Van Winkle impersonation.

He says from the closet, "It's not much, but it's still

a good set up. Free room and board. Four Dominican Brothers take care of the church maintenance, prepare my readings and homilies on the rare occasion I need to do anything like that, and they look after the rectory. Those old boys don't like me very much. Guess they don't approve of my lifestyle."

I say, "Who does?"

"Good point. Hey, if we're leaving and they see you and ask you anything, just tell them you're from below Pier. They're suckers for charity cases like that."

"What, I can't tell them I'm your son? Ashamed to have the bosses see me?"

"Hardly. You just can't afford to be seen yet. Sheesh, you are a paranoid martyr type, ain't ya? Too much like your mother."

"Fuck you."

"And may God bless you."

"Killing a priest in a church would bring seven years bad luck or something like that, right?"

"Nah. But you'd have such guilt." He steps out of the closet and he's not wearing his suit of trade. Black cowboy boots, worn blue-jeans, white button-down shirt opened to the sternum showing off a mouse of pepper-gray chest hair, a black leather overcoat partially cinched at the waist, and what I have to assume are night-vision glasses. The lenses take up most of his face. His hair is slicked back too, like he's going nightclubbing or something.

"Do you always dress like this?"

He smiles like some kind of predator; you choose

what kind. "You're just jealous of my skills."

He's starting to grow on me. Like a melanoma. I say, "You look like a mid-life crisis stooge." A fresh wave of hunger pangs attack along with the realization that no matter what I do, no matter what this guy set up for me, I'm in over my head. And no matter how bad off I'll be, it's probably already worse for my mother.

"That's the spirit, kiddo," he says. He walks over to his bed and bends over. I don't move. He shoves his hands beneath the mattress and they emerge with a fistful of cash and a small pistol. He holds the cash up and says, "Passport," then the gun, "and the insurance policy."

The threads and glasses and slicked hair add up to a good look for him. I can admit it. He could be some aging but hip movie star, or even a comic book character. How about Priest-Man? A cross in one hand and a can of whoop-ass in the other. He tucks the gun into his right boot and quick, like it fits, like it's supposed to be there.

"Let's go," he says.

"Goddamn it, I need something to eat. You have any food?"

"The cupboard is bare."

"What the fuck were you doing while I was asleep? We have time for you to get all duded up, but I can't get a morsel to eat? I haven't eaten since Farm breakfast, which was a century ago."

"Buck up, buckeroo. This side trip was necessary. I can't take you into the Zone empty handed, so to speak," he pauses, tightens his overcoat and adds, "and dressed like Father What's-his-face from *Our Town*. What are you bitching about? You took a big old nap. Now come on, we were supposed to meet with your campaign managers ten minutes ago."

28

IN THE ZONE

He let me sleep a long time. It's night again, but not sure exactly when, or even what day it is. I adjust my slept-upon disguise and we're out of the church and into Downtown. Lights and signs flashing and a sea of downtown noise, revving engines, horns, street chatter, and all the ad jingles playing from speakers of unknown origin and coming from the Ad Walkers. Those Ad Walkers work all hours, wearing their silver jumpsuits with flat, holo-screens on their chests and oversized baseball hats branded with company logos. They grab people from the crowded streets and force them to watch their ads. People usually break through a lone Ad Walker, but the larger ad campaigns tend to work in gangs and are more successful in trapping quarry. Just ahead is a gaggle of Farm recruitment Walkers with their hands all over a young male. That guy is all done. They have one arm pinned to his chest, the other in a chicken wing, his legs tangled in their legs, and his head in a headlock. He'll have to watch every one of their ads before they release him back into the wild. My favourite Farm ad is the one that says, "Do you have what it takes?" as it shows some muscle-bound stud scaling the Upshore Cliffs, and when he reaches the top, he stands overall-clad in front of an army of overall-clad clones looking ready to kick some ass for Farm.

Papa Padre turns to me and says, "Those guys get real aggressive during the evening commute. Gotta keep it moving, and quick." We kick our pace up a notch, actively working at not getting hassled or sidetracked, or in my case, arrested and/or shot.

I think about ditching Father Fuck-up right here. I could easily get lost in this crowd. But what then? I have no money and nowhere to go. I don't believe his kaka story about campaign managers and me running for Mayor. Not for one second. I do believe one part of his tall tale though: me being set up as some sort of patsy.

My father says this out of the side of his mouth and despite the crowd and all the noise, I hear it. "I know what you're thinking, but you can't run now, kiddo. Nowhere to go."

I choose the I-will-hate-you-silently technique of nonresponse.

He says, in concert with one of the giant ads playing on a holo-board above us, "Don't hate me because I'm beautiful."

Would the psychic priest see my fist colliding with the back of his skull before it happens?

We pass under another holo-board that spans the width of the street. This one showing a clip of a busty young mom driving a continent-sized global-warming-on-4-wheels SUV dropping off her nerdy son at school, but all the kids think he's cool because of his pimpin' ride.

We swim upstream, passing packed coffee shops and cafe nodes. There's a ton of suits working through the crowd. I assume most of them can afford City-approved stun guns to scare off the Ad Walkers. Buses as big as whales struggle down the cramped streets and then beach at street corners. Cabbies and cops knife through the traffic. We're just two blocks from the Zone and across the street is a Pier Wagon. Four cops swinging light-batons spill out of an alley with a stunned and flash-burnt homeless person in tow and stuff him into the van. At least I'm supposed to assume the person is homeless given the deployment of a Pier Wagon. There's a wind and a buzz above us, something flying overhead, its spotlight cuts through the night and fog and shines on the van and then randomly on the buildings. A group of kids applaud the Wagon show, before sprinting away from three Ad Walkers and their Toy-Taser ads. Most of the adults walkin' and workin' these streets turn their backs and tend to their own business. They know better. They know that they're only one paycheck away from being loaded into a Pier Wagon.

We turn right and my father says, "We're here. Watch yourself."

The Zone. It's a dead end street that's closed off to traffic. Holo-boards broadcast condom and natural male enhancement ads, spotlights and laser anime and neon signs hang off gutted and converted brownstones and leer through giant glass windows of the newer sex shops. Ad Walkers and Baiters wearing cat-suits (some red, some black, some flesh-coloured) and microphone headsets stand in front of their respective places of business barking and selling their wares to a backbeat of loud and fast electronic music, the same kind of crap they played at us during Farm social night. It's almost enough to make me check the overalls I'm no longer wearing. Other vendors and dope dealers aren't relegated to the sidewalk shadows in the Zone. They set up camp in the middle of the street.

A pulsing sea of people jam the Zone but I don't worry about being recognized here. It's the type of place where folks agree to be anonymous. My father sure has been recognized, though. Men and women shout his name and he shoots them back a nod or a smirk, super hip super cool padre that he is. More than a few folks pat him on the back and whisper in his ear. No one gives me an I-see-you-and-acknowledge-your-existence glance. I like it that way.

We walk past the *Voyeur Dome, 2on1, The Animal Farm*, and countless other places toward the dead end, funneling into the *Boutique*'s rounded and metallic façade. A blue, cursive neon sign hangs above a blue awning that stretches from one side of the street to the other. When I lived in City, this place had the rep of being the cleanest and safest and therefore most expensive joint in the Zone. As kids, we used to sneak into the Zone's back alleys but would always get chased off by bouncers and other security.

There's a line of people contained within velvet ropes. No idea how fast this line moves, but I would guess it'd be hours before some of these people get in. My father grabs my shirt and leads us to the front. There's some booing and hissing in our direction but electronica music overwhelms the rabble's complaints. Three Hulk-sized bouncers wearing headsets and an assortment of weapons strapped to their belts man the front door. Each goon visibly recognizes my father, and they even crack a smile as he uses some of his passport to line their palms. They let us in.

I say, "Come here often?"

He says, "Yes and yes, and oh yeah."

I almost wish that I knew or . . . cough . . . loved my father well enough to be disgusted at his double-entendre response.

There's a clear, bubble-shaped booth straight ahead. An older woman sits inside, smoking two cigarettes at once, purple lipstick smeared all over the filters, as if the cancer sticks had been dipped into a plum. The smoke stays trapped in the bubble, forming clouds around her head and clinging to the clear walls. She exchanges money for colour-coded key-chips.

"What do you think, kiddo? Time for a quickie? Sonya is my favourite."

This is where, if I had any guts, I'd punch him in the face or whatever body part opportunity might present. But I have no guts. I'm too tired, hungry, and lost to have any. I say nothing and sidestep the booth.

He knocks on the bubble. The woman waves her cigarette hand and raises her skin-curtain into a smile, showing us more purple lipstick on her teeth.

We're allowed to pass through an *employees only* door, and we walk up a metallic spiral stairwell, four flights and then four more. We emerge into a corridor with no doors and smooth, metallic, tube-shaped walls. Florescent lights above have a blue tint, like the neon signs out front. My father's boots crack like gunshots on the black linoleum floor. After maybe twenty steps there's a door on our left. It's flush with the wall and it's the kind of thing you can only see if you're looking for it.

I say, "What have you gotten me into?"

My father says, "No worries. Stand here and look handsome, like me."

29

PERV LIKE ME

The door opens and there's classical music playing. Piano and violins sound canned and tinny in the metallic hallway. There's a big boardroom with mahogany (just like the Arbitrator's room back at Farm) desks and molding. The floor is hardwood. Flickering flat-screen monitors fill one wall and giant bay windows take up the far wall. Greeting us are a youngish woman and youngish man in matching, dark blue business suits and white, button-down shirts displaying their matching socio-economic and ethnic backgrounds, and their matching hands folded in front of their bodies with matching heights and matching hair length and matching skin tone and complexion, and matching smiles that should be reserved for greeting a Messiah, not a patsy.

I shouldn't walk into this room. But I'm doing it anyway. I should be doing this: leaving. Instinct is telling me to fly baby fly and then hide out somewhere, become anonymous, find some shit job in City and lay low and look for my mother my own way on my own time, but I'm not, I'm telling instinct that I know what I'm doing, telling instinct to bugger off.

The suits say, "This is fantastic, Father, really," then, "You getting him here in one piece," then, "Amazing. Stupendous," then, "Your service will not be forgotten."

I don't know which person in a suit spoke first, their voices fall into the same gender-neutral but falsely exuberant tone, and the words come out so fast I can't lip read to see who's saying what. They each reach for something on the back of their wrists and the music's volume fades into the background of the big room.

They say: "You are truly a prince of City, Father," then, "We should be propping you up to be Mayor," then, "Ha ha," then, "Ha ha." They exchange a glance and walk toward us with extended hands. Everything they've said and done has occurred during the time it took for us to walk through the doorway.

Padre says, "Yeah, yeah, yeah, nice to see you, God bless, mazeltov. Kid, meet Chris Zrike and Kris Cotter. They're to be your campaign managers."

"Wonderful to meet you," then, "Pleasure is all ours." They both pump my hand, and even their handshakes feel the same.

"Come in," then, "Make yourselves comfortable," then, "Drink?" then, "Food?"

There's a catered spread just to the right of the entrance. I say, "Hell yes," and dig in. Cheese, fruit, rolls, cold cuts, and some fancy chicken-tuna-potato-salad type finger sandwiches. I swallow three whole without chewing. Then two more. There're sweating bottles of beer, pitchers of water, and coffee. I drink. I eat. Repeat. And at this point, I don't care if it's my last supper.

Padre says, "Don't you know it's impolite to binge alone?"

I look up from my feeding frenzy and notice my father is over by the huge bay windows, standing and talking to the suits. To my right is a wall of flat-screen monitors. Some screens are in colour, some in infrared.

Filling those screens are the *Boutique* clientele, the Janes and Johns, and they're all fucking like mad. I can tell who are the buyers and who are the sellers as the sellers have blue hearts branded on their shoulders. There's no volume to go with the wall of naked and animated flesh.

The canned classical music floats around the room like a commissioned ghost. Almost looks like the fucking-folks are wrestling. Maybe some of them are. All the colours from the sexual rainbow are represented here. There are some rooms where I don't really know what's going on nor do I care to. And holy shit, there's a guy in a duck suit (what is it with those fucking ducks?) getting his groove on with a doe-eyed, spread-eagled *Boutique* beauty.

The group pow-wow is still over by the windows, and I hear, "We apologize for that," then, "Turning down the volume is the best we could do."

I shrug.

Padre says, "See, I told you he's a perv like me. He doesn't care."

I grab a bottle of distilled water and meet them over by the window. I get a panoramic view of the Zone. The surging crowd is enclosed by towering brick and concrete structures, their giant neon-signed holding pen.

I say, "So what's the story here?"

"It's simple," then, "The Mayor grows weary," then, "A bout of ennui," then, "He wants some competition," then, "To get the old political juices squirting again," then, "So per his request: an election," then, "He needs an opposing candidate," then, "We'd like that candidate to be you."

I watch and damn it, those suits talk so fast I still can't figure out when one is talking or not talking. Really, they're pissing me off and I'm thinking about Farm again, how these two soulless freaks are the engineered animals now and there are some hidden speakers somewhere in this room speaking for them. That said, if they're the animals, I'm not sure what that makes me.

I say, "You, and I mean all of *you*," and I glare at dear old Dad, "have to know I don't believe any of this, or trust any of you, and the only thing I'm confident about is me ending up dead somewhere while people sing Hail to the Chief."

"We're giving you the straight scoop," then, "No funny stuff here," then, "Of course, we can't guarantee your safety," then, "Just as we can't guarantee our own safety," then, "Exactly, on our way home we could get hit by a taxi," then, "Or a bus," then, "Probably a Pier Wagon," then, "My goodness, maybe we should stay here," then, "Ha ha," then, "Ha ha."

I say, "Father Dad, are tweedle-dum and tweedle-dee telling the truth here?" which is probably a tweedle-dumber thing for me to say. The more prudent act would be to wrangle Father ESP away to a quiet corner and ask him about what vibes he's getting from the manic duo. Prudent schmudent. I want to make things difficult. I want to make everyone in the room, especially him, squirm. I might be their patsy, but I ain't easy.

There's a delicious silence, then Dad says, "I cannot tell a lie. They're feeding it, whatever *it* is they're feeding you, to ya straight."

He's lying. He's telling the truth. I have no clue. I can't read him. I don't know him well enough to read him, and he hasn't taken off his night-vision glasses yet so I can't see his eyes.

He adds, "I'll leave you folks to chat it up. I'll be over on the couch, serveilling the surveillance if anyone needs a priest." He pats me on the shoulder oh so fatherly-like and smiles as if to say, *if you gonna play games with me I got your checkmate right here, dumbass.*

The suits chime in. "We understand your position," then, "This all seems so strange," then, "Counter-intuitive," then, "Logic defying," then, "But rest assured, there is a plan," then, "And it's a solid plan," then, "Been worked on and honed," then, "And fine tuned," then, "For months."

I say, "I haven't been a wanted Farm-escapee for months."

"No," then, "You haven't," then, "But we've been searching for a candidate now for months," then, "You're the right one," then, "You're perfect."

I look back to the couch, to my father-the-father, and goddamn me I want him to save me now.

He isn't even looking over at us. He's reclined on the sofa, arms spread apart, whistling and talking about someone's ta-tas.

They say in unison, "Read this letter from the Mayor."

They stick an envelope in my hand, my name in calligraphy, wax sealing the flap. I open it.

30

Δ LETTER ΔBOVT Δ FRIDGE

The letter, dated yesterday, written in an olde English style, complete with random ink blots and stains:

Dear Possible, Future, Mr. Mayor.

How does that strike you? Probably as wild fantasy given your current societal position as a wanted terrorist. By the by, I've seen bootleg footage of your escape, thrilling stuff. It should hit the streets any hour now, which will make things that much more unpleasant for you, but ah, that's life in the big City. Nevertheless, you becoming Mayor is still a possibility, made more so by my insisting that my top two political strategists head your campaign. All I ask is that you fight to the end.

Do note, I am asking you to fight. I expect you and your campaign managers to try and win this election. Take the high road, low road, mudsling, whatever you need to do to defeat me. I can take it, and I will be fighting back just as hard. I fear the lack of political competition through these most recent years has made me staid, stagnant, complacent. A hotly contested election is what City and myself need. The press and interwebbers will eat it up. Not to mention campaign donations and tee shirt production and the like. We'll be a boon to the economy, regardless of outcome! Democracy! It'll be beautiful. I hope you're as excited as I am.

Of course, I expect to crush you like a bug, however, if you simply fall down on your sword before me, I'll ensure you experience the fate that usually befalls a terrorist, a la your chicken-suited ally.

Before I wish you luck, let me tell you a story. When I was a boy (yes, this old warhorse was a boy once), there was an old woman living in the South End projects who had a refrigerator that kept her food cold despite the motor having burnt out years prior. The little light bulb inside didn't work, but she didn't care because her food stayed cold. Gossip and grapevine led hundreds of neighbours, local hangers-on, and even a selectman or two to her humble apartment and into her dingy kitchen to see the miracle fridge, and she always kept a visitors' supply of hot-dog finger sandwiches in that fridge, despite her dire financial situation. As word got out, more and more people came. Some people threw their loose change inside the fridge, like it was some kind of wishing well or one of those fountains in the mall where children foolishly throw their coins. Others took pictures with the old

woman and the fridge. Others brought their own
magnets to leave on the metal doors, the magnets
inscribed with missing loved ones' names or little
prayers. Others called her a fraud and a sham and
searched for evidence of battery power or alternate
fuel sources, and when finding none they claimed
the air inside the fridge was no colder than the air
in the apartment. A group of University scientists
examined the fridge and found the temperature at
a constant 39.4675 degrees Fahrenheit, then spouted
all sorts of theories about electromagnetism, quantum
physics, and environmental conditions they couldn't
prove, yet they still proclaimed another victory for
science. At last count our esteemed City University
Press has published thirty-six scholarly articles on the
refrigerator. Then there were the various religious
leaders proclaiming the wonder appliance as proof of
the mystery of God.

Regardless of who made the pilgrimage to her
refrigerator, she let everybody in to see for themselves,
and they all asked her what she thought about her
miracle appliance. Her response was always the same,
"Don't know and don't care. Keeps my food cold."

Isn't that a wonderful story? All true! Why tell it?
I told it because this story relates to your newborn
campaign. You may think you have no shot as a
Mayoral candidate because of the terrorist and Farm-
escapee stuff. But never underestimate the power of
the public to see what they want to see, either in
their political candidates or their kitchen appliances.

For what it's worth, City officials eventually confiscated the refrigerator in order to run more tests. The results of which are classified. But if you do defeat me and become Mayor, I'll take you to see the fridge myself. That daffy machine still works like a charm. In fact, I might have to put a bottle of City's best champagne in there for the election's victor!

Good luck and may the best man win.

Yours in Mayorality,

A. S. Solomon

31

SHIT END OF THE STICK

Solomon has been Mayor of City for as long as I've been alive and I can't remember who was the previous Mayor or when that was. He's always been there. Heck, I don't remember the last time we've even had a Mayoral election that wasn't uncontested. And now I know that Mayor Solomon is unquestionably out of his mind.

I fold the letter back up but can't force the stupid parchment back into the waxed envelope. "Um, this guy is nuts."

"He told you the fridge story," then, "Yes, of course he did," then, "Ha ha," then, "Ha ha."

My father is still sitting on the couch, enjoying his peep and porn shows.

I say, "Yeah, he told me about the magic refrigerator."

"That's our Mayor," then, "You gotta love him."

Still can't get the letter in the envelope, so I throw it on the floor. "Let's pretend any of this is legit for a second. How is it you guys can whip up a new election like this?"

"Recall election," then, "It'll be announced tonight," then, "Along with your candidacy," then, "In two weeks there'll be ballot questions," then, "One will decide whether or not to continue subsidizing no-kill animal shelters," then, "Another question will relate to decreasing transaction taxes in the Zone," then, "Another ballot question asks to revoke the 100 foot Ad Walker-free buffer around schools and churches," then, "And the final question will ask if there should be a recall election," then, "If the voters choose yes, they will then have two choices for Mayor," then, "You and Mayor Solomon," then, "You'll be labeled as an independent," then, "We didn't think you'd mind."

"Oh, I get it. This isn't ennui on the part of the Mayor. He's done something wrong and is being recalled and you guys are here to set up a patsy to lose. I'm your perfect candidate because there's no way I'll win."

"No, no," then, "No, no," then, "This is all by decree of Mayor Solomon," then, "Sure we bent his ear," then, "Did some persuasion," then, "Some convincing," then, "But the important thing is," then, "He believes it's all his idea," then, "He'll explain to the citizens tonight," then, "We're going to make you a legit candidate," then, "Spin your soon-to-be infamy into celebrity," then, "A true politician," then, "A folk-hero," then, "Someone who could actually win."

I can't say I ever expected or wanted to be part of a

conversation like this. My suitably intelligent and all-encompassing emotional response is: "Yeah, right."

"Really," then, "Most view Mayor Solomon as imperial and God-like," then, "But the numbers show he's too God-like," then, "Out of touch with the common man," then, "Grapes of Wrath sort of thing," then, "Yup, losing his humanness factor," then, "All the polls say so," then, "We can take advantage of that," then they say in unison, "We have a plan."

They lead me to a table and sit me down. There are stacks of contracts and papers, and if they were talking at me fast before, they've gone into warp-drive. Their voices drone along with the classical music and the hooting and laughter of my father on the couch, but I don't hear any of it. Life was so much easier at Farm.

"Hold it!" I yell. They stop talking and stare at me. For a crazy moment, it even seems the writhing naked flesh on all those screens stops. "What if I decline your candidacy nomination?"

"You walk out of here," then, "Public enemy number one."

"I only escaped Farm to look for my missing mother."

They both shrug, looking bored, like I'd asked them the simplest, plainest question possible, like I'd told them something utterly ridiculous. "Become Mayor," then, "Then you can find anyone you want," then, "You're not going to find her from jail," then, "You're not going to find her if you're dead."

My father shouts from the couches, "You're being conscripted! What an honour!"

I get up and walk over to him and say, "Can't you grant me asylum or something in your church?" As soon as the words are out of my mouth, I want to stab myself in the pancreas for begging him for help.

He shakes his head and says, "Nope. My church hasn't been allowed to grant asylum for decades. Us Catholics get the shit end of the stick in this town."

In the end, there really is no decision, is there? I've spent the last three-plus Farm years as an automaton taking orders, what's a few more weeks? So I spend the next hour signing contracts and pretending to listen to their coffee-on-speed speeches and directives. They have me read and sign off on my official platform, my campaign promises, which are very vague and speak only to the nebulous idea of sweeping change and the common person's perspectives, to get an outsider in City Hall, and similar kinds of bullshit.

A youngish Asian woman with a hand-held vid-cam enters the room. Her black hair is tied up beneath a black, logo-less baseball hat. She says nothing and takes stills and vid of me sitting and standing in different positions, then shoots some vid of me walking. My father heckles me the whole time, saying shit like *my, what a pretty pony*. Everyone but me laughs with him. My campaign managers (I'll call them *the CM* from now on) tell me that they'll be able to make ads from this simple footage. They tell me about all the holo-board space they have and the elite team of seven Ad Walkers ready to go. They record me saying that I approved this message, whatever this message is, whatever the message they want it to be. Yeah, I'm the voiceless animal now, with the CM fixing to pump in the fake sounds.

A few more shots, a few more smiles, a few more ponderous and solemn leader-type facial expressions into the camera and the CM say, "That's a wrap," then, "Very good, very good," then, "We're on the path to victory now," then, "No one can stop us."

I say, "Yeah, great, I'll be sure to save a spot on my cabinet for you folks."

They laugh, but then flip through three-hundred pages of contract to show me where I already promised such positions of power in the event that I do win the election. And oddly, I find this comforting. I mean, I don't find the monstrous, what-did-I-actually-sign contract comforting as I'm sure somewhere in there they now have legal claim to my spleen and kidneys, but it does make me feel better that these two parasites have something to gain from my success. Man, I'm as phony as they are.

I say, "So what now?"

They tell me. To be safe, I still need to go into hiding. No telling what whackos might do to me when the Farm escape vid is released. I'm to go with my father-the-father under City, down into the Pier, more specifically to his charity, simply called Home, set up adjacent to the old Dump; a fabled mountain of refuse that suddenly isn't so fabled. Melissa Madsen—

the intrepid cameraperson—is to accompany us and document my helping the discarded for the TV show.

I say, "What TV show?"

The CM say, "This is the best part," then, "Our secret weapon in this campaign," then, "The Mayor doesn't even know about it," then, "He's going to flip when he finds out," then, "Yes, this will scare him," then, "This is our coup," then, "The major network," then, "City Broadcasting Company," then, "Is giving us a nightly one-hour show for these two campaign weeks," then, "Reality TV, of course," then, "Called 'The Candidate,'" then, "They're excited," then, "Given who you are and where you'll be it'll be the highest rated show of the season," then, "Maybe the decade," then, "And for us we'll get all that free air time," then, "All that free publicity," then, "You can't buy exposure like that."

My father gets up off the couch and slaps me on the back, hard enough to force the air out of my lungs. He says, "My son, the TV-star-Mayor guy. I'm so goddamn proud, I could just shit."

Then, there's that crashing elevator sound again, an explosion (I'm fast becoming an expert on explosions, aren't I?) outside of the *Boutique*. This sound is muzzled a bit, but still snaps hard against the almost-sound-proof bay windows. The screens on the wall shake and tremble and go fuzzy for a second. But the people on those screens keep fucking.

We all step toward the window to look out into the Zone. There's billowing smoke and a column of fire near the Zone's entrance. Twisting and projected bodies and body parts splatter into windows two or three stories up. The mass of people squeezes around the fire column and presses up against the assorted storefronts, looking for cover. A significant percentage of the crowd pull little white gas masks over their mouths and noses. The gas mask contingent don't seem to be panicking, but rather waiting out whatever it is they're waiting out. About a half-dozen of the shops dropped their automated metal gates over their entrances to keep people from rushing inside. Some people try to scale the gates but they fall quickly, shaking their hands in pain. The gates must be electrified. Makes sense to me. The smoke rises and spreads, and flashing lights poke through the cloud. Other than the faint sound of sirens, I hear only the classical music still playing in the room.

I say, "What is going on?"

The CM say, "Terrorists," then, "Which group?" then, "Who knows?" then, "Though nothing out of the norm," then, "This happens in the Zone every two weeks," then, "Like clockwork," then, "Melissa's partner was killed a few months ago," then, "So unfortunate," then, "But nothing for you to worry about," then, "We have a private car for you out back in the loading dock."

I look at Melissa. She nods, acknowledging something. The CM don't look at me while speaking, but outside at the smoke and damage and death. They have bemused smiles on their faces. They could be watching a child putting silly things in her mouth. They could be watching a neutered dog humping people's legs.

To keep from screaming and then accusing them of blowing up people for whatever purpose that is their purpose, I say, "Private car. What is a private car, anyway?"

My father says, "Hey, maybe those were your FART peeps down there."

Melissa starts the camera rolling. I feel her zooming in on my face. Sweat breaks out and I'm itchy, allergic to the camera lens. I say, "They're not my peeps." There's really something wrong with me now. Instead of being rendered speechless in the face of more senseless death, I'm bickering with this guy like we're kids arguing the merits of Cookie Monster and Big Bird.

Melissa says, "Can't use that," and stops filming and whispers into some sort of hand-held recorder.

The CM say, "Melissa's the best," then, "Came highly recommended," then, "A pillar in her field," then, "A true professional."

Father says, "What do you mean they're not your peeps? Said so on TV. TV said you and the FART gang blew up your two-faced buddy and high tailed it out of Farm."

"Fuck you, you fucking sham, you fucking hypocrite, you . . . you . . . ." I swing at him, he ducks and hides behind Melissa.

He says, "Did you get that on tape?"

"Missed it," Melissa says. "My fault. Won't happen again."

The CM say to Melissa, "No problem," then, "You'll get it next time."

Father says, "Man, I set him up for some true righteous indignation that the voters would've swallowed faster than their homogenized Farm milks and you missed it. Am I the only one here keeping our Mayor-to-be's best interests in mind instead of our own career advancement, hmm?"

A SPIDER WITH YELLOW WEBBING

They never bothered fixing or replacing my apartment's elevator after the crash and Mrs. Lopez's death. They just draped the elevator doorway with CAUTION tape. I pretended a big yellow spider lived in the elevator shaft and spun her yellow webs over all the doors so people would leave it alone.

It was the beginning of summer, a few months after the accident. Mom spent those months watching TV or looking for a new job or taking long naps in my bed, sometimes staying there with me at night, sometimes not. I spent more of my days with my friend Jimmy, just the two of us running around the apartment building, especially on my floor. We'd pretend we saw the yellow spider and leave it dead flies we'd find in the windowsills of our bedrooms. The game was younger than us, but we didn't care because everything else was older.

There was one day when we were reasonably sure that everyone on our floor was out somewhere and we dared each other to step inside the web and act like we were trapped. Jimmy went first but didn't stay in the web long. He pulled himself out of the tape, mumbling something in Spanish, breathing heavy, and blinking back tears. I didn't make fun of him for being scared. Instead, I jumped in, took his place. I rolled myself up good, even covering most of my head. I worked at it, getting all tied up and tangled. I wanted to be in there tighter, more secure, and suspend myself off the floor if possible.

Jimmy clapped and laughed and screamed. "Somebody help, the spider is comin'."

I imagined her legs tickling the walls of the elevator shaft, carrying her bulk down, toward me. She'd bring me inside and the shaft, her lair, would smell like death, like Mr. and Mrs. Lopez's apartment did after the funeral, that dusty dry smell not of rot but of something missing, of neglect, of something that they had tried to preserve. The spider wouldn't eat me right away, but stick a gentle fang into my arm and put me to sleep. Not a deep sleep, more like a waking doze. I'd still know everything that was happening around me. Then she would wrap me up tighter, into a warm cocoon, rub my belly and back, cozy up real close to me, so close I wouldn't know what was cocoon and what was her, and whisper sweet lies about how everything would be okay and I'd listen and want to believe her. Then she'd leave me there, hanging and swaying in the warm but dead shaft for days and weeks and months. I'd miss her when she was away and I'd miss her when she sat silently next to me. I'd long for more of her sweetly whispered lies.

"Hey," Jimmy said, and he pried the tape off my face as he pulled me out of my spider daydream. The tape sagged and drooped because I'd stretched it all out. "I've got a dare for you."

I was both relieved and mad at Jimmy. "What?"

"Lean against the doors with all your weight and close your eyes, and I'll count to ten and then press the button."

"Why?"

"Maybe the doors will open. Maybe they won't."

"They won't open."

"I dare you."

I could've said no. It was obvious Jimmy was trying to make up for his near tears while in the tape. "The doors ain't gonna open. That's dumb."

"Then do it."

"I'm doing it."

Although it was a hot summer day made even hotter in the third floor hallway with its trapped and cooked air, the metal elevator doors were cold against the bare skin of my arms. It was too cold for any spider to be in there. Too cold for anybody.

Jimmy peeled his long bangs off his forehead. "Close your eyes and I'll start counting." He hovered his finger, already pointed out, just above the dark elevator call button. The button was black and cartoon big.

I closed my eyes, listened to him count, and pressed my back hard against the double doors, sticking my spine right on the rubber where door met door, trying to pry those suckers open with my vertebra, with my bones. If those doors did open there was no way I'd be able to catch myself from going in. All the weight I had was pushed up against the doors. I kept pushing even after he got to ten and pressed the button.

33

WHEREVER IT IS WE'RE SVPPOSED TO GO

The CM press buttons and open the rear-doors of the elevator car. They file out fast, like Farm's hummingbirds, and then they have a hovering conversation with two bouncers.

After, the CM say to me, "They'll lead you to the car," then, "Good luck," then, "We'll be in touch."

Then to Melissa, "We look forward to the dailies," then, "Keep the camera rolling."

Then to my father, "Keep him safe," then, "Don't work him too hard down there."

They scurry back into the elevator chatting to each other in low tones. The hummingbirds are full of nectar.

My father says, "I'll sure miss them. Didn't even get a chance to try and convert them. I'm a sucky missionary, you know."

Melissa hangs a card around her neck: some sort of television credential with CBC holo-logos and official looking signatures. She says, "Rolling."

My father says, "I knew you were going to say that. I'm psychic, you know." Fucking guy is flirting with her. Mom is homeless, deported, or dead and he's flirting with the cameraperson. The goddamn priest is old enough to be her father!

You know what I mean, goddamn it.

The bouncers take us through an employees' changing area (and we are ignored by most of the changees but there are a few who flash their tits and wag their dicks at the camera, and my father yells, "I see you've already been blessed, my children!"), then through a small and empty cafeteria, to the shipping and receiving docks out back, three of the four truck bays occupied, then out a door and once outside I choke and cough on the acrid smoke from the bomb, or maybe it's just the daily/nightly/minutely output from the City Works smoke stacks only a few blocks away.

There's an idling black limousine parked adjacent to one of the empty docking bays, one of those SUV hybrid-limousines that probably has more interior space than the dorm room in which I'd spent my Farm years. The bouncers open the door and Melissa gets in first, keeping that camera aimed at my coughing and eye-watering face. This camera stuff is going to get old real quick.

I climb in and the filtered air inside is a saviour. My throat unclenches and I let cool, clean air into my lungs. There's at least twenty square feet of walking room inside, and tinted windows, white shag rug and lamps and appliances and multiple flat-screen TVs. My father climbs in next and sits across from me, sits with Melissa. He pats her knee and smiles. Of course he does.

I'm alone on a big white-leather bench seat. I notice my father patting his boot, presumably checking on his gun, his insurance policy. Melissa is as expressionless as her camera.

I get the urge to fuck with Daddy-dearest. Embarrass him on TV, if I can. Don't care if that helps or hurts the polls. I say, "Your little toy still there, Padre?"

He says, "You'll find out when I shoot you in the ass. Is there a mini-bar on this berg or what?" He finds a fridge and dives in. "There better be more than just wine, or I'm going to be very put out. Look at this junk. Orange juice? What, are we going to get fucking scurvy or something? Ah, here we go." He pulls out a bottle of a murky brown liquid.

A driver appears at our door. He wears a cap and an overcoat that strains against his chest and belly, both of which distend out so far that if he fell face-first, he'd automatically roll onto his back like he's wearing a reverse-turtle shell. My father hands him a note. The driver reads it. Then there's a look on his face. The look: is this chocolate or shit on my hands?

The driver says, "You sure?"

My father nods.

Driver says, "We can't leave until the ambulances and cops clear out of the Zone," and walks away, as if that is a sufficient explanation. But it's not sufficient for me. Not even in the neighbourhood of sufficient. I mean, are the cops still after me? Is that what he's implying? Couldn't they set this up so I don't have to go into hiding? If I'm going to be the CM's puppet candidate, I want to get some candidate treatment and privilege and entitlement. Yeah, I'm a fraud.

Padre offers Melissa and me a shot of whatever it is he's drinking. We both pass. He shrugs and we sit in the idling limo. Waiting to go wherever it is we're supposed to go.

Melissa quickly explains that one of the features of *The Candidate* show will be a 'confessional' segment. Me, my father, or anyone else who end up a player in our campaign will talk one-on-one with the camera, confessing to the audience. She says it's standard fare for reality television. This appeals to me. Reality television having its own code of conduct, a strict set of rules and regiments amid the supposed reality and chaos.

Melissa says, "Pretend you're not here and listening to any of your father's confessional." Then she aims the camera at my father and says, "You're first, and talk about something juicy."

He says, "What are we going to talk about? Prep me, baby."

Melissa shuts off the camera and preps him. I'm indignant! Appalled! And not that I needed any more evidence that I'm the dog and pony of this dog and pony show, but here we have it. She tells him she wants to hear about why he left my mother and me. She wants him to talk about his God-gig and where we're going.

I say, "Forgive my naivety, but isn't this supposed to be spontaneous and, um, real?"

Melissa says, "We're on a tight schedule and I've got certain shots and pieces I have to get for the network. You know, bonus incentives and the like. If it helps, think of this as a docu-drama instead of some schlocky reality show."

"It doesn't help."

Sweet as Farm's engineered and uber-processed honey, my father says, "Whatever you need from me, Mel. You just name it. I'm here to help."

So much for that reality TV code of conduct. And I'm thinking about joining Father Fuck-up with a drink now.

Melissa says, "Whenever you're ready, Joseph."

Joseph. She calls him by his first name. Oh, bartender?

He clears his throat, adjusts his night-vision glasses, and runs his hands through his slicked-back hair.

"Rolling."

"I alternate weeks between my Church and the Pier. When in City, I do morning and evening masses Monday through Saturday, only a handful of old biddies attend those, and then three Sunday masses. More folks attend the Sundays, but it doesn't take a mind reader," and he pauses and points at his temple with his right hand, "to know that most don't want to be there. You've got the brats Grandma dragged to the service, they kick the pews and fold the prayer booklets into funky shapes, then there're the cold-fishes, the ones that just sit there and don't say the prayers or sing the songs during mass, their faith doesn't extend past the weekly ritual, the Sunday habit they just can't kick even though they don't believe in it anymore. Those people depress me. They're too much like me, I guess."

He takes off his glasses and closes his eyes. Goddamn, he's hamming it up. Feigning anguish and deep thoughts. I'll give this family-deserting priest some anguish.

He throws the camera a quivery smile and says, "Ah, but that's Catholicism. It's all about taking the bad with the good.

"When I'm not in City, I work and live at the charity I set up down in the Pier: Home. I'm not going to try and describe it." Another dramatic pause. "You'll see it soon enough. I'll only say that my life's work, and my dedication or even obsession with Home, is why I left my family, your future Mayor, and his mother, all those years ago. I know I'm less than perfect, especially in the husband and Daddy departments, but Home ... it is who I am." Two tears, one from each eye roll down his cheeks. He's a one-man special effect.

He puts his chin in his chest and wipes his eyes. Then he looks up laughing and slashing at his throat, giving Melissa the international *cut* sign. She puts the camera down.

He says, "Tell me that was gold, Mel. I know it was."

She says, "Pure gold, Joseph."

"Nice! Nailed it."

I have a lot of people inside of me. They're all me, of course, but they are different. There's a seven year-old who was crushed to hear there was no Santa, the angry teen who thought signing up for a stint at Farm would save his mother and him, the nine-year-old who loved to climb those fire-escapes even after catching mom and dad in the act of fucking, the six-hours-ago guy who still wants to kick this Mayor-scheme to the curb and go off on his own, the twelve-year-old who saw Mrs. Lopez's dead body, the two-days-ago guy filled with despair at his elongated Farm service, riding with Jonah toward the perimeter fences, and dreaming of escape.

In that huge crowd inside me there is that little pre-pubescent kid, the one who he abandoned. That kid takes over and says, "I hate you. You know that, don't you? I just really hate-hate-hate you with everything I have."

My father says, "Don't player hate, congratulate!" Then to Melissa, "My bad. The camera missed another one of those outbursts. This one's on me, Mel. I should've told you to keep your camera rolling. Live and learn."

34

FIVE NVMBERS DEEP INTO THE CONFIRMATION NVMBER

We're still idling in the limo.

Melissa says, "Mr. Mayor, you want to follow this up with your own confessional?"

"Fuck you, too."

"Fair enough." She turns the camera back on. "Joseph, you two don't look like father and son."

"Because I'm white and he's black?"

Melissa isn't flustered. She says, "Besides the obvious, Father."

She calls him Father when the camera is on. I think about what I should call him, then I stop thinking about him when I see Melissa's smart phone hanging in a holster on her utility belt. Is finding Mom as easy as a cell phone call?

My father says, "He has my spirit, my *joie de vivre*, and my eyes, and possibly my mouth. Otherwise he looks just like his mother."

Melissa says, "Where is she?"

My father looks at me. Glasses back on. "That's the

sixty five thousand dollar question. We don't know, do we?"

I say, "Can I use your phone, Melissa?"

She unholsters it and tosses it over. Camera, of course, now pointed at me. Hope she gets my best side.

My father sings, "Who ya gonna call?"

I say, "Somebody. Police, maybe. Report my mother as missing."

"I knew you were going to say that. Don't do it, kiddo. If you report her as missing, that's as good as listing her as homeless, or dead."

I look at Melissa for some sort of visual confirmation or denial on her part. But she's all about the camera now. I try talking to her. "What do you think, Melissa?"

She says nothing. Right, she's part of the background now. *Cinéma vérité*, my ass.

I say, "I want to know why her apartment is empty."

"I told you she's fine. She left, is all."

"You know this for sure."

"We already talked about this. I haven't spoken with her since before you left for Farm. But I know she's okay. Trust me."

"Yeah, trust you." I stand up and walk toward the front of the limo, away from him and Melissa. She gets up and follows me. Dad stays put. I dial information and ask for the police department, not an emergency line. I follow automated directions skipping past menu options that include curfew schedules, updates to anti-terrorism laws, street blockade schedules, Ad-Walker complaint-lines, homeless sighting hotline, and ways to make donations to the policeman's ball fund. Finally, it's press 9 for the *report missing persons* line.

I tell the police secretary my mother's name and her former address. Camera still rolling, I say to Melissa, "You're not going to broadcast my mother's name and address, are you?" She gives me an off-camera thumbs-up. Which is great. Only, I can't tell if that's a yes or no.

The secretary says, "No, we will not broadcast your mother's name and address. That's not how we do it."

"Sorry, I wasn't talking to you."

"How long has your mother been missing?"

"Four, maybe six weeks, I guess."

"You're guessing?"

"No. Yes. I don't know the exact amount of time, but it has been substantial. It's a long story, alright?"

There's a measure or two of silence on the other end. I feel the guy's eyes roll. He says, "We need your contact information."

I say, "Is there just some homeless list we can check or something?"

My father groans and says, "My God, throwing your own mother under the bus like that. Glad she's not here to see this."

I mouth a silent shut-the-fuck-up at him.

The secretary says, "We do not give out that information over the phone or to the general public.

For your missing persons report to be activated I need your contact information."

I lean away from the phone and say to Melissa, "Psst, what's the number on this phone?"

She gives me a thumbs-up again. I don't like Melissa.

I can't tell this guy I have no address or number, so I give him my mother's old address and a dummy phone number, and a dummy name, too. The police won't be able to contact me, but maybe I can check back with them.

He says, "Your report will be processed in three to five business days. Take down this confirmation number."

I dance around the limo, frantically signing my name in the air.

My father, Mr. Supposed-to-be-ESP says, "Why is he asking for the check? This ain't no restaurant."

The secretary is five numbers deep into the confirmation number before Melissa tosses me a pen. The limo starts with a jerk and I fall flat on my face, the phone still pinned to my ear. I write the thirteen digit and letter code on the back of my right hand. The secretary repeats the number and I got it right. Then he says, "You can enter this code on the phone or on our website and check the case's progress. Thank you for calling City Police."

I hang up, roll onto my back, and toss the phone back to Melissa. It rings the instant she catches it. She checks the number and answers it. She only says, "Hello," then listens for about ten seconds, then hangs up.

My father says, "Police tapped the phone?"

"No. Turn on one of the TVs. You're going to be on the CBC."

35

COMMON DECENCY COMPELS ME

The news anchor says, "Farm has just now released a video of the terrorist attack. Common decency compels me to say that the following video contains disturbing images and I invite you to look away."

What the news anchor really means is: Come one come all and look at the glorious and gore-ious death and destruction because I know you want it and the only thing that I could do to make you possibly crave it more is to feign through that hoary old decency and dignity sermon-on-the-mount and tell you to look away.

Then there's a dead donkey on the screen. Full colour. It's missing an eye.

My father says, "That's icky!"

The camera zooms in on the empty socket, for what effect, I don't know. Maybe security camera-guy was a wannabe film student, focusing on the gritty realism and nihilism of the moment: the empty eye socket of a dead thing that some might argue was never really alive in the first place. All I know is that Jonah was right. I'm swallowing that donkey's eye.

The news anchor talks over the video, giving names and places and times and other stats, but I don't really listen. I focus on the video. After the eye-socket zoom, it gets choppy, full of cuts, showing obvious signs of editing. There's a flash of Jonah and I getting out of our ATV and walking to the donkey. We get a clear shot of the back of Jonah's head. Then the front.

My father says, "That schmuck has two faces! Brilliant stuff."

Another cut. Jonah and I are laughing. Then I walk to the back of the ATV. Camera zooms on my face and freezes. I'm looking over my shoulder. It certainly looks like I'm waiting for something to happen. Then something does happen. The explosion tears into the ATV and Jonah. The donkey and Jonah are on the right side of the screen, and then they disappear, exiting stage right. The video rewinds, then goes slo-mo. A spot shadow highlights the explosion's epicenter; the donkey's ass. Then the explosion grows. At this slow speed it creeps, like suds leaving a washing machine. It hits the front of the ATV. The hood peels back like a banana, then tears up into shrapnel, and the shrapnel slides into Jonah's head and body before Jonah jumps off screen. Then another edit, showing me putting on a duck head then climbing into the Chicken's Jeep and driving away. That escape scene fades into a mug shot of me that fills the TV. They animate it and rotate my head so the viewing public can get a 3-D image of my fugitive ass.

My father says, "Well, that wasn't too bad, now was it? No such thing as bad publicity."

The androgynous anchor comes back on, but is brief, sending the live feed out to the Mayor's press conference.

36

STATE OF THE CITY ADDRESS

I look out the limo's tinted windows. We're cutting
through the financial district. Stone and brick and
mortar buildings buried beneath neon signs, holo-
boards, and giant vid screens. On every board and
screen is Mayor Solomon's press conference. There's
an army of him. He has a handlebar mustache.
Just like BM's. Melissa tells me that the mustache
is relatively new. He's Teddy Roosevelt without the
Teddy part. He's the late-in-life, bloated version,
replete in what looks to be vintage clothing, a
costume community theatre might stock. He checks
the time on his gold pocket watch, then slips a hand
inside his vest, somewhere between his barrel chest
and beach-ball stomach. His podium is outside,
standing at attention on the marble stairs of City
Hall. Filling in behind him are assorted men and
women in suits.

He starts his speech with "My fellow country-
men . . ." then stops to shake the hands of everyone

standing behind him. We get a wonderful view of the Mayor's cotton-wool-blend-covered ass as he does this. Then we get a shot of a large, boisterous, presumably appreciative crowd cordoned off at the bottom of the City Hall stairs. Upon returning to the podium, Solomon waves at the crowd, then continues, "Myself and the assorted City Selectmen you see standing with me, acting as your tireless servants, have petitioned and scheduled a recall election, complete with a number of referendums, the details of which will be made known to the public via the various media outlets."

On cue, a news ticker at the bottom of the screen rolls by, detailing the ballot questions, date and time, polling locations for the various City sections and districts.

"In two weeks, we will add a glorious new day to democracy, a day that has been long overdue." He pauses. We, the TV-viewing audience hear an ovation. There is only polite applause in the background. "After years of running unopposed, I'm recalling myself. Political muscles must be exercised, or like any other muscle they will atrophy and wither. I intend to whip our collective flabby and cellulite-ridden political bodies into shape."

He stops and goes for another round of handshaking with his cronies. We see another shot of the penned-in crowd. There's a bomb explosion somewhere in the middle and bodies go airborne. The camera doesn't linger. When Solomon returns to the podium, he doesn't offer any further explanation or reason for the recall election (the first such recall in sixty years according to the news ticker). I wonder if anyone at the press conference will be allowed to ask, or care to ask for a better reason for the big recall to-do.

The Mayor goes on to detail the prosperity under his many years of leadership. Then he drops my name. The crowd boos and there are more bomb explosions.

He says, "This man is the candidate found, funded, and backed by an exhaustive City-commissioned search for the fledgling Opposition Party. Under ordinary circumstances I would refer to the OP's man as a worthy candidate. After all, I oversaw the commission to find the bloody fellow. But these are extraordinary times, my friends, and in this early round of political competition, I'm here to declare the OP candidate is scum. An accused terrorist wanted for the heinous, treasonous crimes most recently committed at Farm."

The rest of his spittle-flying, fist-pounding-on-podium speech rails against FART and all other terrorist groups, and vows to go forward with the recall election and all other City functions and events despite their horrific and unabated acts. It all sounds so very reassuring. Wild applause and a few more bombs, then Mayor Solomon leaves the podium without taking any questions.

My father is asleep. The empty glass of scotch leaks out of his hand. It lands on the shag rug and rolls with the limo's momentum. Melissa's smart phone rings. All she says is hello, then hands the phone to me.

The CM.

"Congratulations, Future Mayor," then, "Game on."

37

SWEEPING IT VNDER THE RVG

The limo parks behind BankCity Center. There's some sort of sporting event going on, or maybe the Ice Capades. We wait for the semi-random police check point at Cedar Street to go away. The CM tipped us off. I don't know who tipped them off.

While waiting I've seen my mug up on the stadium's holo-boards. There've been two ads for *The Candidate*. Simple ads: black background and a red logo, the letters fashioned from governmental-looking documents, the C might be the Declaration of Independence all twisted and rolled up, but I can't be sure, and good goddamn the show starts tomorrow night, primetime, and every night at primetime until the election. I've also seen three campaign spots. Apparently, I'm the candidate for change, taxing the upper class, better schools, and environmental control.

See. That proves it. The CM are in the bag. There's no way I'll win on that platform.

Apparently, I'm also the candidate who thinks that Solomon's two billion dollar cuts or outright elimination of social programs like school lunches, food stamps, Special Supplemental Nutrition Program for Women, Infants and Children are bad. My political spots are full of all those nice Solomon administration stats, but nothing about his magic fridge. At the end of each spot you get my mug and canned voice telling everyone that I approved the message. And you know what, I find myself wanting to vote for that guy up on the screen; he says some nice things.

We've been sitting for forty minutes. Melissa has forty minutes of me doing nothing on tape. So I spice it up, and dial the police again. Plug in the thirteen-character case code, feeding it through the automated system to see if they've started work on my mother yet, even though I know they haven't. The automated verdict: case approval pending.

My father is still asleep. I pick up the empty scotch glass and balance it upside down on his crotch. Melissa doesn't film that. She gives me a small hand-cam, the size of my palm and tells me to go do a confessional while we have the free time. Melissa climbs out of the limo to go chat up the driver.

I take the camera, sit it on top of a mini fridge, and stare into its eye. Here it is. This is my confessional. I open my mouth.

What is there to say? You know, I feel pressure to make an impressive opening. There're so many ways

I could go with this. I could talk about Mom and how the summer after Dad left, I'd come home after a day of running through hydrants or stealing candy from the sidewalk markets in Annotte and find Mom napping in my bed. Door and windows closed, shades drawn. It'd be so hot in the room and the smell of her sweat was a door behind my door. Sometimes she stayed there, sleeping through until morning. I'd eat cereal for dinner and watch the TV shows I wasn't usually allowed to watch. I never left the apartment though. I pretended she was sick and I had to protect her. I'd stay up late and end up sleeping on the couch, or the floor in front of the couch, but never her and Dad's bed.

I don't say any of this in my confessional. I let the camera run and tape me and my silent open mouth. It feels right.

When the limo finally starts again, we drive through the one section of City I've never seen, the North End. The North End extends the farthest out over the bay. It used to be City's industrial and textile center but fell into ruin over sixty years ago, so the history goes. After ruin came the fraternal twins of abject poverty and epidemic crime rate.

It's harder to see out the limo's tinted windows because there are no neon signs or Coke ads or newswires here. Only one in four streetlamps even seem to be functioning. Outside the limo is a graveyard of slums and empty factories, the skeletons of City's closet. Broken glass on the sidewalks, dented but full garbage cans, chairs without legs or backs, an overturned baby carriage, burnt out cars. Rats and anorexic dogs dart out of the limo's path. This is where some homeless try their luck at evading police sweeps, where fringe gangs have their wars.

When I was a kid, the parental threat was if you didn't clean your room, you'd be shipped off to the North End. And that parental threat is finally coming true for me, since it's where my father is taking me.

Speaking of that fraud, I've appointed him to be my deputy campaign manager. I think it suits him well. He now answers the phone and handles almost all the communiqué with the two-headed CM monster. So far, they've called every minute on the minute. After our quick pit stop at the BankCity Center, it has been a steady stream of Dad-relayed numbers and stats and ratings and polls and projections. Right now he's giving me the latest on what TV talking heads and bloggers have to say on everything and anything relating to me. He gives me the CM's suggestions on changing strategy and tactics. I wave my hand like a seasoned Caesar and let Father Politics decide for me.

Without warning or ceremony, the limo stops. Dad says, "Last stop, folks." He pulls out his pistol, says, "Safety first," opens the door and gets out.

Melissa doesn't say anything. Since my confessional she's gone quiet and ensconced herself and her camera into the background.

I climb out into a stiff, salty wind, and my feet hit dirt. On the other side of the limo is a lumpy boardwalk with a rusty railing. We must be at North End Point. I jog onto the boardwalk and lean on the railing, rust flakes off at my touch. I've been told that at one time this was a beautiful place with a small grass park and a spectacular view of the water. I don't see much now because of the omnipresent smog and cloud cover but I hear the ocean below and beyond. It sounds gentle and far away.

Our fleeing limo breaks my reverie. I'm not above admitting I'm a little sad watching the cruise-ship comfort on its thirty inch rims back up and leave me standing on poverty's decaying boardwalk while holding a crumbling railing.

Father ESP says, "Might as well be holding your dick. Come on, no time for sight-seeing. Over here." Just ahead of where the limo is parked is a thick, one-bar iron gate that stretches across the street. Anyone can step over or under it, like my father is doing now.

We walk down the middle of the street with the boardwalk on our left and condemned factories on our right. Two blocks down we hang a right onto another street. No name but a sign says *Dead End*. There's nothing okay about this corral. Decaying buildings are on all sides now. I'm afraid to look behind me. I start thinking about how this whole mayoral campaign is really bullshit and I'm going be left here in this industrial graveyard to rot.

"Jeez, lighten up, kid," my father says.

I'm getting sick of his ESP stuff.

He says, "I'm taking you where I said I was taking

you. I might be a lot of things, but a liar isn't one of them."

Can't say I ever dwelled on the whole hiding-out-below-City aspect of the campaign, but I'm dwelling on it now, and it's scaring the piss out of me. Mostly it scares me because I believe that I'll find my mother down there and won't be able to do a thing for her. It doesn't help that the wind funnels into our quaint dead-end street and makes those carnival fun house sounds that are only scary when you're not in a fun house. Father ESP whistles a circus tune now.

Up ahead, only fifty yards or so away, is the dead end. A hollowed-out office building, its front façade missing. Still damn dark out here but there are more functioning street lamps on this end of the street. Inside, flaps of insulation and stripped wiring hang from lumpy ceilings and there are black lumps that look like tumours but must be the old office furniture.

"Watch your step."

I didn't notice my father had stopped walking and I had gone ahead. Three steps away the street disappears. A huge rectangular hole that spans across the street and to the frontage of the hollowed out building.

"What is this?"

"The Old Dump chute. Or I should say, the new one. This is a temporary chute that connects down below with the old one."

"They still use the Old Dump? I thought that was illegal."

My father laughs at me. I'm sure I deserve it.

I say, "Using the Old Dump makes about as much sense as me running for Mayor. I mean, I snuck into City by stowing away inside a garbage truck on its way back from Territory Dump."

He says, "Actually, it makes more sense. Territory Dump is miles outside of City. Think about how much more gas one truck uses on a ride out there. Now multiply that by how many trips a day a truck needs to make, and multiply that by how many trucks City uses. Take that figure and multiply it by the number of days in a year. Add on top the cost of running the environmentally regulated processing and recycling plants because we gotta keep Farm and the breweries and, of course, the golf courses clean, and you get the picture. So much more cost effective to just sweep it all under the rug, don't you think?" He pats me on the back. "Something you'll need to consider when you are Mayor. Walk this way." He walks to the left, following the perimeter of the chute.

I crane my neck and take a peek down the gaping hole, and there is a definite garbage stench wafting up. "Don't people see full garbage trucks coming out here to the North End and then leaving empty?"

"People know City still uses the Old Dump, but like most things, they don't care. Or they don't care enough to want to act. That's where your guy Solomon knows his politics. You can make people accept anything as long as they're not willing to act. There's a lesson there, for sure." Dad cups Melissa's camera in his hands, forcing the lens to focus on his mug. "Well, do any of you care out there? Anyone keeping score with *The Candidate* home-game?"

38

TVNNEL OF LOVE

He leads with his gun. "Gotta be careful here. Never know who's lurking around the door."

The chute is behind us and we're inside that hollowed-out building on the first floor. The carpet has tears and worn spots. The bowed ceiling is up higher than it looked from the street. This used to be the main lobby or foyer of this building. We step through broken and overturned chairs, desks, some torn and accordion-style waiting-room magazines. Melissa's camera has a spotlight and my father tells her where to point it. The light finds a black metal door, seemingly standing by itself in the middle of the foyer.

I walk around to its side and there's more of the black metal, or maybe wrought iron, that tunnels into the floor, and I have to assume below City and into Pier. No sir, I don't like this door. It looks so final. Someone needs to tell me again how all this is supposed to help me and Mom.

There are some electronic bleeps. My father is working at a numerical code-box just above the handle. He types in a ridiculously long number. He stops and says, "Shit!"

"Can't you just use your special mind powers to open the door?"

"You're a funny guy." He punches at the numbers again. This time there's a loud click then some pneumatic hisses. He grabs the handle and opens the door slowly for the dramatic benefit of Melissa and her camera. She gets it all. He says, "We're gettin' there, kiddies."

I take a peek. What I see first is what I see second and third and on and on . . . I see down, City's maw, the gullet of the giant who wanted to eat that beanstalk punk Jack, a tunnel with no light at the end, the path to nowhere: the City codified and regimented and legalized nowhere.

My father says, "You are such a drama queen. Strap on some balls and let's go." He steps inside and in plain sight of the camera, I give the middle finger to the back of his head.

Father Psychic Friend says, "Not very Mayoral. If you listen closely you can hear your poll numbers dropping."

I step inside. The walls and stairs are made of the same iron as the door. Our shoes click and clack on the stairs. There is light in here. Light bulbs housed in wire-cages hang off the ceiling, one every five feet, an upside-down breadcrumb trail. The ceiling is a foot or so above my head so I don't have to duck, but my scalp gets flash fried when I walk under one of those bulbs. The tunnel is wide enough for two to walk side-by-side, but we go down single file with camera-Melissa as the caboose. After an initial steep descent the stairs give way to a smooth ramp and the tunnel levels out, the angle of depression almost negligent.

I say, "Are we there yet?"

"It'll take us a solid hour to get to where we're going." He steps to his left and stops. "You lead. I got some info to give to our viewing audience." He slides in between Melissa and me and plants a two-handed shove on my back.

"We could do without the tour guide spiel," I say, but he doesn't listen. He starts flapping his gums. Talks about how his parish and charity efforts raise funds to keep this tunnel, the last of its kind below City, in commission to help serve his mission and blah, blah, blah. I don't fucking care and I stop listening. I really have a hard time believing that this guy has followers. That he has folks who believe in what he has to say and believe in him enough to give him money. Likely he's fleecing his sheep somehow. He's all scam and nothing but the scam, always has been. But I keep going down with no real idea of where I'll end up.

39

CAUGHT CLIMBING DOWN

I was sitting in the hallway, back against my apartment door. I kept nodding off, falling in and out of sleep while waiting for them to come back. Didn't sleep much the night before.

As I was starting to think they wouldn't come, three other kids who lived in the building ran down the hall right behind Jimmy. Those other kids giggled and whispered. Jimmy had a crowbar tucked inside his jacket, the handle sticking out near his waist. He was always finding things he shouldn't.

Jimmy said, "Shut up or we'll wake his mother." I doubted they'd wake her up. Like me, she hadn't slept much the night before.

We scurried down the hall and to the elevator, tearing away the last of the CAUTION tape. It was the end of summer: one week before school started back up and only a few months after our yellow-web-spider-in-the-shaft games. Nobody was afraid of that spider anymore.

Jimmy said, "You ready?" I'd grown noticeably taller than him at some point during the summer. I'd mentioned it to him a few days earlier. His answer was to swear at me in Spanish and say that he still had two parents living in his apartment. Back then, everything we said was true.

He said, "You really gonna do this?"

I answered Jimmy and the group by pulling the crowbar out of his jacket. That shut up all the whispers and giggles. I pretended to weigh and inspect the metal bar and made a *not bad, not bad* face, like I was a pawnshop broker inspecting someone's wedding ring. I placed the curved crowbar tip on the rubber jam between the elevator doors and then I pushed with everything my getting-to-be-not-so-little body (that was what Mom had said about me the night before) had. The crowbar sank between the doors, maybe a quarter of the metal swallowed up.

Jimmy helped me pull on the bar. There was an awful high-pitched metal sound that bloodied our ears as the doors separated. We let go of the crowbar and it fell down the elevator shaft. It crashed and rang like a tuning fork on the lobby floor.

I said, "Whoops," laughed, and tried to shimmy my body between the elevator doors. I only got my left arm and shoulder through. I squirmed back out and we pulled and pushed on the doors, managing to open them a body-width wide, or at least, my body-width wide. I stuck my head in and looked down at the bottom landing, the lobby. The lobby elevator doors had been removed along with the ruined elevator car and the ruined Mrs. Lopez. The landlord had only seen fit to cover the doorway with a nail-fastened see-through plastic tarp. Us kids had undone a flap and had played in there all the time. We'd been in there earlier that morning, climbing up the sides of the walls, using the stilled gears and brakes, cable grooves, and wall studs as handgrips and footholds, daring each other to touch the elevator doors on the floor above us. The climbing had been hard because there was only the light of the lobby and it'd made us mostly blind in that shaft of darkness above our heads. I'd been the only kid who touched the second-floor doors. Then I'd made the bet about climbing down from the third floor. No one had egged me on or triple-dog-dared me. I'd just thrown it out there on my own.

I'd hoped to see more from up there on the third floor. But I didn't see anything defined on the walls, just the lobby light at the bottom. I did see the crowbar lying there three floors below me. With its curved tip pointing north, it was a question mark.

I said, "See you dirtbags in the lobby. And you better pay up."

I was still convinced this would be easy. Going down was always easier than going up, no matter what anyone else told you. The only tricky part was how you got down.

Hugging the door with my right side, I swung my left foot out, then down in search of a foothold.

Didn't find one. I patted the other side of the door but it was as smooth as the outside. Feeling along the door's top I found the track on which the doors slid. I latched on and squirmed inside the shaft. As soon as I disappeared from view of the third floor, I heard a few *whoo-hoos* from the kids and then crazed footsteps beating their path to the stairs. I wondered if Jimmy stayed up on the third floor in case I needed help or if he ran downstairs with the rest of them. I almost called out his name.

I couldn't see anything and the how of my down was not going to be easy. I groped my way to the sidewall, limbs shaking already. I did find the same metal bars, wall studs, and gears I'd used earlier that morning, but every move was a guess, extending my limbs in every possible direction, usually finding nothing and when I did find something it ended up hurting me. I scratched up my legs and arms pretty good on the studs, and those gears chewed on my fingers and toes. I banged my forehead on a stud near the second floor landing, or where I thought the second floor landing should be.

Sometime during the climb down, the gang got to the bottom and cheered me on. Jimmy was with them. I couldn't decide if I wanted to cry or just let go and land on them. This wasn't what I wanted. I stayed where I was, fingers wrapped around something metal and the tips of toes looking for stable footing like dogs continually sniffing out an area that confused them. Then the kids got louder. I was exhausted and I estimated how far above the lobby I really was, hoping that I wouldn't break a leg or something if I just let go, hoping I had enough strength to push away from the wall so the shaft innards wouldn't tear me up some more on the fall down, hoping one of the kids would move the crowbar so I didn't have to land on it. That was it. I was just going to let go. Let go.

The kids went quiet. Their plugs pulled. Something clamped around my waist and pulled me down. A nasty cut on my palm opened up when Mom grabbed me. Her hands went from my waist to my arm and she pulled me through the plastic tarp, yanking on my arm hard enough for some familiar burning pain in my shoulder. I stumbled and almost fell.

She said something I didn't quite hear, though it sounded plenty angry. I stood there in the lobby, blinking my eyes into focus. Everything was bright again. My shoulder ached and hands bled, and I was embarrassed, hoping Jimmy and the boys were long gone but knowing they probably weren't. My mother stood there with her hands on her hips, wearing her pink terrycloth robe, not tied all that tightly.

She saw my bleeding palms. Her face went through so many expressions, I thought she might be having a seizure. Then she rubbed her eyes quick, and came back with an angry look. A Mom look. It'd been months since I'd seen that look. She tried it on and it seemed to fit, and what had happened the night before, I got the feeling that it was a relief for her to still be able to be mad at me.

She said, "You stay out of that goddamn elevator shaft." Despite her words, her voice was softer than her look. She tightened her robe and pivoted. Then she walked away, past the other kids cowering in their hiding spots, and to the stairs. She didn't make me go with her back to our apartment.

I stepped back into the elevator shaft and kicked the crowbar out. The rattle of metal on linoleum echoed. My injured hands were damp and stinging, but I still wanted to climb back up to my floor.

40

HOME IS OVER THERE

We've been silent during most of the trip down. It has certainly been the longest time I've had since Farm to be inside my own head without everything and everyone crashing in on me. Hopefully, I'm far enough ahead of him so his ESP vibe, or whatever it is he can or can't do, won't work. He hasn't said anything to me and I've tried mentally baiting him, thinking happy thoughts about me giving him a hotfoot, which is odd because I've never given anybody a hotfoot, nor do I remember even thinking about giving someone a hotfoot.

So, after dwelling on the fantasy of toasting Father Hotfoot's tootsies and Melissa and me and the rest of City having a healthy chuckle at his expense, I've spent most of this me-and-my-own-head time thinking that my father orchestrated this whole thing. Everything: me being a patsy candidate, the TV show, the jaunt below City, maybe even the donkey bomb and Farm escape. I'm thinking somebody is lining the pockets of his priestly pants. I'm thinking, despite his protests to the contrary that he's lying through his pearly white teeth. Really, who can trust a priest with teeth that white? They must be caps. I don't have his ESP but everything sure feels like a lie. And now I'm thinking about Farm, the Tours, and the voiceless animals again, and I guess I'm trying to figure out when and if dear-old-Dad is using his real voice and when he's just lip-syncing. The biggest lie is that he doesn't know where Mom is. She's below City, living in the Pier, and he won't take me to her, or maybe he will take me to her but then leave us again. Why not, right? Practice makes perfect. Shit, I probably should give him that hotfoot.

Okay, maybe I'm better off without all the in-my-head time. I can try and think and guess at his motives all I want, but ultimately it's a useless exercise. Useless because I don't really know anything.

Well, I know this now: he didn't lie about our trip taking the better part of an hour. I don't know if we've hit the bottom of this metal tube but we are stuck in front of another black, cast-iron door. I don't like the looks of this door any more than I did the first one. I'm starting to feel like Jonah again, God's Jonah, not my Jonah. I'm in the gullet of some leviathan and it's no fun and I want out but I'm pretty sure that I don't want my *out* to be the exit on the back end.

I'm a few paces ahead of Melissa and Dad. I get to the door first and rap my knuckles on it. Shave and a haircut, two bits. There's a flash of silver down by my feet. A quarter. This likely means something but I don't know what and it makes me nervous and excited. I pick it up.

"Hey, I found a quarter."

My father slaps my back and says, "Congratulations. A few more bucks and you'd be pulling down City's minimum wage for this hour. Isn't that fantastic!"

Ever the brilliant deductionist, I say, "Hey, why would people need money down here?"

His face folds in on itself and he snorts. Apparently I'm the dumbest of dumbfucks for asking this question. "Just because they're homeless and deportees doesn't mean they've stopped being consumers. You've got a lot to learn if you're going to be Mayor." Then he sets his fingers dancing on this door's code panel. "I've always been told that I had magic fingers."

I should ignore him, but the camera is on, and I get the vibe from Melissa that we've been quite boring as of late. I pocket the quarter and I say, "I bet that's what all those altar boys used to say."

"Hey, good one!"

The door opens. I can't really describe what I expected to see. But what we get isn't it. We step out into a room with florescent track lighting, blue carpet, and a station of desks with computers. We step out into a fucking office, something you'd see in Farm headquarters, just like the room where BM interviewed me. Except this time there are two guys with guns, their laser sighting painting a nice red hole on our chests.

One of the armed men says, "Welcome back, Padre."

The other one herds the three of us in and makes sure the door closes.

My father says, "Boys, meet my son."

The guards break up laughing, so does my father. Can't say I enjoy being a living joke.

The bigger of the two guards says, "Well, then, he's got my vote."

"That's one," says my father. "See, your deputy campaign manager is already raking in the votes."

There are no windows in the office, which is really just a guard's station set up to monitor the tunnel, but there is another door: an ordinary, wooden door. Nothing fancy or ominous, and yet the outside, or the Pier and Dump and millions of desperate and suffering souls are just beyond it. All that somehow kept out by an ordinary door.

The gun-toting guards serve us cappuccino and biscotti. They cross their legs when they sit down and my father makes fun of them. Melissa checks her smart phone for messages and my father chats the CM up on his cell. I'm surprised those phones work down here, hundreds of feet below City. The signal has to pass through all that City blacktop and concrete and then through the Pier's wooden posts, struts and support beams, and likely through all the homeless people down here. Isn't technology amazing!

My father hangs up and says, "Onward." He collects our cups and dishes and dumps them in a mini-sink, then walks to the door and simply opens it. Again, nothing fancy; just a knob twist, then a pull, then one foot up and then down, and he's outside.

I pause in the doorway. There's the rush of an ocean breeze. Its coolness and smell and sound hit me. And then I look, really look out.

I get a taste of vertigo, my knees go rubber, and I latch onto a railing just outside the door. Spread out before me is a living Escher painting. Denuded sequoia trees serve as the giant support posts for City and they are as big as anything I've ever seen, or even imagined, thicker than skyscrapers, their height disappearing into a cloudy darkness above. Struts and beams, both horizontal and angled span across the distances between the posts, some are wide enough for four lanes of two-way pedestrian traffic while others are as skinny as a flagpole. There doesn't seem to be a pattern or reason to the construction of any of it. I see a spider web and then I blink and I see spokes in a bike tire, I blink again and I see the gnarled inner branches of a rose bush. All this I see in every direction, until darkness. And all over everything is humanity and their adaptations and appendages. There is some light down here; a collection of street lamps that stick out from the posts at odd angles like hairs that refuse to be combed down. Bridges made out of rope or metal or plastic or wood or something or anything else and there are ladders shimming up posts like vines of ivy and other ladders are all rungs, pieces of metal or wood or plastic affixed to the posts. There are people climbing and walking on everything. So many people. Clothed in rags or not at all, old and young, healthy and infirm, and everyone has something in their arms or in tow. A few hundred feet directly in front of us is the heart of this anthill and maybe where the queen ant lives, but I certainly don't ever want to meet this queen; the Dump. Streetlamps mark the perimeter of this sprawling mountain of junk. I smell it now, too. Mixing in with the ocean smell is a tinge of rot and decay that's too Farm-like to ignore.

My father says, "Home is over there, by the Dump." He waves a follow-me hand and walks down a rickety staircase made of mixed and mismatched pieces of metal and wood that hugs the circumference of the giant post to which the guard station is moored.

Melissa comes up behind me and says, "Holy shit."

"Well said," I say.

I walk and we reach the bottom of the staircase after the equivalent of maybe three flights. One more door to pass through, this one chain-linked and electrified, says my father. The stairs end on a horizontal support beam thick enough for five, maybe six people to walk shoulder-to-shoulder without having to worry about falling off. I look down and the ocean is only ten feet below us. The water is dark and calm. I thought it would be colder down here than in City, but it isn't. I'm not sure how that works but I'm not going to ask him about it.

There's a buzzing sound, some static-filled communiqué from one of the boys in the guard station, and the electrified door swings open. Still playing the effervescent tour guide, my father tells the camera that this guard station only monitors the tunnel and its access stairwell for potential escapees. They turn a blind eye to anything that might and does happen everywhere else. Why should the guards be any different than the rest of us?

41

BLESS YOV, FATHER!

We sit in the small staff-only cafeteria of Home. The three of us are the only ones in here at whatever time it is now. There's a bowl of cold chicken soup in front of me.

My father says, "So, what do you think? I'd offer a drink but I'm all out of sacramental wine."

I say, "I don't know." To get here, we walked past thousands of people crawling and living on Pier's posts and beams. Then thousands more while we skirted the Dump perimeter. All along the way people called out to us, or more specifically to my father-the-father. *Father! Father! Help me, Father! Save me, Father!*

He told me and Melissa that he'd walked this gauntlet countless times and it seemed everyone was Catholic when the chips were down. Then he waved a non-committal hand at some people, others got a salute, others got a quickie stations-of-the-cross, some a simple bye-bye or a hand puppet. He told us it didn't matter what he did and that it all worked because none of them knew any better. I hated him when he said it. Then he gave the middle-finger to a group of older men sifting through some trash. They responded with laughs and a hearty round of *Bless you, Father!*

He says, "Took four years of fundraising and two years of construction to get this place up and running."

Home is only one level, but almost the length of a City-block. Like the guard station, the building is attached to a post, though there are also cement footings attached to some other beams and struts. I haven't seen it yet, but I'm told Home's back end leads directly into the Dump.

I stir my soup and chunks of Farm chicken float to the surface. I say, "What do you do here at Home?"

He doesn't answer my question. He's talking to Melissa. Telling her about how Dump's base sits on the ocean floor, and how underwater wires and netting surrounds the base perimeter and acts like a sieve. Telling her how the salt water, with a little help from City Pharmaceutical's all-natural additive (that's how he put it), helps the trash to degrade quicker and then disperse and disintegrate into the ocean. Telling her that's why he never eats seafood when in City.

I say, "Is this place a soup kitchen? A shelter? Is this a weigh-station? Are you trying to rehabilitate the homeless and get them back up City side?"

He tells Melissa that the entire homeless population lives off Dump. At least, the homeless population that makes it this far. The homeless are usually dropped at a point far away from Dump and they have to climb and crawl their way to it.

I say, "So this is a hospital, then?"

He tells Melissa that even though City government knows all these people live off Dump, they still use the all-natural additive. When ingested, the all-natural additive breaks down the immune system, exacerbating and accelerating the spread of disease in an already disease-prone population. Tuberculosis, cholera, hepatitis, influenza, pneumonia, typhoid, malaria. It can't be said that the all-natural additive does not do its job: breaking down the world's largest compost heap.

I say, "So this is the place you abandoned us for. This is your calling, your reason, and you haven't said a goddamn word about what Home actually does." And right now I don't care how callous I sound, how selfish. Here's a man discussing the plight of thousands down here and I'm the kid who wants to know why this place was so important that he had to leave me and Mom.

He looks at me, and I feel Melissa zooming in for my reaction shot, and he says, "No, this is not a hospital. Yes, this place is why I left you and your mother. This place is a home for the dying."

42

MORE THAN YOU COULD POSSIBLY KNOW

I didn't believe that white-collared fraud until he took us to the Wing. It looks like a hospital. There are beds and every one of them occupied with a coughing or unconscious person. There are bedpans, IVs, feeding tubes, catheters, white linens. But this isn't a hospital. There aren't any monitors. There's nothing beeping or flashing. No flatlining EKG or iron lungs. Nothing to unplug. Nothing that can save people from dying. There are no doctors here, no nurses. Only the terminally ill and my father's volunteers. He introduces me to ten or so of them. I lose count. I've already forgotten their names. I'm not forgetting on purpose and I'm not trying to be mean. I'm just not ready yet.

My mother isn't in any of these beds. I've looked.

I do know that all the volunteers, with the exception of my father, are City deportees. The cynic in me believes they're only volunteering to be fed, that they're about as much of a volunteer as I am. I know I'm not being fair but I'm sure they're used to it.

We stand at the foot of a bed that cradles a middle-aged woman. Middle-aged is my best guess. It's hard to tell with the feeding tube, puffy face, matchstick arms, pale skin, deep, watery breaths. It reads tuberculosis on her chart.

My father says, "We can't save them. But Home is where we care for the dying. Our mission here is to make these people feel loved, wanted, human before they die."

We stand and watch the volunteers in action. They clean bedpans and empty catheters. Only some are wearing rubber gloves. No one wears surgical masks to prevent any respiratory ailments. They change sheets. They wheel dead bodies out and wheel barely breathing bodies in. They sit at bedsides, holding hands and rubbing the foreheads of the dying. They smile and laugh and talk to them all.

Father ESP taps his temple and says, "She's on her way out." He leans over the middle-aged woman's bed and whispers her name. Her eyes open. The whites aren't white. They're as red as a crayon, capillaries burst from her unrelenting coughs. She tries to say something. The feeding tube in her nose has a pink tinge.

He says, "You don't have to talk. I know."

The woman stops trying to speak.

He says, "I love you. You are important to me and everyone else here."

I wonder how many times he's said this to someone. Out of all those times he said that, I wonder if he ever meant it. I still hate him and I want him to sound rehearsed, but he doesn't. He sounds like he means it even if it's something I've never heard him say to his wife or son.

"You matter. You will be missed." He turns and looks at me. "Isn't that right?"

I'm sweating. Does this mean my body is crying and I'm just too much of an ass to follow suit? I'm supposed to say something. What can I possibly say to this discarded woman that wouldn't ring hollow? She knows better. She knows better than I do that no one loves or loved her. Maybe what my father is doing is wrong, trying to give an ounce of dignity and hope to the hopeless.

Melissa punches me in the back. I turn and she's flailing her free arm at the bed and the woman. Now is not the time to be thinking about her motivations, though I think she is crying behind the lens.

I step toward the bed, take a deep breath that isn't so deep, a breath conscious of where it is, and then I say, "I will mourn your passing more than you could possibly know."

I think she died before I got it out. My father told me I did a good job anyway. He told me that before I could tell him that I didn't think I could do this for the two weeks preceding the election.

Melissa pulls the camera off us and goes right to her smart phone. Melissa says yes and no into the phone between long stretches of time. My father and I don't say anything as he walks me to the sleeping quarters. A long linoleum hallway dumps us into a suite with four doors.

My father says, "Take any one of those three." Then he disappears behind the fourth door. I hear it lock.

Melissa sticks her phone in my ear. It's The CM. This is what I hear:

"The premier episode just aired," then, "The last ten minutes were a live feed," then, "Congratulations," then, "The ratings are through the roof," then, "Insta-track polls show you gaining by as much as ten points," then, "Of course that brings your total to eleven points," then, "Ha ha!" then, "Ha ha!"

43

23VI4900-I

Melissa isn't here. She positioned a camera on a tripod and it's filming me now. This is what I am doing:

I'm in my room lying in a cot with her phone cradled to my chest. I can't sleep. The walls in here aren't thick enough to keep the crashing sounds out. City must be making a deposit to Dump. There's a rattle of debris on Home's roof and one loud thud, then it stops. I wonder how many people were hurt and how often it all comes crashing down on their heads. There likely isn't any warning from above.

I am not going to make it here. It's still two weeks before the election.

I dial the police hotline number. No need to turn on a light to see my mother's thirteen character case code still tattooed on my arm because I've memorized it. I punch in the code and this time there's a new voice and message saying, *please hold for the next available agent*. I sit up fast, ready to sprint to wherever it is I need to sprint to because they know where my mother is. They know where she is!

"Hello, City Police."

"Hello?" I speak in a hushed tone. I'm not sure why speaking in my normal tone seems wrong while alone in this dark room. "Do you know where she . . . um . . . my mother is?" Fucking A, listen to me. When did I become this helpless and pathetic?

More loud crashes. The fuckers are dumping more trash on us.

The agent on the phone says something but I don't quite hear it. I thought this person said *I have no idea where your mommy is, you wuss*. But that can't be right. I say, "Sorry, could you repeat that?

More crashing. Trash lands on the roof right above my head, the cot and floor vibrate from the impact. Burnt-out TVs or dishwasher asteroids falling on my ass. I say, "My neighbours are moving furniture or something."

"Case number, please."

"What?" This is an I-heard-you-but-don't-quite-believe-what-you're-saying-to-me *what*.

"Case number, please." The agent is clearly annoyed with me and the continuing ruckus. Everything in me sinks all the way into my toes. I give the numbers. I hear a flurry of computer keys. Then a return of the automated voice. "Thank you for calling City Police. If you'd like to make a donation to any of the Policemen's Ball charities please press one, otherwise stay on the line for your requested information." There's a click, a hint of hold music, then I hear,

"Case denied: invalid reported information error: 23UI4900-1."

I stay on the line. The message loops until the phone hangs up on its own. How convenient.

It's only a few hours before my first morning shift at Home and I won't be able to sleep now. I mess around with Melissa's smart phone, and find myself on the Internet. The City NewsWire has the following headlines:

FARM UP AND RUNNING AT NORMAL LEVELS

FORTY-THREE FARM WORKERS ARRESTED ON CONSPIRACY CHARGES

FIFTEENTH SUICIDE BOMBING IN A WEEK BRINGS DEATH TOLL TO 1344

DOW REACHES A NEW HIGH (MAYOR SOLOMON PREDICTS GOLDEN ECONOMIC AGE)

SLUMPING CITYTODAY MORNING SHOW TO GET A 'MAKEOVER'

THE CANDIDATE WINS RATINGS WAR ON OPENING NIGHT

On the front page of NewsWire there's a link to the footage of my Farm escape. I download it and watch. I hoped seeing it on the small phone screen would make it seem less real, but it's not working that way. Nothing works the way we want it to. Watching this vid hurts. I watch it back-to-back-to-back and I will continue to do so because I don't know why it hurts. I don't miss Jonah. Honestly, I don't. At least, I don't think I do. I'm sorry he died so horribly, but there hasn't been a moment since that I wished it was me instead of him. To me, that means I don't miss him.

After watching the donkey explode and kill Jonah for fifteen minutes, and after three years of living and working and then blowing up with Jonah, I find myself mercifully drifting toward sleep, but also remembering this:

It was my first month at Farm and Jonah was still filling me up with his conspiracy theories and life lessons. He'd once tried so hard to be the father figure he knew I didn't have. During a lunch break, after toasting my one-month anniversary, he hit me with his theory behind why homeless life might not be so bad. How once removed from the money and guns and corruption and bullshit of City, the homeless could create a kind of primitive utopian society. Everyone caring and looking out for one another because they had to. That made sense, right? They had no choice if they wanted to survive. Wasn't it possible that the homeless would be okay, that it was what they ultimately wanted—to be ignored and alone and just out of the way? Maybe it was good for them, and they were happy and they weren't getting hurt. They were different than us. They were equipped for homelessness. They could handle it. They were meant for it. They deserved it.

No one at the lunch table really argued with Jonah. They wanted to believe what he was saying. I know I did. How else could we live with ourselves, otherwise?

44

HANGIN' WITH QVAZ

Days and nights bleed together because there isn't any drastic brightening with morning or darkening with night down here. I mark the passage of days by cot-time and phone calls from the now rabid CM. I've been at Home for a week. I still don't know where my mother is.

My Home partner is a man my father has dubbed Quaz, as in Quasimodo. The reasons for his nickname are obvious if not utterly cruel. He doesn't seem to mind my father giving him the nickname. I feel like a shit-heel whenever I call him Quaz, but he won't offer his real name. So fuck him.

In this first week, Quaz and I have honed a routine. In the morning we clear Home's roof of trash with push brooms. Then Quaz, me, and Melissa (of course Melissa follows us wherever we go) search Dump for the dying. We always find more than enough to fill any empty beds at Home. When I don't think Quaz and Melissa are looking, I'll ask people if they've seen my mother.

The search is the worst part of our day and our day is a cornucopia of worst parts. Death is everywhere—horrible, painful, and undignified. People fall off the posts and beams, or they jump. They drop like a tree might lose its leaves. If the bodies don't land in the water, they become a soon-to-be scavenged carcass. Picked over by other people and water rats so big they should be called something other than rats. I've seen people crushed by falling trash and a few lost underneath a landslide of refuse. Disease, vermin, and decay are thicker than the fogs that sweep through here. As we walk and climb through Dump and Pier, trailing our gurneys behind us, everyone begs us to take them Home, to feed them, clothe them, take care of them. Gangs of younger males physically threaten us but have yet to follow through on those threats. Most go from begging to offering all manner of sexual favours or clung-to heirlooms and personal trinkets. My father wasn't lying when he said the homeless were still potential consumers.

Upon returning Home, we spend the afternoon caring for these terminally ill people, talking to them, telling them we love them and that we care about what happens to them. Home's stated mission is to convince our patients they are not being cosmically or karmically punished and that they deserve our love and care. We are rarely successful. Although, Quaz is especially good at this aspect of his job. He kisses them all on the forehead as his greeting. He has no fear of catching their diseases or viruses. Me? I'm deathly, morbidly, shit-scared of Hepatitis C. It kills at least half our clientele. In my limited experience, it is by far the messiest and quickest disease passing through here. Vomiting, diarrhea, yellow skin that cracks and bleeds, and it's so very contagious. I wear latex gloves and wash my hands and face so many times my skin is raw and ashen.

Before dinner we clear out the morgue. The morgue is a large, empty room in the back of Home. Throughout the day, staff simply stack the dearly departed against the walls. By the time we get there the room is SRO and full of the unmistakable smell and heat of rot. We bring the bodies out behind Home to a somewhat cleared area of Dump, incinerate the bodies, and send the ash to the water below.

Tonight, as the ashes fall, Quaz mumbles a little prayer in a language I don't understand. I assume it's a prayer. Given that my father-the-father runs the show here, I expected more God-squad kind of talk than I've been hearing.

I say, "Where'd you hear that?"

He says, "Nowhere." He doesn't look at me when I talk to him, even though we've cleaned vomit, blood, and shit off each other for a week now. He closes the incinerator hatch, his Popeye forearms black with ash. He says, "I made it up."

I say, "It sounded nice."

"Thank you. I want to say something important to the ashes. Something that's never been said. But when the time comes, I can't think of anything. So I just let the sounds come out and hope I get lucky."

I nod my head. This makes more sense to me than anything else I've heard since I've been down here.

Quaz straightens as much as he can, pushes some of that black hair out of his eyes and looks at me. One eye is bigger than the other and his mouth slants, so I can't be sure, but I think he's smiling at me. He says, "You know what Father says when he's out here with me?"

"No."

"He tells me a joke, to try and make me laugh. He says, 'Quaz, I have a joke for you. Do you know what someone who lives in City says to these ashes?' I say, 'I don't know, Father,' even though he says this to me all the time. He says, 'Those assholes, they all say *no fuss, no muss.*'"

45

COME ON AND SEE THE SHOW!

"Where've you been today? They cancel the show?"

Melissa has been AWOL for a few hours, which was fine by me. Gave me a chance to search for my mother by myself. And she didn't get to videotape me leaning up against a post and puking on my shoes after I stepped on a desiccated torso and head (though by appearance, not a matching set, as if that matters) during the morning run for bed-fillers.

She doesn't turn off the camera. She never turns off the camera. "*The Candidate* has been the highest rated show for eight straight nights."

"I know that. The CM call me every night with the stats."

She pulls her black baseball cap tight over her eyes, then takes a bite of a BLT. Mid-chew she says, "I was out with Joseph, filming."

"Is that code for you guys were out staging your own version of *Thorn Birds*?" It's my turn to be the asshole. And I'm okay with it. I don't like Melissa. I don't like a lot of people and I'm probably not very likable myself, but I don't like her. I don't like that she's making a mint off this mountain of human suffering. I don't like that she doesn't do anything down here but point that camera and watch and watch and watch. She watches like she's not really here, like she has no other moral responsibility to affect the here-and-now. She's nothing but an impotent and omniscient eye, documenting and detailing everything but changing nothing. No, I don't believe anything will change down here because of her and *The Candidate*. *The Candidate* isn't journalism or a documentary. It's a show. A show isn't real. A show panders. A show entertains. A show covers its eyes during the ugliest parts. If you don't like a show you can change the channel and watch something else, probably a sitcom about beautiful rich people or flip over to the news where they tell you how the days' events affect the beautiful rich people or click and there's another *reality* show about beautiful rich people.

Melissa says, "I know you don't like me, but I'm going to tell you anyway."

"Why do you say I don't like you?"

"Your disdain is obvious."

"I don't think that's true. I think I hide it very well."

"Joseph told me you think I'm akin to a social parasite."

"Of course he did. I don't like you because you call my father by his first name," I say and get up from the lunch table.

"Do you want to hear about where I was or not, Mr. Mayor?"

I do. I want to know about the exploitation flick she made with Father Love-'em-and-leave-'em. I sit back down.

Melissa says, "This morning, Joseph tipped me to a bunch of men in suits carrying duffle bags and guns climbing on the north side of Dump. He told me they come about once a week. He told me about what they did. I didn't believe him. So I went out and interviewed one of the suits. Didn't take long to find one once I knew where to look. We reached a binding verbal agreement to disguise his voice and black-bar his eyes should the tape ever be viewed, which isn't likely. I know who and what I am down here. Anyway, I got lucky and found the leader of this particular group. He's an affluent City businessman and he agreed to take me on their Expedition, as they called it. They had water, food, drugs, alcohol, even money in their duffle bags. They offered it to anyone and everyone in return for blow jobs. They turned away no buyers. I filmed it all. Later, this Expedition leader boasted that he sometimes took down groups who recruited serviceable females and young boys to be their pet prostitutes hidden away in the abandoned buildings of City's North End. He said in a month he's even taking down a Mayor-approved group of doctors who will trade duffle-bag goodies for blood. If it goes well, maybe they'll come back for organ donation. He said none of this was a secret. He said waste not want not." Melissa goes back to hiding behind her camera. She says, "For what it's worth. I don't like you either. You're like a dog being led by the scruff."

I say, "I know that. I've always been the dog. But I'm still helping people down here. You? You aren't in the background, you are the background, like everyone else."

Melissa stands and says, "Zooming," and walks toward me, slow, like an animal stalking its prey, not that I've ever seen a real animal stalk real prey, just what they show me on TV. "You're only here because you have to be."

"So what? You're not telling me anything I haven't already figured out."

She comes closer with the camera. Her progress is slow, but inexorable. If I stare, I can't see the movement. I only notice the shrinking distance between me and the camera after not paying attention to it. She says, "I'm just making sure you understand that I'm the only person at this table who volunteered to come down here." Melissa keeps going with her manual-zoom, the camera and the lens makes contact with me, right between the eyes, and she keeps pressing and pushing and zooming.

46

SOMETHING BLVE FOR PVSSY

It's my ninth day down here. The CM call right before Quaz and I do our bring-out-your-dying sweep of Pier and Dump.

They say, "We need a big night on *The Candidate*," then, "Only three days until the election," then, "Your numbers have leveled off," then, "You're still behind by 15," then, "Polls say the people still don't identify with you," then, "You need to do something tonight," then, "Something new," then, "Something bold."

I say, "Something blue?" but they don't laugh. "I'm just trying to make it through each day without succumbing to a drooling and pants-shitting insanity. If me being surrounded by horrifying government-sanctioned death and suffering isn't entertaining enough for the Nielsen families, then fuck them."

They say, "That's the spirit," then, "Show the camera that fire," then, "You've been like a zombie for the past three days," then, "Very boring," then, "Very un-Mayoral," then, "The I-just-want-to-find-my-mommy shtick isn't working," then, "Makes you seem weak," then, "Ten percent of the respondents in last night's insta-poll said you were a pussy," then, "Harsh, but you did come off pussy-ish last night," then, "We're not going to lie to you," then, "That bit where you paused to wipe your eyes," then, "Very pussy," then, "People aren't going to vote for a pussy," then, "But, we'll take some blame, too," then, "We knew we shouldn't have aired that segment," then, "Should've cut it," then, "But don't dwell on this," then, "You can and will fix this," then, "You have to show some fire," then, "Some righteous indignation," then, "Some angst," then, "You have to inspire the people," then, "You want them to want to call you their master and overlord," then, "Not a pussy."

Pussy? I can't talk. I'm so angry my tongue has hardened into a fist. I grunt into the phone. I growl. I seethe. Last night I finally acquiesced to Melissa and gave her a real *confessional*. Me talking one on one with the camera. I used it like a milk box. I asked the camera if anyone had seen this missing woman. I didn't have a picture, of course, but I described my mother and gave her name and old address. Then I told a quick anecdote about her taking in a stray cat despite our abject poverty. The fleabag hated me, took dumps on my bed and bit and scratched me at all opportunities. It hid under the couch in the TV room and if I was wearing shorts when I walked by it'd dart out from under the couch and shred my legs, then go back under the couch. I didn't tell Melissa's camera that part of the kitty tale, of course. Okay, a lame story. I'll admit it. I was just trying to think of something quick to tell that would make my mother a real, live human being for all the TV-watching chimpheads out there. She's not just a homeless or missing person; she's not an abstract label.

They say, "You still there?" then, "You're mad, aren't you," then, "We don't mean to offend," then, "But politics is a bitch," then, "You have to start growing a thicker skin," then, "Or you'll be eaten alive," then, "Crying over Mommies and kitties won't play in City."

I choke the phone and what I first say to them is this: "I wasn't crying. When was I crying, goddamn it? What the fuck? I wiped my eyes after I sneezed for Chrissakes!"

They say, "That's not how it looks on the vid we saw," then, "There wasn't any sneeze," then, "We saw all choked up," then, "We saw I-can't-go-on," then, "We saw pussy."

Goddamn Melissa. She must've fucked with the tape, edited it to make it look like I was fighting back tears. Which I wasn't. And now I'm thinking I must be a pussy because I'm arguing with the twin sociopaths not about how they've reduced the plight of humanity in the Pier to *boring*, but about how I wasn't actually crying.

They say, "Solomon is using it against you," then, "Running new ads about how you abandoned your mother," then, "He juxtaposes clips of you wiping your eyes and him flexing his arms and showing his fists," then, "He says that this proves you don't have the moral fiber to be a leader," then, "Our numbers show it's a more damaging tact than harping on your Farm escape and terrorist links," then, "That got stale quick for him," then, "He overplayed it," then, "That's right," then, "Because criminals as Mayor we can have," then, "But not teary-eyed pussies."

I want this election to go away. I'm sick of them treating me like anything other than a patsy candidate. I say, "How's this for thicker skin: Fuck and You. If you motherfuckers were standing in front of me now, I would wrap one hand around each of your throats and squeeze until your heads popped off. Then I'd take a couple of cameras and stuff them down your necks until the fucking lenses poked out of your assholes. And voila, a reverse colonoscopy, and an appropriate political point of view for the TV audience."

"Ha ha!" then, "Ha ha!" then, "That's our guy."

47

WHISTLE WHILE YOV WORK

Quaz and I decide to search the levels above Home to change the routine if nothing else. I will not admit to searching a new area because the CM want me to liven things up. I will not admit it. This is just another day in the daily search for the dying and my daily search for my mother, which hasn't gone anywhere. Despite the continued failure and what Father ESP says, I know she's down here somewhere.

I split from Quaz and climb a level above him. Every person I find, I ask two questions: Are you feeling okay? Have you seen my mother? I follow up the second question with a brief physical description. No one says yes to both questions. I climb a bit higher, into a shadowy and gnarled section of beams and find a dirt-old woman sitting in the crook of the cross section, perched like a bird. She fusses with paper, cloth, and the other garbage that makes up her nest. I visually scan her dried husk of a body for any obvious signs of terminal illness.

I'm a regular Florence Nightingale.

"Are you feeling okay?"

She says, "Don't come too close! I'm scared." I try to tell her that I won't hurt her, that I'm there to help, but she continues. "I'm so scared I can't do nothing anymore. Nothing but sit in this corner. It's terrible. I get the shakes and shivers. See?" She holds out her hands, and they are shaking. "I can't sleep. I can't close my eyes from the worry. I'm worrying myself to death, worrying City and all this wood that's everywhere will come crashing down on my head." She slips into another language, Russian, maybe, but I don't know. Doesn't matter because two things are clear: she doesn't need Home's help just yet, and she's too out of her head to be of any help to me. I not-so-subtly try to slink away.

She says, "Wait! You need to know it's all going to come crashing down, squash us, drown us, mix us in with water and wood, and buildings and blood and bones. I try to tell them, but no one listens." She talks faster than the CM and worries her nest the whole time. "That's the truth. I don't know much, but I know that. Someday it's all going to come down. Someday soon."

Maybe I should take her back to Home, let someone else decide if she can stay there or not. I offer. She shakes me off and throws a can at me. I duck and cover, and slink away without asking her if she's met my mother down here. I'm not that desperate even if I am that desperate.

Quaz hooks back up with me on the way down to his level. I tell him about the old woman. He laughs and tells me that she threw a colander at him two weeks ago, and then we continue our search.

We find a man lying on a wide, four-lane beam. Heavy foot traffic passes him by, no one cares enough to lend a hand, or even kick him off the post and into the water. He's a skeleton inside a plaid cardigan sweater and gray nylon running pants. His skin is yellower than butter, closer to lemon. Hepatitis C, in spades. I don't want to touch him, but Quaz throws Mr. Hepatitis over his shoulder and hump. Mr. Hepatitis is awake but unresponsive. He doesn't resist. Our climb down to Home's level is a struggle with Quaz catching the brunt of it. His arms and legs are shaking as we stagger into Home.

"Welcome back, boys," my father says. I don't really see much of the old man these days. He pops in and out of the Wing to greet newcomers and to say bon voyage to the out-goers. Literally, that's what he says to the deceased as we wheel them out, *bon voyage*! It's no fancy eulogy or last rites, but appropriate, I think. Otherwise, he's the administrative guy, the string puller who stays in his office and on his phone or computer. Only, when I go looking for him, he's never in his office. He's in his room, behind a locked door. The great and powerful Oz. If I sound bitter about this, I don't intend to. I'm starting to almost understand what and why he sacrificed for this place.

PAVL TREMBLAY

We put Mr. Hepatitis in a bed. His eyes open and they're egg yolks. I ask him his name. He shakes his head, which is something very painful to do judging by facial expressions. He says something in a language I do not understand. Quaz recognizes it as a Hindi dialect. This means we have to find an interpreter. My father the father comes to see our new roomie and he approves our finding and bringing in an interpreter for our newest patient. We can offer our interpreter food and shelter for as long as Mr. Hepatitis is alive. This is not written in any sort of contract. Quaz goes out on an interpreter search by himself. Padre stays. Melissa stays, of course and ad nauseum ad infinitum. And I stay with the new patient even though I am petrified of him. He is a balloon filled to burst with his illness.

My throat is dry and lips clamp tight. Breathing is shallow. My body is on Hep C yellow-alert. So when I try to say universally reassuring things in a universally reassuring tone of voice, I know I'm not convincing. He talks but I don't understand. He sounds afraid, or maybe he's agitated, angry. I can't tell.

My father says, "Comfort him, will you, please?"

"How?" I say, but I know the answer.

"Pretend for a second that you're not afraid of him. Smile. You know, whistle while you work." He actually whistles the tune.

So I'm supposed to be an oh-so-cute dwarf now, whistling while I work, and I imagine myself as one of the dwarves mindlessly whistling while I shorten my life span by breathing in diamond dust and those gases that killed the canaries (they won't be whistling anymore!) or get crushed in a cave-in while in the last hour of my twelve-hour, minimum-wage shift, *In the mine, in the mine* . . .

Father ESP says, "Lighten up and get a grip, Dopey. This isn't about you. Fine, don't whistle then. Just hold his hand, cradle his head, hug him, do something, Mr. Mayor." He says all this in a light, airy tone, like he's talking to a precocious toddler who is deserving of the highest praise.

I want to say *you do it. You give comfort to Typhoid Harry, I'd like to see you give comfort since I never got to see you do it back in the day, you know, when you were my father.* But he's right. This isn't and shouldn't be about me. So I give Mr. Hepatitis my bestest smile, reach into my pocket and pull out some latex gloves.

My father says, "Gloves. Jesus. You're being a pussy again." Then he walks away, grumbling to himself.

I take the latex gloves and make a balloon with udders, a fake cow. I make another one and bat them in the air above my head. I force some smiles and even a small chuckle but it sounds hateful. So I stop and grab this guy's hand. He's two-thousand degrees warm. He sweats and shivers. I talk. I don't lie and tell him he'll be okay even though he doesn't understand me. I lie and tell him that I love him, like I'm supposed to. Then I ask him if he's seen my mother.

He bolts upright and throws up all over me. All. Over. Me. Green bile tinged with some pink in my hair and on my face and clothes and hands and arms, and I'm a dead man unless someone turns a scalding hot fire hose on me right now.

My father is back. He says, "Oh, son?"

I stand up, dripping incurable virus and disease. He tosses me a damp facecloth.

He says, "You'll be fine. Clean yourself up." He walks away whistling.

48

THE MORNING AFTER THAT NIGHT (BVT BEFORE SHE CAVGHT ME IN THE ELEVATOR SHAFT)

The morning after *that* night (but before she caught me in the elevator shaft) we were up with the sun. It was orange again, not yellow, and unwelcome. It still came through our windows, regardless. I usually got up early, but she didn't. Mom scrambled eggs and hummed a song that I didn't know. Its melody had a lilt, but some abrupt, sharp changes. I sat at the kitchen table with a glass of frozen-concentrate OJ and an empty plate. When she finished her song the eggs were done. Then we had breakfast together. None of this was normal.

We sat as far away from each other as possible at the little kitchen table. She issued smiles that were afraid of me. She gave me eggs too, but I wouldn't eat them. I told her my stomach was a little too grumbly for eggs. So she made me a bowl of Frosted Farm Flakes instead. I only ate a few spoonfuls. My spoon was an old Spiderman spoon: half-metal and half-rubbery plastic. I wore only my Spiderman underwear. I was getting too old for Spiderman underwear, but it was the only clean pair I had left in my drawer. She wore her pink terrycloth robe. The robe she always wore around the apartment. She tried another smile. I told her she had eggs in her teeth. I thought she might cry, but she laughed instead. A big laugh.

Why was she laughing? Her behaviour was as perplexing to me then as it always had been. I had always craved the attention of my parents, those omniscient gods who acted with motivations and reasons I didn't understand, but I didn't question. As I grew up my gods became fallible before my faithless eyes. What was more confusing or depressing than watching your gods become human?

She still laughed while she picked egg out of her teeth. She made a joke about being a classy babe. I laughed a little with her, wanting to join in, to still be a part of her team. Then I dropped my spoon into the still-full cereal bowl and wrapped my skinny arms around my folded legs, hugging my knees to my chest.

She asked me if I was done. I told her I was.

She wasn't laughing anymore. Her hands disappeared behind her head, making sure her hair stayed tied up, then she tightened her robe belt, and she was still so very young. She said I could leave the table and that I could eat a Farm Pop Tart if I was hungry later.

I climbed out of the kitchen chair. I was still so very young but getting older. I left my god (the only one I had left) sitting at the table, and ran to the living room and the TV. Ten minutes into the cartoon and its neon violence, I listened to my god put the dishes into the sink. She wasn't humming her song anymore. Her slippers shuffled past the living room and then down the hall. She went to her bedroom and closed the door. Then I listened to my god crying herself back to sleep. Eventually, I stopped listening.

49

THE LONG SLOW GOODBYE

Bright and early, only not so bright, and it's the day before the election. For days, the CM have called me every two hours with numbers and updates. They tell me I'm closing in on Mayor Solomon, but I need a spectacular finale to *The Candidate* for a real shot at winning.

Quaz has been missing for two days and I assumed something happened to him on his search, but today he makes it back with an interpreter in tow. And, apparently, the interpreter's name is Peter.

While my father gives Peter the once over, I pull Quaz aside and I say, "A homeless white guy named Peter speaks Hindi?"

Quaz shrugs his shoulders. At least, I think he shrugs his shoulders. He can't really achieve that kind of body language with his giant hump. He says, "I looked everywhere. There were others who spoke Hindi, but he was the only one who would come back with me."

I say, "Why?"

Peter says, "I couldn't help but overhear. I can answer that." He smiles then cracks his knuckles. Peter is middle-aged, wears a stained golf-shirt and khaki pants. He somehow managed to keep his beer gut in good standing and has a nice comb over. "For twenty-five years I managed Barter Brother's toy-making plant. The plant employed a significant population of Hindi speaking folks, so I had to learn the language. Five years ago CareCo bought us out and closed the plant. Two-weeks severance and then kicked to the curb like everyone else. Can't say I blame them, though. Business is business.

"Anyway, let me answer your question. No one else came back to Home because the Hindi-speaking Hindus believe this guy is being punished for sins in his previous life. Of course there are plenty of Hindi-speaking Muslims and Hindi-speaking Christians and even some Hindi-speaking Jews, but they believe he did something to fall out of God's good graces. Basically, everyone thinks he must've done something to deserve his horrible death."

I've had enough of this Peter guy already. Peter certainly sounds like a plant manager, like my old buddy BM. The sound: a pompous, self-absorbed asshole who isn't even capable of feigning realistic empathy.

My father-the-father nods and says, "Sounds about right. Consistent with those God-fearing dopes who fill my church. They believe God only punishes the guilty. The saps."

I say, "Quaz, couldn't find any Hindi-speaking agnostics or atheists or druids?"

Quaz says, "I did, but they all thought this guy would be better off with an assisted suicide."

Peter interrupts. "Can't say I disagree with them. Would ease his pain and save you guys time and funds."

My father says, "Ah, I see you found us a Hindi-speaking Capitalist!"

Peter says, "Amen."

Padre and Peter share a laugh, then exchange a few more pithy aphorisms about religion and suffering and capitalism. Their smug labelling and know-it-all-ness while standing at the foot of Mr. Hepatitis's bed makes me want to vomit.

"Okay." Peter rubs his fat hands together and adds, "So where's the grub? I'm starving."

I say, "You eat after you help us talk to this guy."

I tell Peter that Mr. Hepatits is fading fast. That he has vomited on me three times. That he's too weak to eat solid food. We had to snake a feeding tube through his nose. He was too weak to protest. He likely only has a day, maybe two left in him.

Mr. Hepatitis is awake and Peter tries to chat him up. I pull Quaz aside and ask him how he knows this guy can actually speak Hindi. Quaz tells me it doesn't matter, because he was the only one willing to come back.

Peter says, "I'm a little rusty with the particular dialect this guy uses, but I can understand him."

I say, "What did he say to you?"

"Not much. He wouldn't tell me his name. He doesn't like the tube in his nose."

"Tell him it's a feeding tube. It'll help him keep his food down."

Peter talks, Mr. Hepatitis nods slowly. Then he says, "Okay, what next, boss?"

My father walks away without a long slow goodbye. Or even a quick one.

I pull up a chair near Mr. Hepatitis's head. Peter maneuvers behind me, but not very gracefully. He bounces the back of my head off his gut. I tell Peter to start translating everything I say to this man.

I grab Mr. Hepatitis's hand (sans gloves) and I say, "You are loved. We love you. I love you."

Peter interrupts, "Whoa, whoa, whoa! Just what kind of place you running here? I didn't sign up for this." He backs away holding his palms up, like I had a gun pointed at him.

I should go ape-shit on this guy. Throttle him. Beat him about the head and neck. But I don't have it in me. If I'm going to communicate with Mr. Hepatitis, I need him. I say, simply, "You can leave now, without lunch, if you're not comfortable with me treating this man with dignity."

Peter says, "What's for lunch."

"Hotdogs and beans."

"Real hotdogs?"

As if there were actually any such thing as a real hot dog, but I answer, "Yes, real hot dogs. As many as you'd like." Peter scurries back into position.

I say, "Okay, from the top." And I tell Mr. Hepatitis that he matters. His life is and was important. I tell him he is loved. Or more importantly, that he is deserving of our love, our care. But he doesn't believe me. In a voice that is breathy and high pitched, he speaks to Peter.

Peter translates: "I am being punished."

I say, "For what?"

There's a long pause. Some laboured breaths. Then, quiet, and unsure, some words that Peter takes and chews up and spits out. "I don't know."

I say, "No, you are not being punished. You've done nothing to deserve this. Can I have your name please?"

I wait for Peter to translate and Mr. Hepatitis to respond. He speaks, this time gesticulating with his marionette arms. "I've done something to piss off the universe."

I look at Peter. Brow furrowed so hard my eyebrows might rip off my face.

Peter says, "Well, that's the gist of what he said. In not so many words."

I say, "No more *gist*. I want a word-for-word translation or no hot dogs for you."

"Slave driver, sheesh."

We continue in this manner throughout the morning hours. Mr. Hepatitis still insists that he's lower than dirt and isn't deserving of anyone's love or care, but slowly, we share details and information. I explain to him as best I can what the pinkish stuff is in the feeding tube. He tells me he doesn't know what's happening to his wife and two children who were left behind in City. I tell him Home's mission statement. He tells me he made a complete mess of things in City. I tell him he could tell me why he was down here if he liked, but it doesn't matter because I won't judge and I will still care for him and I will still talk to him. He tells me he misses drinking soda and eating French fries. I tell him my name. He tells me he doesn't miss TV. I tell him that I fear my mother is down here. He tells me his name is Feroz and he too fears for my mother. Before Peter and I break for lunch, I tell Feroz that I'm running for Mayor. Feroz wishes me luck and tells me I can't be any worse than anyone else.

Peter and I eat a hurried lunch. Peter consumes a frightening amount of hotdogs. There's no way he'll be able to keep all of that down.

We go back to Feroz's bedside. We've been gone twenty minutes and he looks worse, but upon our return Feroz gives me a smile. He's yellowing and weakening and disappearing before our eyes, but a smile is a smile is a smile. This smile is a good sign. It isn't fake or hiding cruel or deceitful thoughts and words behind it. This smile means everything. It's all I can ask of him.

Peter doesn't notice because he's still working through the last of his hotdog-o-rama feast, his payment.

Feroz speaks. Peter gives me: "Did you enjoy your lunch?"

"Yes, I did, actually." I smile. Feroz returns it. Maybe I can send Peter on his merry way. I likely don't need him anymore. Feroz and I are smiling, and communication is that simple. What's complex is that I want him to die, to have a merciful end to his suffering; and I don't want him to die, and I don't want to see Feroz stacked in the body room and I don't want to see Quaz stick his body in the incinerator. I know which of my he-dies he-doesn't-die wishes is selfish.

Peter still stuffs his face full of hotdog. He must have hidden a couple in his pockets. The sound of him chewing fills the room. I look at Peter and say, "A real hard-working interpreter you are." I point at Peter and smirk the isn't-this-guy-a-jerk smirk for Feroz's benefit.

Peter says, "You'd be nowhere without me."

Melissa's smart phone goes off. I almost forgot about her. Almost.

She says, "It's for you."

I wave the back of my hand twice. Brushing her and them off. Feroz is teaching me that I don't need words to communicate anymore. I'm saving my words. They're too important to waste.

She says, "It's your campaign managers, and they insist."

I haven't talked to Melissa since the doctored crying-tape incident. More brush-off hand waving from me.

She says, "They think you're turning into a pussy

again and they need something spectacular for tonight's finale."

I break my code of silence. "Tell them I'm firing their worthless asses."

Melissa doesn't tell them anything. But Feroz says something. Peter doesn't translate for me, but says something back to Feroz. Then I watch Feroz's smile die. At the risk of hyperbole, it's one of the worst things I've ever seen.

I grab Feroz's hand. I feel him trying to pull away from me, but he's too weak. He won't look at me. "Peter, what did you say to him?"

"Um . . . nothing?"

"What do you mean, *nothing*? You said something to him, what the fuck was it?"

"He asked me what you said to her and I just repeated it."

Through clenched, enamel-dripping teeth I say, "What. Did. You. Say. To. Feroz?"

"Wait a minute." Peter closes his eyes and whispers Hindi to himself, a bad actor trying to remember the lines he just fucked up beyond recognition. "Okay. Oh, shit. Maybe I screwed up the dialects. I tried to tell him you said the person you were on the phone with was worthless." Peter stops eating hotdog. "Shit. Maybe Feroz thinks you were saying that he was worthless."

"Really? You think so, Peter? What makes you think that? Is that your years of managerial expertise shining through?" I look at Feroz and I know if he could turn his head completely around until his face was buried in the pillow, he would. "Get over here and tell him you fucked up!"

Peter moves his bulk closer to Feroz. Fucking mustard stains on his gut and all. He talks to Feroz. Who knows what he is saying. Feroz ignores him. Completely.

Melissa's phone goes off again. I jump out of my seat, try to grab her camera, but miss because of her sidestep. I say, "Shut off that phone."

Peter is still talking at Feroz. The phone still rings. Feroz is still dying. Everyone down here is still homeless. My mother is still missing. Everything will come crashing down soon. I've never felt so helpless.

"That's enough," I say to Peter. He stops and slides past my chair and then me, taking care not to brush up against me. I send Peter away. He apologizes and keeps on apologizing and that full-of-hotdogs-and-nothing-else buffoon dares to leave me with, "I was just trying to help." As if good intentions somehow absolve his disastrous incompetence. I don't answer him. I don't look at him. I ignore him. Because if I pay any attention to him, I will kill him. He leaves.

I sit on the edge of Feroz's bed. I can't tell if he's closed his eyes to keep from looking at me or if he's unconscious. A yellow discharge leaks out his eyes. My weight forms a valley in the mattress, forcing Feroz's body to turn toward me.

Feroz is dying and I know I'm his unwitting killer even though his body was already dead before I met him. His blood pressure drops. There's blood working upstream in his feeding tube. Blood in his colostomy bag. I hold his hand. His skin hot enough to burn through to the back of mine. Hot enough to turn me into ash. I hold his hand and I talk to him. No interpreters. I tell him I'm sorry. I tell him that I lied to him but he probably knew that already. I tell him I don't know if everyone is deserving of love or care or dignity. I tell him I don't know that everyone's life has intrinsic value like it says in Home's mission statement. I tell him I think there are plenty of people who are walking piles of shit. I tell him I do not know what the value of his life is. I tell him I care about him anyway. I tell all this to him over and over and over and over and over and over and over and over.

And I give him his long slow goodbye.

50

ALL COMING DOWN

Quaz and I know this drill. We put Feroz's body on a gurney. I have not pulled the sheet over his face. There's nothing to hide anymore. We load the shelf underneath the gurney with a box of Feroz's soiled sheets and IV lines and feeding tube. We go through the body room and out the back into Dump and to the incinerator.

There's a gaggle of teens and kids out back with us, picking through the trash, asking us for handouts. All we're carrying is the dead. Once they figure that out, the teen boys shout at Quaz, call him a slave, and make fun of his hump. Quaz shouts back at them. I notice Melissa and the camera retreat to the safety of the body room's doorway. She's still filming. Quaz takes the box of Hep C infected medical supplies off the gurney and I unload Feroz into the incinerator. There are flames. His body goes in. I'll miss him and I'll think about him. I close the hatch. I think about Quaz's prayer technique, and I give it a try, but nothing comes out. There's really nothing more to say.

Quaz is behind me with the box o' Hep C that we need to incinerate. Someone throws a bottle and hits Quaz in the head. The cool, calm, Zen-like Quaz I've lived with for almost two weeks goes absolutely bat shit. He growls and grunts and drops everything and runs out into Dump. Yelling and screaming and crying and trying to catch one of the scurrying teens.

I jog a few steps away from the incinerator and toward where Quaz ran to and I yell, "Quaz, relax. Come back! You're going to get hurt." Then there are rustling sounds behind me. Melissa cries out from the doorway and from behind her camera. I turn. Near the incinerator are two young children. One boy wearing a superman sweatshirt and jeans. One girl wearing a surprisingly clean summer dress; it's blue. They have dumped the box o' Hep C and they sit criss-cross-applesauce in the debris. Their little hands are wrapped around the feeding tube, one tube-end is in each of their mouths. They suck and search for food. I hear them sucking, their hunger, their tug-of-war over the pink remnants. Tube-food mixed with mucus and bile and blood. Their throats move when they swallow.

This is despair. I see it in front of me. I hear it in Quaz's screaming rage. I hear it in Melissa's quiet tears very much in the background. What am I supposed to do? What are any of us supposed to do?

I yell, "Drop that!" and run over to the children.

The boy takes advantage of the girl's momentary surprise at my voice. He snatches the tube from her. He has the treasure all to himself now. He takes off into Dump clutching his prize. I give chase for ten hard, climbing steps. But then a toaster oven lands on my next step.

I look up and see the oddly shaped raindrops of garbage falling out of darkness and bouncing off the latticework of posts and beams. I look up and see oversized roulette balls bouncing around looking for black or red, or some lucky number. I look up and I know we're in one of those glass snowballs and everything is all shook up. There is more screaming from everywhere around Dump. Take cover is the hue and cry. I hesitate and the boy is too far ahead of me. Something large lands near him, maybe on him. I can't tell. I let him go. I run back toward Home. Everything is falling apart around me. It's all coming down. Mattresses and TVs and engorged green garbage bags and plastic milk bottles and beer cans and dinner trays and tires and armless mannequins and confetti streams of paper and cloth and a red bigwheel missing its bigwheel and broken lamps and nightstands and computer screens and microwaves and I'm not sure but something that looked like a broken elevator car crash lands behind the incinerator and there's so much more bent and mangled and unrecognizable debris, the sloughed, dead skin of City and this isn't right, there is too much to be just a garbage dump and *soon* must be now because City is finally crashing down on top just like that old woman said it would. I dodge and duck, manage to stay upright and running, and the girl is two steps away, hiding under Feroz's Hep C box. Instinct and inner logic are arguing within me again. Logic says I should leave her here, that I can't save her, that I can't save anybody, that she'll suffer less if she's crushed under a falling refrigerator and that I might be better served staying out here with the girl and trying to catch the matching washer-dryer set with my head. I give in to instinct this time. I grab the girl. I grab her and run inside Home. Quaz, on my heels, follows me in. We're all in the body room. Melissa is leaning up against a back wall. Death and rot on either side of her. I stand with the girl in the blue dress in my arms. I'm facing the camera. The lens stares. I stare back. Neither of us blinks.

I know it's too late, but I stick my fingers down the girl's throat until she gags and vomits. She doesn't fight me. I repeat until her gags are dry heaves.

I say, "Let's wash up and take our guest to dinner." My words sound too normal.

The camera shuts off. I know this because I watched its red light die.

51

ON *THAT* NIGHT

On the night before my mother caught me in the elevator shaft, on *that* night, Mr. Lopez died. He was lonely. He had never been the same after Mrs. Lopez died. He'd stopped taking his walks and he'd stopped leaving kids Tootsie Rolls.

On that night, Mr. Lopez killed himself. No one saw it coming; my Dad-the-psychic wasn't there to warn anyone.

Everyone who was in the building, didn't matter what floor they were on, heard his antique handgun send an antique bullet into the roof of his mouth and then into his brain, and out the top of his head. The bullet kept going into the ceiling and through a floor and then embedded into the leg of the kitchen table of the person who lived above him. Had Mr. Lopez lived to tell a joke about the prowess of his antique handgun, he would've said, "See, they don't make them like they used to."

No one was joking in the apartment building

after we heard the shot. No one was joking when the police and coroners arrived, and they arrived loudly complaining about the broken elevator. The landlord was MIA and my mother was the only person in the building who had a key to the Lopez apartment. After Mrs. Lopez had died, Mr. Lopez had given my mother a key so she could check up on him. I'm not sure if she had ever followed through on checking up.

I was up past my bedtime, sticking my head out the kitchen window, trying to hear what was going on upstairs. There wasn't much to hear, but someone said they should throw the old bird out the window. At first, I didn't know what they meant by *the old bird*. Initially, I thought Mr. Lopez had a pet they were going to set free. I was a stupid kid.

When Mom got back from the Lopez's apartment, I asked, "What did you see?"

She expected the question, and she answered it. Her answer started with, "Poor Mr. Lopez," and forevermore, she'd only refer to him as Poor Mr. Lopez. She said, "Poor Mr. Lopez was at the kitchen table, still in his chair. He'd moved every picture in the apartment into the kitchen and taped them to the walls, counter, table, and refrigerator. It must've taken him a long time. There were a lot of pictures."

I was confused again, thinking my mother had stated the obvious. That, yes, it had taken Mr. Lopez a long time, his antique lifetime to take and be in all those pictures. But then my tired, up-past-my-bedtime head caught up with the rest of Mom's words. I didn't say anything.

She said, "Are you okay, bud?"

"Yeah. Just sad."

"Me too."

I'm sure she expected me to ask why he did what he did. But I didn't. I sat and drank a glass of water, kissed Mom's cheek, wished her goodnight, went into my bedroom, closed the door, and crawled into bed.

I was hot. Real hot. A City day's worth of summer heat and sweat collected in my little room. The open window did nothing to help. I stripped down to my underwear and kicked the blankets off the bed.

I don't know how long I lay there awake thinking about poor Mr. Lopez and Mrs. Lopez. It didn't seem like long before Mom knocked on my bedroom door, then opened it. She was hot too. I could tell because she was only wearing white underwear and a tight white tee shirt that ended above her bellybutton. The whiteness nearly glowed against her dark brown skin. She shut off the kitchen light and everything was total darkness for a little bit, but I got used to it.

Still in the doorway, she said, "Are you okay?"

"Yeah, Mom."

"I don't think I am. Would it be all right if I slept in bed with you?"

"Yeah, okay."

I split up my two-pillow stack, leaving one for her, folding one in half for me. Then I rolled onto my side, facing away from where she would sleep. She got into bed slowly, as if she was sneaking in, afraid of waking me. I was awake. Her body absorbed the bed. I tried to stay tucked away, my own island, but there wasn't enough space.

She lay on her side, facing me. I felt her breath on the back of my head and neck. Then soft kisses in the same spots. Then her arm folded over my body, her hand resting on my belly. Her skin was hot, even hotter than the room, hot enough to burn through me, hot enough to turn me into ash. She pulled me close, and pressed against my back and legs. No more island. She rubbed my belly and then my bare chest, and all over. She was crying.

I wasn't crying. I thought about Poor Mr. Lopez finding me spitting down the elevator shaft, and I thought about him sitting alone in a room full of pictures. I thought about who and what were in all the pictures. I thought about how he made himself as still and as past as the images, and that thought scared me.

I was in her hands, and she asked me to flip over and face her.

I thought about all the things people I knew did to loved ones or because of loved ones. That thought scared me too. And I flipped over.

52

BLOW UP EVERYTHING

On my door, there's a knock. It's light, but not hesitant.

I was asleep on the floor without a pillow or blanket, trying to forget that I was alive. I had no dreams. I am awake now. My right arm is numb and stinging with pins and needles. I try to shake it out. I have no idea what time it is.

I sit up and see the girl in the blue dress is still asleep on my cot. She's curled up into a tight ball with the blanket. She ate two plates of chicken wings and fries at dinner. She didn't answer any of my questions. She didn't speak at all. On the way to my room, she fell asleep in my arms.

There's more knocking. I whisper, "Go ahead, open the goddamn door."

It's Melissa. She says, "Come out here, please."

I limp outside my room. My whole body aches like I've been sleeping on the floor for months, but judging by Melissa's appearance (still wearing her clothes and hat from earlier, but no camera) I don't think I was asleep for very long.

"This is my last official act for *The Candidate*." She hands me her smart phone.

I say, "The CM are the last people on earth I want to talk to."

Melissa shifts on her feet and fiddles with the phone and her fingers. She doesn't know what to do when she's not watching other people, which really doesn't make her any different than most. Maybe I should feel sorry for her. But I don't.

She says, "I know that. You don't have to talk to them. I had them leave a message instead." She gives me the phone and walks away.

I shut the door, then think better of leaving the girl all closed in by herself. So I open it a crack, wondering if the light from the hallway will reach her.

The phone is a grenade in my hand and I want to throw it and blow up everything. But I don't throw it. I bring it up to my ear. The phone tells me to press 2 to hear the message. Nothing good will come of listening to this message. I know this. But I do it anyway.

53

PANDERING WINS BABY

This is the message on Melissa's cell phone:

"Wow," then, "Wow," then, "I think I'm having an orgasm," then, "Me too," then, "Let's share," then, "Ha Ha!" then, "Ha Ha!" then, "That was magnificent," then, "You were a stud tonight," then, "A Greek god," then, "Goosebumps," then, "A real live action hero," then, "A walking-talking summer blockbuster," then, "You performed beyond our wildest expectations," then, "You're making us look like geniuses," then, "Tonight's finale was the highest rated primetime show in twenty years," then, "The insta-polls are all too close to call," then, "Solomon is panicking," then, "You should see it," then, "He's going for a last ditch smear campaign," then, "He's running a bit from the show," then, "Showing you not going after the boy in Dump," then, "But it's not working," then, "Not even a blip on the screen," then, "No one is talking about that," then, "Everyone is talking about you and the girl," then, "You're going to win," then, "Can't get over that final shot," then, "You standing there holding the girl," then, "Brilliant," then, "There isn't anyone in City who hasn't seen that shot by now," then, "Sure, some of the TV critics have panned the finale," then, "That's to be expected," then, "They'd complain about water not being wet enough," then, "Some are calling the show and specifically that final shot *pandering*," then, "Which is fine with us," then, "They're not wrong, really," then, "But who cares?" then, "Because pandering is good," then, "Pandering wins, baby," then, "Pussy no more," then, "We have a real shot at winning this thing," then, "The Pandering Mayor, maybe," then, "But not a pussy Mayor," then, "Congratulations," then, "Good luck to us tomorrow night," then, "See you soon, Mayor."

54

WORD FOR WORD

I wake up on the floor again. This time it's the next day. My first thought is that today is election day. My second thought is that I hate myself for thinking that first thought.

The girl is awake in bed, just staring at the ceiling. I ask her if she wants breakfast. She doesn't answer but she doesn't fight me when I bring her down to the cafeteria. I don't carry her this time. We walk. She holds my hand.

Melissa and Quaz are already in the cafeteria. Father-my-father isn't there. We eat. Quaz tells me the executive order of the day is that I'm to have the day off from my regular duties. I don't argue. Melissa promises to keep an eye on the girl. They ask me where I'm going.

I tell them the truth. Or maybe it's a lie. I'm not sure anymore. I tell them I'm going to look for the boy. They don't question me.

I'm almost certain this is my last day here.

Maybe I'm getting a touch of ESP. I have to look around for Mom one last time. Out in Pier and Dump I crawl over trash mountains and descend into trash valleys. I ask people about my mother, they beg me for help. We tell each other sorry. I pass the morning hours this way, walking Dump and not seeing who I want to see. Then I climb posts and beams next, first going down a level or two and sticking my hands in the ocean. I've never touched the ocean before. It's very cold, and the salt stings my lips when taste it. I don't linger close to the water. Instead, I climb, going as high up as my body will take me. In these higher levels of Pier the posts are slick with fog condensation. No one is up here. The last person I saw was maybe five or six levels below. I didn't know that person either, as if I really know anyone. I'm alone. And I've reached a point where I can't see through the cloud above me, but I haven't reached Pier's ceiling. I haven't reached City's floor. I don't know if I could. I get the sense I'm still miles away from City. Dump is at least one-hundred feet down. It doesn't look any better from this height.

While up here, I consider and indulge the following fantasy: The CM know where my mother is, in fact, they have her, keeping her safe for a *The Candidate* follow-up or reunion-type show, and I can just see it; there's Mom appearing from behind a curtain or from off the set or the green room and she's all tears and smiles and so am I and so is the audience, now that's pandering! And, dammit, I hate the fucking fucker that I am all over again for thinking like a TV producer, for wishing my life was a perpetual media stunt.

Back to reality. I climb down. The urge to jump never hits me because it'd be too easy. I'm climbing down. I'm climbing down with a purpose, and unlike the rest of my Dump-walking morning and Pier-climbing afternoon, I have a final destination in mind.

One level above Home. She's there. In the crook of a post and beam. Still that bird in a nest. Still fussing with the paper and cloth and other nest materials. I watch her and I know before she speaks that nothing really changes.

I say, "Hi, again."

She says, "Don't come too close! I'm scared. I'm so scared I can't do nothing anymore. Nothing but sit in this corner. It's terrible. I get the shakes and shivers. See."

She's saying what she said to me the first time. Word. For. Word. I remember.

"I can't sleep. I can't close my eyes from the worry."

I don't know what to do. Maybe I should leave. Maybe I should stop listening and just pretend to believe my CM fantasy, pretend that everything will really be okay. Maybe I should say something, something to interrupt her, stop her from saying it all over again. Maybe if I can stop her from saying it all over again everything will be different.

"I'm worrying myself to death, worrying City and all this wood that's everywhere will come crashing down on my head."

I say, "I lied to everyone back at Home. I'm not looking for the boy. I know he's gone."

"Wait! You need to know it's all going to come crashing down, squash us, drown us, mix us in with water and wood, and buildings and blood and bones."

"Can I ask you a question?"

She keeps talking. "I try to tell them, but no one listens."

"Can I ask you a question?"

Her same words. "That's the truth."

"Please?"

"I don't know much, but I know that. Someday it's all going to come down. Someday soon."

She stops talking, but doesn't throw a can at me this time.

I say, "I think you're the only person down here I didn't ask yet." And I am Father ESP's son, because I know she knows. She's going to tell me. "Do you know what happened to my mother?" I rattle off her name and try to cram in the memories of what she looked like, how she talked, and how she walked into as few words as possible.

She looks at me. Really looks at me. The wrinkled curtain of her mouth opens, and one word comes out, dryer than sandpaper. "Sorry."

I want to paint the wooden posts and beams with my own blood because I don't know what she means. It could mean nothing. It could mean everything.

She's talking again, looping back to the beginning.

"Don't come too close! I'm scared. I'm so scared I can't do nothing anymore. . . ."

I turn my back to her. Tears that only have a vague notion of what they're all about fall off my face. I walk away and climb back down toward Home, but she's loud enough that I hear her finish up.

55

THEIR STORIES INSIDE

I return Home. It's dinner time, only there's no Quaz or my father or Melissa or the girl in the cafeteria, just some of the other staff. I ask around. Quaz works the incinerator but no one knows where the rest of the gang is.

You know, Father-my-father is never around like he said he would be. He's never here when I need him. Despite promises to the contrary, he's offered no help since he stuck me down here. And he did stick me down here. I understand that my playing along, my following, my refusal to rebel or even ask the right questions equates to complicity.

It's more than high-time to get some answers from him. He's not in his office, so I walk to the sleeping quarters and his door is shut. It's always shut. I try the knob and no dice. It's locked. It's always locked.

He says, "I'm busy."

"Open the door. We need to chat."

I wait. I don't hear any sounds of movement.

"Go away."

"Where's the girl? Where's Melissa?"

"Melissa went back to City and took the girl with her. She's going to adopt her."

I rest my forehead on the door. Good for Melissa. Helping the person in front of her and all that. My moment of warm-fuzzies is ruined by this behind-the-door proclamation:

"I didn't tell Melissa that the girl will not survive the year, though. You probably think I should've told her that. I'd rather Melissa live with a little hope even if it's only for a year. I'd rather that girl spend her last days in City than down here."

This feels typical and appropriate for us, a meaningful conversation through a door. "You don't know what I think or thought and you never did. Now, open the goddamn door!"

He says, "Fuck off. I'm praying."

That's it. Backpedaling until my body is flush against the opposite wall, I throw myself across the hall and shoulder-first into the door. The wood isn't strong and cracks and splinters in the jam. The door flies open but rebounds, bouncing back into me as it hits something.

"All right, come in."

Books. There are books everywhere. Thick bookcases line all the walls. Thick books fill those bookcases. There are stacks and piles of books on the floor and on my father's desk and under his cot. Hardcover books with cloth covers. The covers only have solid colours; there's blue, black, brown, yellow, red. There is nothing written on the covers and nothing written on the spines.

He says, "I knew you were going to do that. I already ordered a replacement door."

I shut the splintered door behind me and find the stack of books the door rammed when I pushed it open. I pick a book up and flip through it. The pages are white, and empty.

"Are all these books blank?"

My father is a hunched figure behind a solid oak desk. He has a pen in his hand. Fingers stained with ink. He uses a kerosene lantern for light and it smells a little funny, unnatural even.

He says, "No. The books on the shelves have their stories inside."

I wade over to a bookshelf and pick out the book tome at random. There are indeed words and stories inside. Handwritten.

"You wrote all this?"

"Yes."

"Why?"

"Read one of the stories to me."

56

EVE'S STORY

SHE FENDS FOR HERSELF

Eve is quiet and introverted. Not beautiful in the classic sense of physical beauty but beautiful in how she carries herself; confident in her own abilities yet sheepish of where she fits in. Her parents both work long factory hours and Eve is the youngest (two other children out of the house already) and is left to fend for herself at night, something that grows and feeds her independent light. Eve is intelligent and does well in school although she hates the social aspects, the institutionalized competition and usurpation of her independence and identity. She works hard more for the pride of her parents than her own, and manages to earn a scholarship to City University. She lasts two years but drops out. Then two more years of searching, of activism (though she grows cynical of the intentions and motivations of her fellow activists), of confusion over sexual identity. Eve emerges from her tumultuous youth as a social worker. She's very good at her job. She buys a house on the outskirts of City with Jenn, her partner. They would marry if they could. She revels in her sibling's children but does not desire any of her own. Her father has a stroke and lingers too long. Her mother dies of breast cancer, and Eve loses a breast to a mastectomy a decade later, but survives. She survives long enough to outlive Jenn by five years although she'll spend most of those five years—years that she'd describe as happy and productive, but lonely—idly wishing she hadn't.

57

TOE-MAY-TOE, TOE-MAH-TOE, LET'S CALL THE WHOLE THING OFF

He says, "I don't remember who the original Eve was anymore. Maybe two years ago she was a freckle-faced teen and a heroine-addicted prostitute with AIDS when she died here. Maybe for a week all she said to me was 'don't touch me' or 'fuck off' but in the weakest of voices. I choose not to remember that. What I'll remember about her is what you just read to me."

I skim more stories in the book, but don't read them out loud. There's one about a guy who is a three-times-married bank teller. There's another about a truck driver who dies after he falls asleep at the wheel. There's another about a part-time nurse who has two miscarriages but has a healthy child on the third try. There's another about a woman who has two autistic children and one healthy one. There's another about a writer who euthanizes her terminally ill husband and is unable to write another word for the rest of her distressingly long life. There's another about a factory worker who doesn't lose his job until after twenty-five years of service, but manages to eke out a small and pride-swallowing existence thanks to the kindness of friends and family. There's another about a landlord who has a tenant stealing his credit cards and identity, but he rebounds financially and buys more low-income apartment buildings. There's another about a girl who could never escape the ghetto and spent too much of her life taking care of her morbidly obese mother. There's more and more and more. Each story is written as one long paragraph with a title. Some stories have more happiness and triumphs than others. Some stories have more sadness and tragedy.

I know what this is, but I want to hear it from him. "What is all this about?"

He still sits in his chair, behind his desk, holding his pen, surrounded by stories. "Everyone who's ever been at Home deserves a better ending. Even if it's a sad ending, it's better than what they got."

"You're the only one who will read these alternate endings."

"These people are forgotten by everyone else. But they'll live on, at least for a little while longer, through these stories, through these memories that I make as real as I can. In reality, it's all any of us can hope for."

Fictional stories, new memories as reality. I can't argue. Reality is only as real as memories. I put the book back and grab another one. I read more stories.

I say, "You knew I was going to meet Feroz and then see those kids, didn't you?"

"I cannot tell a lie."

"This whole room is full of lies."

"You say lies, I say lives. Toe-may-toe, Toe-mah-toe, let's call the whole thing off."

This room is too much. I'm splintered into parts. Part of me loves my father for what he's doing down here. Another part of me hates him and thinks he's pathetic.

I say, "All this was your idea, wasn't it? Making me a Mayoral candidate, the TV show, bringing me down here, even breaking into your room and reading your stories. Why?"

"You're not going to believe me. I am sorry you had to go through all that with Feroz, and then the little boy and girl. I couldn't stop it. I never could. I never can."

"Where's my story? Or my mother's? Are they here?"

"I don't have to write those stories."

"That's right. Because you already authored those stories, Dad. Everything that has happened to us, to me and Mom, would not have happened if you hadn't left us." And I'm thinking about the night Mr. Lopez died when I say this. That night happened to us.

"You don't know that," he says.

I say, "Neither do you."

He laughs. "Okay, okay. You really think I'm withholding where she is, don't you? You haven't once believed me when I've said that she's okay but I don't know where she is."

"I know you know where she is."

He says, "You're right. I do know where she is. I'm not going to tell you. You'll find out on your own."

I take a book, an empty one, and tear off its cover.

He shrugs. Again, his damn know-its-all-coming shrug. Then he tosses me a smart phone; it was Melissa's. He says, "You're going to get a call from the CM in an hour. They're going to tell you that you are the new Mayor. You are going to use your newly elected position to, finally, find your mother." He watches me. In his eyes am I a snake ready to strike or a slug that he's going to sprinkle with salt? "So, do you believe me now, kiddo? Do you believe in anything?"

I don't answer him. It's my turn to read the future. I'm going to leave him sitting in this room with his ink and empty pages, his chosen reality, and I'm going to disappear into mine.

He says, "Would you like to write something for Feroz or the little boy before you storm off into the sunset?" He offers me a pen.

It would be so easy. Giving them their lives back. I take the pen out of his hand, pick up the book I tore the cover off, and on the first blank page I write:

He believes his parents love him even when they do bad stuff. He works in a land of mute animals to escape one of them. He learns about suffering and dignity when he tries to find one of them. He eventually understands and forgives the actions of one of them.

Do you know or care who the one of them is at the end?

I say, "Sorry, I cheated and wrote into a second paragraph. It's something to remember me by. You pick a title."

Father-my-father takes the book and reads it. He says, "You'll be back. I guarantee it. You can believe that. Who else am I going to get to read all these stories?"

I take a blank book and tuck it under my arm. A souvenir. The cell phone rings in my pocket.

He says, "Whoops. Looks like they're calling earlier than I thought they would. Can't be right all the time. Right?"

I walk away with the ringing phone in my pocket, empty book cradled to my chest.

He yells behind me, "Hey, Mr. Mayor, don't fuck with Home's funding. And shut the goddamn door on your way out."

58

CINDERELLA WANTS THE PVMPKIN BACK

9:30 PM.

I emerge from Pier in the North End and the CM scoop me up into a limousine. I want to wash and change my smelly, dirty clothes but they won't let me. I want to tell them where they can stuff this election but I don't say anything, which makes me think I don't really want to tell them where they could stuff the election. I want to win. I confuse myself.

10:17 PM.

All three major City networks declare me Mayor although only two percent of the precincts have reported. Faster than a McDonald's burger, I become Mayor. The CM pour champagne for us. I drink it too fast and the bubbles go into my sinuses.

10:43 PM.

Solomon delivers a concession speech, still all smiles, still declaring a great day for Democracy, still with his Napoleon hand in his vest. While leaving the podium, he tosses his pocket watch into a throng of supporters. I start into a second champagne bottle.

10:51 PM.

CityNews reports that Solomon is granting me a full pardon from all terrorist charges related to my Farm escape and chooses to vacate the Mayoral position immediately, forgoing his optional one-month, lame-duck period. I am full on drunk.

10:52 PM.

Television pundits agree the pardon and waiving his right to be a lame-duck is a wonderful, graceful gesture that will go far to ensuring his legacy as one of City's most beloved and important Mayors.

11:11 PM.

City Counsel announces plans for a Solomon Statue and dedication.

11:17 PM.

City Counsel announces plans for a minted Solomon coin.

11:23 PM.

McDonald's unveils the Solomon Burger.

11:27 PM.

City Press announces Solomon has signed a book

deal for a record-breaking ten million dollar advance.

11:33 PM.

City Hall and the financial district are cordoned off and the sidewalks barricaded for the inauguration and parade. All sidewalk garbage cans are cleared and roadside metal detectors set up.

12:01 AM.

I'm standing in the giant marble foyer of City Hall. It's dark, with only the emergency lights on. The room is full of closed office doors, empty staircases, and marble columns, Pier-like columns. The CM talk on two cell phones at the same time. I'm not listening, and only thinking about standing up. I wait to be sworn in as Mayor. To be inaugurated. I really fucking hate it when my father is right.

I stand behind the grand oak doors of City Hall. Twenty feet tall, thirty feet wide. Thick doors, but not thick enough to muzzle the roar from the streets, from City. I'm to be their Mayor. Who am I really? I've graduated from being the dog to being Cinderella, a Cinderella who wants her pumpkin back at midnight but doesn't get it.

Those thick doors open and there is a great, unending roar, and spotlights, cameras, flashing bulbs, and a thousand and one questions shouted at me and I don't think I can answer one of them. The CM usher me, Mayor in-ten-and-counting-seconds, Mayor still-wearing-his-homeless-chic-threads, through the sea of press and toward a judge. I repeat his words. I am Mayor. It's as easy as that.

12:11 AM.

My midnight inaugural parade of City. Behind the sidewalk barricades and endless line of armed soldiers and police is City. As many people as I have ever hoped to see at once. They are here. They cheer. They scream. They dance to the upbeat electronic music my cavalcade pumps out. They point, laugh, cry, love, hate, eat, shit, love, steal, fuck, lie, kill, and die. And I wave at them. My waving image is on all of the City holo-boards and ad streamers, my face swallowing up entire City blocks. There are clips and stills of me holding the little girl in the blue dress. Pier is right under my feet. Pier is a galaxy away and I let myself believe I'm a made-up story in my father's book.

Helicopters and their spotlights fly overhead. I have bodyguards. They hold a finger to their ears and listen to someone else. Government-trained snipers lean out of windows and walk the roofs of the buildings we pass. Everyone is here. The CM tell me they all love me. The CM think I'm dumb enough to believe them. But out here, in front of all these people, it is almost believable. Almost. People stand on mailboxes and they fill the side streets and hang out the windows next to the snipers. Parents hold up their children, their children hold up sparklers and flags. There are veterans in full garb, dangling their shiny metals. There are balloons and pretzels and cotton candy and fireworks. I'm handed a microphone. Say something, anything. I say, "Thanks for coming out," like I'm some old has-been rock star thanking his fans for shelling out good coin for my third Final Tour Ever Tour. The crowd responds: an explosion of sound that I didn't think could get any louder. We roll into the well-lit financial district and people wear *The Candidate* tee shirts and hats and people hold out pens looking for autographs, looking for something. Live bands play music and there are other sound stages set up for all the late-night talk shows. I allow myself to look for my mother, to see if she is standing on any of those sound stages, waiting to reunite with the new Mayor. We keep on rolling. Me standing in the Mayor-mobile, ankle deep in confetti and I say, "Thank you," again into the mic and this time there's a rush against one of the barricades and there's no way there aren't people being injured or crushed to death, but we drive past, slow, at our predetermined Mayoral speed. Then there are other explosions besides the fireworks. From the sidewalk and from one of the side streets I hear that animal growl and then there is smoke and bodies and parts flying through the air, my human-flesh ticker-tape victory parade. Donkey explosions on every block. I try to yell, "Go home, please. So no one else gets hurt!" into the microphone but it's been shut off. I throw up a belly-full of still bubbly champagne over the side of the car. The parade continues at the same speed.

SWALLOWING A DONKEY'S EYE

The crowd still stays and screams and crushes and explodes. Someone says in my ear *we'll be home soon, Mr. Mayor.* I still try to yell to the crowd but I know no one can hear me. And I know the pumpkinless-Cinderella has become Nero with a dead microphone.

59

IT MEANS SOME ASSHOLE WAS JVST THERE

It's my first official day on the job. My first official day in a suit. My first official day alone in the Mayor's office.

I stare at my closed office door. It's hard not to imagine Pier and all those people living and dying right outside that door and I wonder what my father is writing into his books now and whose turn is it to be forgotten and then replaced with fiction. I suppose I should focus on being Mayor.

Here is my office: There's a refrigerator next to my file cabinet. It's the elephant in the room. I hear it humming but I'm not ready to take a peek behind it to see if it's plugged in or not. Some things are better left as mysteries. That pig of a man Solomon left the place a mess. Twinkie and Ding-Dong wrappers and empty soda cans everywhere. All kinds of kitschy stuff clutters his desk: one of those plastic long-necked birds drinking out of a cup of water, those clacking metal balls on strings, slogan-filled coffee mugs, pens and over-sized pencils branded with company names and logos. It's almost hard to believe people somewhere worked and sweated and slaved to manufacture utter pieces of crap like this stuff. People working to make crap, this I do believe. I push all that junk off the desk and into a trashcan to make room for my empty book. On the walls there are pictures of Solomon shaking hands with celebrities and dignitaries and cutting ceremonial tapes and throwing out ceremonial first balls. In the middle, in the spot of honour on the wall is this plaque:

> ## A MODERN AXIOM:
> IF THE TOILET SEAT IS WARM,
> IT MEANS SOME ASSHOLE
> WAS JUST THERE.

The pictures have to go, but I think I'll keep the plaque.

The CM share an office next to me. They'll need a name change because, as stipulated in our contractual agreement, they're now the Assistants to the Mayor. At least, that's what they told me in the morning briefing. How about I call them the Ass-May? Works for me. I'll make it official with my Mayoral signature later.

In the briefing the Ass-May told me I'm supposed to do a brunch with Shriners and then make live appearances on a slew of radio stations. Then coffee with public transportation union leaders, then cocktails with Young Republicans and a five-hundred-dollar-a-plate dinner with Young Democrats, then a late-night talk show stop. Sounds like a full day of Mayoring.

First things first. I call the Chief of Police. I tell him the Mayor knows of the giant, public DNA and location database they keep, and the Mayor wants to know where his Mommy is. Chief tells the Mayor that he'll get back to him post haste. It's as easy as that. Now I'm thinking that I'm afraid to know where my mother is. That it can't be good. That Father ESP's *you'll find out on your own* sounded more ominous than hopeful.

I pick one of Solomon's pens out of the trash. This one has *Tony's Sub Shoppe* and its address on the pen. The thing is even shaped like a submarine sandwich, rubber and lettuce leaves bend under my fingers. I put my Home souvenir, the book from my father's room, on the empty desk. Maybe I should take a page out of my father's book and write me up a happy ending for me and my mother.

I write:

I find my mother.
She is happy and she continues to live in happiness for the rest of her days.

I tear that page out of my father's book, crumple it, and toss it to the floor.

I go back to the phone and leave a message for the Ass-May telling them I want Melissa's adoption of the Pier-girl expedited and the Pier-girl's medical care taken care of or I won't be a happy, cooperative Mayor. I try for an intimidating I-lead-you-follow tone, but it comes out sounding like a whiney *pretty please.* I hang up, but I call back and leave another message telling them I want Home's funding tripled. Inspired by this sudden attack of Mayoralness, I pick the BLT-sub-pen up again, go back to the book, open it up to a blank page somewhere near the middle, and write.

60

~~MAYORAL MANIFESTO RHYMES WITH PESTO~~

~~MAYORAL MANIFESTO~~
~~Rhymes with pesto!~~

After the cross-outs, I tear out the page and try again.

OUTLINE OF THE MAYOR'S POLICIES

—Deporting the homeless is morally and legally reprehensible. Ending the practice will be priority number one of this administration.

Nice. I'm proud of that.

—In addition, we will work toward the reintegration of current deportees. Social programs and initiatives will include shelters, educational support, and breakfast and lunch programs for the children. For the adults, professional skills training, affordable housing, health care, and general social service support.

I write more. Pie in the sky kind of stuff that I know won't get done, but I'm writing it anyway.

–City will comply with environmental law and cease its dumping practices under Pier.

–There will be tougher restrictions on emissions and a ban on SUV sales. I will work toward eventually replacing fossil fuel engines with clean-burning fuel alternatives and hydrogen cell batteries.

–Farm will be regulated by the Mayor's office. I will require Farm to publish its engineering programs and practices, along with any and all pertinent pesticide and chemical use information.

–I will end Farm's long-term, binding employee contracts and regulate the working conditions.

–I will raise minimum wage to a living wage.

–Ad Walkers will be pushed back to 500 feet away from schools and residential homes.

–I will work toward a goal of socialized medicine and subsidized higher education.

THIS IS JUST A START!

61

KING FOR A DAY, FOOL FOR A LIFETIME

My policies list fills one side of one page. I add my John Hancock to the bottom. Then I manually copy the list onto another page, sign it, and tear out both pages from the Book of Empty. I leave my office, walk down the busy hall, and toss a copy to the Ass-May's secretary. I stand outside of their office until a City Hall beat reporter recognizes me. It doesn't take long.

The press-man snaps a digital pic and says, "You got anything for me, Mr. Mayor? How about five minutes?"

I say, "I do have five minutes but you can't have them."

"That's no way to start a relationship with the media." He's young like me. Wearing a brown suit topped off with a fedora. He has thin, wispy eyebrows, but they meet just above his nose, making him look permanently angry.

I notice some other people starting to mill around, listening to us. Likely recording us. I say, "You're probably right. You can have this instead." I give him the second copy of my Mayoral manifesto.

Press-man looks at me funny, like I'm the innocent child who just drew a picture of torture and mutilation. He looks over both of his shoulders, making sure no one's perched on his back. He reads it again and laughs.

"You sure about this, Mr. Mayor? I'll tell you what, I'll give you a mulligan, if you want. I'll tear it up and you can give me those five minutes instead. No harm, no foul."

"I'm sure. No mulligans. Print it, broadcast it, disseminate it. Do whatever it is you do."

He flips open his cell phone and smiles. He says, "You're a fool." Those eyebrows almost separating so he doesn't look angry anymore. It's more of a surprised look. Or constipated. I have a crazy urge to bring him to my office to show him the refrigerator and the plaque on my wall and ask him who is the fool? Instead I walk to my office alone. Other media moguls converge on me but I don't give them anything and close the Mayoral door in their faces.

The phone on my desk has a blinking red light. There's a message. It could be a message from the Chief of Police with my mother's whereabouts. It could be a message from anybody. I don't know how to feel or what to believe or what to hope.

I'd left the office with my Book of Empty open on the desk. It's still there, and open. I sit and re-write the happy ending to my mother's story. I stare at the story and at the blinking red light. The two choices are incongruous. The dream of happily ever after versus the blinking red light, a command to listen to this. And I think about red alerts and ambulance lights and other warnings and alarms associated with blinking and red.

I close the book and pick up the phone. The message plays. The message is from the Chief of Police and he knows where my mother is. He tells me. He tells me my personal-universe-shattering news in casual conversational tones and I break up into parts and pieces all over again. There's the relieved piece that is rounded and smooth. There's the so-goddamn-angry piece with torn sections and jagged edges. There's the I-need-to-laugh-for-the-rest-of-my-life piece, light and wafer-thin. There's the sad and hurt piece that is bent and wet. There's the I-really-am-a-fool piece with its odd angles and colours that won't match any other piece. There's the logical piece with square and rectangular edges, easy for fitting, this piece thinking only about how to get to her and how to put myself back together.

But this time the puzzle of me will never fit back together and all of the king-for-a-day's horses and all of the king-for-a-day's men can't put this fool-for-a-lifetime back together again.

62

THE NOTE I SHOVLD'VE WRITTEN

It was early and I was alone in the kitchen, staring out the window. Dirty streets with tumbleweed trash, broken windows behind wire-mesh cages, leaky tar roofs, rusty cars missing headlights, cracked streets and sidewalks, smoke stacks above it all in the background making clouds that didn't take the shapes of fluffy bunnies or god. Our neighbourhood was decaying, at least to the eyes of the eighteen-year-old me. Maybe it was always that way but it seemed worse because I wasn't a little kid anymore, because I knew my mother couldn't protect me from the bad things anymore. But I wanted to protect her and I had convinced myself that was the reason I was leaving.

So there I was. Eighteen-year-old me sitting at the kitchen table, trying to write a note to my mother. I had planned on telling her the night before, but she went straight to bed after getting home late from her night-school class. Who knew what class as she'd changed her focus of study seemingly every week.

But hey, at least she was trying.

I had convinced myself I was doing the same by signing six years of my life away to Farm. It seems I can only be honest with myself after the passage of a significant amount of time. It's safer that way.

The note:

> Mom,
> I wanted to talk to you about this face to face but I'm a chicken. . . .

Of course, the eighteen-year-old me didn't realize the prophecy of this opening statement.

> . . . I knew you'd try to talk me out of it. But this is something I have to do. I need to be on my own and Farm gives me the opportunity to do that and help you at the same time. Through the recruiter, I've already set up a plan where a portion of my paycheck is automatically deposited into your chequing account (yes, I got your account number by going through your pocketbook, sorry). You'll be able to keep going to school, and maybe even work a few less hours yourself.
> The bus leaves this morning. I am sorry to do this to you in a letter, but it's the only way I can do it. I will call when I get settled. I love you.

It got the job done, I guess. But this is the note I should've written:

Mom,

I'm leaving because I can't stay in this neighbourhood anymore. I'm leaving because I can't stay in City anymore. I'm leaving because Mr. and Mrs. Lopez died. I'm leaving because he left. I'm leaving because like father like son. I'm leaving because I can't watch you fall apart anymore. I'm leaving because the Farm recruiter found a sucker. I'm leaving because he simply asked me to. I'm leaving because I simply said yes. I'm leaving because the spider in the elevator shaft is real. I'm leaving because I'm too old for attention even if I still want it. I'm leaving because you tell me too much about you and your boyfriends. I'm leaving because I'm your son, not someone else. I'm leaving because you haven't decided what to do with your own life. I'm leaving because I know what I just wrote isn't fair but I still wrote it anyway. I'm leaving because I can't save you. I'm leaving because you can't save me. I'm leaving because I don't know what else to do. I'm leaving because I'm afraid, afraid I'll never get out otherwise, afraid of you, afraid of everything. I'm leaving because I don't know anything. I'm leaving because I'm sorry. I'm leaving because I don't know you. I'm leaving because I don't know me. I'm leaving because I love you. I'm leaving because I don't love me. I'm leaving because I need to forgive you for that night. I'm leaving because I need to forgive myself for that night.

I left the real note the eighteen-year-old-me wrote on the kitchen table, pinned under a sweaty, mostly empty glass of orange juice. Water beads rolled down the glass and onto the paper, making a circle, and smudging the ink of my signature. I left the glass there and I left the apartment, closing the door so quietly that I knew no one heard it shut.

63

FILLING THE BOOK OF EMPTY

I have a plan.

Back in a limo, but I'm hijacking this one. This is supposed to be the take-the-Mayor-to-the-Shriners-brunch limo. I tell the driver, the same Mr. Rolly Polly who drove us all that long-ago night, to take me to Farm or I'll have him shipped below City faster than he can say *Weebles wobble but they don't fall down*. I'm allowed one token abuse of power.

Fifty minutes of high-rises, intersections, and traffic-lights later, we're through City and rolling down the Farm access road. Trees, dirt, and dust. My Mayor's cell phone is red, Batphone red, and I call ahead to Farm to let them know the Mayor is coming and that the Mayor expects access to wherever it is he wants to go, the Mayor is done sneaking around. The receptionist assures me my visit and tour will be well above satisfactory. I tell him don't bet on it.

The Book of Empty is still with me, only it's getting to be not so empty. I'm writing one word, a different word, for every page. Sometimes I write the word horizontally, then vertically, diagonal, parabolic, concave up and concave down. Sometimes I write the word so some of the letters are higher than the others, but nothing too radical so that the particular word can't be read. I use big letters, small letters, capitals, lower case. I outline some words and some I make bold and block by pressing hard with the pen and retracing the sticks and curves that form the letters. Some words mean something, some mean nothing.

A sampling of the words: insect, mob, duck, reality, fart, lies, words, dog, incompetence, suffering, piss, hole, love, donkey, eye, me, dump, forget, scream, numb. I will give this book to my mother. Maybe it'll fit together and tell her what I need to tell her. Maybe it won't.

In no particular order (do you believe me? do you believe in anything?), here's what some of the pages look like:

ABANDONED

humanity

BELOW

DIGNITY

INCest

regret

64

TAKE A FARM TOVR AND SEE CLETVS

I tense up as we pull through the giant, swinging white-picket fence gate that will funnel us into Farm's main entrance, the tourist entrance. My stomach is full of malformed butterflies, their wings stunted or incomplete or misshapen or spotted with malignant growths, and these freak wings flutter spastically, irregularly, or not at all. I imagine they'll die soon, and that's supposed to be a comfort.

The limo drives down a short gravel road lined with bushes trimmed into animal shapes. The landscapers, dressed in their Farm-issued overalls, stop what they're doing to smile and wave at the limo. Apparently they're okay with the former-terrorist Mayor. They can't see me through the tinted windows, but I want to hide anyway.

The limo stops in front of the reception hall, which is adjacent to the large administration building. The reception hall is red and shaped like an olde tyme barn. Three meet-'n'-greeters sit on a haystack next to the barn's swinging doors: two young and suitably attractive women in overalls and one Chicken. The birth-defect butterflies have a few twitches left as all my years of servitude and acquiescence training and Chicken-experience will be hard to wash out of my system.

The driver opens my door. There's an explosion of sound, some tune with Dixie horns and ragtime piano and jangling bells and barker-shouted lyrics about Farm blares from speakers that are likely hidden in the haystacks around the barn.

> *Farm! You feed us.*
> *Farm! You need us.*
> *Take a Farm tour and see Cletus. . . .*

I bend and yell into Rolly Polly's ear, "Turn off your phone and wait right here for me."

He nods. But I don't buy it.

Chicken takes my hand and shakes it hard, then the women loop my arms into theirs.

"Welcome back to Farm, Mr. Mayor."

"It's an honour to have you here."

I don't say anything and let them herd me into the red barn. Inside, hay mostly covers the tram-tracks and animal stalls have desks, computers, and workers instead of horses and cows. More people, an assortment of desk-jockeys and tour leaders in their animal suits, come and shake my hand and pat me on the back. I wonder how many former Farm employees were really arrested or liquidated because of the Duck-attack and my escape. Well, I am Mayor, I suppose I could find out.

Two people dressed as the *American Gothic* farmers flank me, and flashes flash. A Cow hands me an insta-print of the special moment. The old guy from *American Gothic* leans over my shoulder for a closer look, and he scratches me right below my chin with his goddamn pitchfork. Blood drips off my chin and lands on the knot of my Mayoral tie. I don't know if I can do this.

Pitchfork-guy says, "Whoops, sorry about that, sonny. These glasses are props and I don't see through 'em too good."

Someone presses a rag on my wound and it's so far past the time to take control. I yell, "All right, all right. Everybody just shut up!" The room goes quiet. Thank somebody. Someone turned off the music and everyone looks a little scared, even the people in their animal suits. This is good. A little scared never hurt anyone.

I say, "You," grab the Chicken by his wattle, and pull him close. I tell him where he is going to take me. The Chicken doesn't say anything, but gives a follow-me wing-swipe, that wonderful wordless communiqué that only the privileged few Farm employees get to experience. Can you tell I already don't like this version of Chicken? Chicken 2.0. I think I understand Jonah's natural hatred for oversized poultry.

So the new Mayor dislikes the new Chicken, but he follows the feathered fucker to a tourist tram anyway.

65

HOW ABOVT SVPER-MASSIVE-
BLACK-HOLE HATE

Being so reliant upon a Chicken wasn't part of my plan. I'm trying to be flexible.

We drive through Orchard and I have to trust Chicken 2.0 to take me where I want to go because I don't know where she is. I mean, I know where she is but I don't know how to get there from here. Story of my life.

The Batphone goes off, flashing red and the ring screaming like a smoke alarm. It better not be the driver calling me.

"Hello?"

"What are you doing?" then, "We've never seen a roomful of Shriners so angry."

The butterflies tickle my belly with a couple of death twitches. I say, "Did you take care of Melissa and Home for me?"

"Of course," then, "We took care of each as soon as we got the message," then, "Which was before you stiffing the Shriners," then, "And before the City-wide press release of your 'Mayoral Policies.'"

"I'm sorry about the Shriners, but I found out where my mother is, no thanks to you. And the Mayor has to see her now." I have a plan, remember. The plan includes referring to myself in third person. Besides, I knew this call was going to happen. Trust the Mayor.

They say, "We are speechless," then, "Totally," then, "Utterly," then, "Without word." Their voices sound more dead and robotic than usual. I can almost hear the steel gears turning in their robot-minds.

I say, "So, a press release. What do you think of my list of policies? Should stir things up."

"Why don't we start this way," then, "By telling you what the populace," then, "City," then, "Your constituents," then, "Think of your policies."

"Lay it on me."

"They hate them," then, "Hate isn't strong enough," then, "Maybe nuclear-hate," then, "How about supermassive-black-hole hate," then, "That one might fit."

We drive by some apple-picking ATVs and they stop what they're doing to wave at me. We're close enough to see their forced smiles looking a little more forced, a little more confused because some guy in a suit with a bloody tie is sitting alone in a tourist tram.

I say, "You're exaggerating."

"No," then, "We're not," then, "Your policies have spawned instant protest," then, "Riots in the streets," then, "Riots on the steps of City Hall," then,

"The police and City Guard were forced to use tear gas," then, "Tasers," then, "Rubber bullets," then, "Billy clubs," then, "Hundreds of people arrested and injured," then, "Thirty-two people killed by suicide bombs," then, "All because of how much they hated your policies," then, "More specifically, your homeless policy," then, "You should see the signs," then, "Hear the slogans," then, "Thousands of people chanting: *Hell no, they have to go*," then, "Has a nice, retro-ring to it," then, "Love the old-school activism," then, "Or how about the simple but effective: *Deport the Mayor!*" then, "This is not an exaggeration," then, "Not even close."

I should not be surprised by this, should not be hurt by this, but I am. I'm such a sucker. I say, "As long as I am Mayor, you are not allowed to utter the phrase *old school*."

They say, "That's fine," then, "You won't be Mayor for much longer," then, "We feel it our duty to inform you," then, "Upon our counsel and advice," then, "City Selectmen have enacted emergency impeachment hearings," then, "You and your policy release endangering the public," then, "Coupled with your irrational public behaviour," then, "Is enough to have your mental state declared unfit for the public service position," then, "They're voting on it right now," then, "On live TV," then, "The ratings will be higher than the final episode of *The Candidate*," then, "We'd point out the irony," then, "But we don't believe in irony."

I can't honestly say this was part of the plan. Chicken 2.0 and I are still slogging through Orchard. I'm ready to jump out of this tram and find a poison apple.

They say, "The vote will be done within the hour," then, "We expect it to be unanimous."

I take off my bloody tie, still tied in its Windsor knot, and hang it on a low-lying branch. A noose without a neck.

They say, "The City Supreme Court judges are also hard at work," then, "Overturning Solomon's pardon," then, "We expect your original charges to be reinstated."

I put my hand over the phone and yell to Chicken 2.0, "How much longer?"

Chicken 2.0 says, "Ten minutes, tops."

They say, "We are sorry things turned out this way," then, "We hope you appreciate our candour," then, "You deserved it," then, "It was an honour representing you, Mr. Mayor," then, "If there is anything we can do for you," then, "Anything to make your eventual arrest," then, "Or deportation," then, "More comfortable," then, "Don't hesitate to ask," then, "At least you'll be famous," then, "Historic," then, "The only Mayor to have his administration measured in hours," then, "Instead of years."

We're close to leaving Orchard. The produce-packing buildings are up ahead. Chicken 2.0 veers right to avoid a large mud-puddle and some low-lying branches are only inches above my head. The branches are thick with apples; shiny, red, new, marketable, pre-processed. I take one off the branch, a big one. It is easy.

I say, "You two can do something for me." I slip the apple into an inner suit-coat pocket. Slip is a bad choice of words, just one bad choice in a long, long line of bad choices, but I'm okay with that. I have to be. So I don't slip the apple into my pocket. I force it in. The apple is a foreign, penetrating invader to the suit. There is damage. One end of the pocket tears, threads popping and material splitting. I close the jacket and there's an obvious apple-bulge just under my left breast. This has turned into a nice pregnant pause to build up the drama. If Melissa's camera were still on me, the audience would be fascinated with my apple stuffing, waiting to see what I will do or say next, breathless, at the edge of their seat, insert any other lame-TV-cliché here. They'd know that I was ready to spew forth the perfect response, layered with meaning and dare I say dignity, something they'd remember for the rest of their lives, or at least until the next SUV or beer commercial.

I say, "You two can go fuck yourselves."

The audience would not have been disappointed.

66

A MOTHER AND SON REUNION IS ONLY A MOTION AWAY

After hanging up with the Ass-May, I take advantage of my waning minutes as Mayor and call Farm's main offices and set up my appointment with Mom. No one argues with me or tries to stop me. Chicken 2.0 brings me all the way to the door of the conference room like I'm a delivery, a package, a parcel.

The parcel says, "Thank you."

Chicken 2.0 stands next to the door. I'd like to say he's looking expectant, but I'm talking about a dumbass in a chicken suit, so I have no idea what look he's giving me. Maybe he's a narcoleptic and he fell asleep inside the suit or maybe he's playing with himself, a Chicken choking his chicken, or maybe he's doing something more ADD like trying to touch his nose with his tongue.

"That'll be all, Chicken." I say Chicken like it's a swear. "You can go, but leave me the tram, please. I'll be fine on my own, now."

He says, "Good luck, Mr. Mayor," and steps aside

with a buck-buck and wing flaps. I think that was supposed to be funny or cute. It makes me want to break off his beak.

I watch Chicken 2.0 leave. Then I stare at the conference room door. I have an apple in my pocket and the former Book of Empty under my right arm. I'm not quite sure what to think at this point. I feel like I did all those years ago while standing in front of our apartment door. Why does my coming back here feel like I'm leaving? And here we go, through another door.

The conference room. Same as it was when I was here with the lawyers and then with the Arbitrator. There's the long mahogany table with a small group of plush-backed chairs as satellites. The opposite wall is a giant mirror. My wing-tipped shoes sink into tan carpeting. There isn't anyone in the room. I didn't expect there to be anyone in here.

I walk in, put the book on the table, then I go around to the front so there's nothing between me and the mirror, nothing between me and myself. I see the apple-lump in my jacket; it could be a swollen heart, or a monster-sized tumour.

I say, "I brought the real deal with me this time."

"The real what?" Speakers in the ceiling, subwoofers in the floors. The voice is modulated. Deep, digital, metallic pitched. Same as it ever was.

"An apple." I open my jacket and pry it out, tearing away the rest of the pocket. "This time it's new, not rotten, or fallen. This time no one seems to care that

I've picked it. I haven't bitten it yet, either."

I hold it up. Its red is the brightest thing in the room. Under the florescent ceiling lights, it's almost too red, like someone painted it and tried too hard for red.

The Arbitrator says, "I don't understand."

I say, "Neither do I. I don't know what this apple is supposed to mean. Just like I don't know why you didn't tell me you were *you* the last time I was in here talking about apples, Mom."

There's no weighty or dramatic silence. She kicks in with an instantaneous response, as if she studied and prepared for this. "You lied to me when you were here last time, too."

"What? I thought you were just the Arbitrator."

"Why does that matter? You shouldn't have been lying, regardless. I thought I brought you up better. I thought I made it obvious it was me, your Mom, as the Arbitrator."

"How the hell was I supposed to know you were the Arbitrator?"

"I gave you some pretty obvious clues."

"Clues?"

"I told you I was a woman and then asked you about Christianity."

"Some clues. Gee, I must be a moron to have missed those. Plain as the nose on my face, as clear as day, right as rain . . . ." I can't stop. I'm angry, real angry, and I want to bury her, stone her to death under a rain of clichés.

She interrupts, and that digital-metallic-deep voice is so very, maddeningly calm. "I know, you're right, but I had planned more clues and I was mad that you were lying to me. Besides, it was my first case. I had to try and not be obvious. Farm was testing me by having to deliberate my son's capital case."

"You achieved not-obvious. And thanks for not killing me, Mom."

There's silence, but there isn't. The buzz of florescent lights, the hum of air pushing through the vents. We're arguing like any other parent and now-adult child. It's almost comforting how we're able to pick back up so naturally. It's also so fucked up that I want to run screaming from the room because there is nothing natural about this.

Voice still modulated, proof of the unnaturalness of everything, she says, "I know you're angry. I am sorry. I didn't mean for you to find me this way."

"Can you shut that fucking thing off and come out here?" I'm yelling at the mirror. My arm wants to throw the apple through the mirror and into anything else the apple deems appropriate to destroy. Death by apple, for real this time.

"I can't come out there. Not even for the Mayor. I'll lose my job," she says with her real voice. At least, I think it's real. It could be a copy of a copy of a copy like Farm's animals. What hope do I have when that makes sense to me?

"I have a million things to say at once, but I'll start by saying I'm glad you're not dead or homeless," I say, stopping short of telling her I care about her. Instead, I add, "That would've sucked."

She says, "Thank you, and I know you were worried." She sounds older and weak, trapped in the speakers and behind the walls. "I watched your show. You were so sweet when you asked the camera if anyone had seen me."

I sit on the table and stare at my well-shoed feet; it feels like something a son should be doing while having a confrontational and uncomfortable conversation with his mother. "How did you get here?" I hold out my arms as a visual aid. The mirror-guy does the same.

"It's a long story."

"Make it short."

There's no pause on her end. She launches into her short story. "For six months before you left, I was taking night classes: law. I don't think you ever knew that."

"Nope."

"I tried to tell you."

"I don't remember that either."

There's a tongue cluck, or it could be interference in the radio relay, who the fuck knows. She says, "When you left I kept up with the classes, the money you sent home helped, of course, and I was ready to take the bar exam a couple of months ago. I was going to surprise you with that."

"Well, the timing's off, but I am surprised."

"Not sure why, but the Dean of Continuing

Education took in interest in my situation and set me up with an interview for the Arbitrator position without me knowing. I showed up for the final review class for the bar exam and there were Farm representatives waiting for me. I didn't know what to think, initially. They ended up making me the proverbial offer I couldn't refuse. They hired me. They hired me because I was willing to leave City, willing to become anonymous, willing to disappear for six years. Just like you."

That hurt. So I fire back. "And Farm would be able to control you and your decisions, right?"

She says, "Again, just like you."

"This isn't just like me. When I left I at least told you where I was going."

"I couldn't tell you where I was going. The Arbitrator's anonymous identity is contractually obligated and legally binding."

"You didn't have to tell me that you were an Arbitrator. A call or a note to tell me you moved and you were okay. That would've been enough. Instead, I get rumours, terminated bank accounts, and an abandoned apartment."

"I know. I was trying to work out a way to get that information to you. I tried relaying a cryptic message through a tour leader, she was a Duck I think, but I know that didn't work out, it didn't seem like she understood what I was trying to tell her, and then you figured out I was gone too quickly. I wasn't expecting you to check your financial records because we missed a phone-call night."

"I checked my records because that woman, the Duck said she knew you and told me that you were living with a drug dealer and about to be evicted from your apartment." I describe the Duck a. k. a. piss-girl to my mother. I leave nothing out.

She says, "Why would she say that? There was no drug dealer and I wasn't evicted, not even close. I simply left for Farm. That's what I told her."

My head is a messy kid's bedroom. Piles of dirty laundry, broken and forgotten toys erupting from a splintering toy box, torn posters dripping off the walls, sheets twisted and mattress tags exposed on the unmade bed, mostly empty cups and a film of dust on the dresser. How am I supposed to clean all this?

She says, "Sounds like she was just messing around with you."

I want to change the subject. I want to change everything. I say, "Right. Anyway, did you know I spent the last two weeks with my father?"

Mom says, "I know. I told you I watched your TV show, remember? Which means I don't have to ask how your father is doing, because I know."

I say, "I don't think you do. I spent all that time with him and I certainly don't know the how of his doing."

"Be that as it may . . . Hey, something just occurred to me. Maybe Farm saw that I'd tried talking to her at lunch once, and they had that Duck say those things about me to you to lead you down the false path, to ensure they kept me and my whereabouts anonymous." Even though Mom is nothing but a voice through speakers, and me without the benefit of the near infinite-in-number visual communication signals we receive when talking to someone face-to-face, I know that Mom is proud of herself for solving the piss-girl problem, although the implications about her employer are darker than burnt toast.

I say, "I don't doubt it. And to say she led me down the false path is the understatement of a lifetime." I don't know what to say next. I wish she'd come out from behind the mirror. I'm sick of talking to the great and powerful Oz-people of the world.

She says, "This wasn't and isn't easy, you know, but when my six years are up, I'll never have to worry about money again."

"You didn't have to worry about money before. I came here to take care of you financially. I left to help you." I know I'm lying to her. Does that make the lie worse or better?

"You left for yourself, and that's okay."

There's another silence. I flip through the former Book of Empty. Pages whiz by. I see a cartoon of dancing letters and random images that coalesce for an instant before breaking up into chaos again.

She says, "I don't blame you for leaving. I never did. I understood. I was happy for you."

Would asking her *who's lying now* be too cynical?

She says, "Can't you just be happy for me? I have a

career now. A place of my own. That apartment was always his. Now, I don't need anyone else's money or charity or help. I'm not dependent upon anyone."

"Other than Farm, you mean."

She says, "I was happy you won the election. I voted for you via absentee ballot."

I laugh. So does she. I get up from the desktop and walk to the mirror. I'm very close.

I say, "I don't think I'm going to be Mayor for very long." I don't say it very loud. A confession, layered with poisonous shame.

She says, "That's nonsense. You'll be a fine Mayor." I smile at the Mom-as-cheerleader praise. Hollow praise, insofar as it comes with the parental territory, but still effective. "You'll get used to it. You can get used to anything." That last sentence is the saddest thing I've ever heard come out of my mother. And because of it and how she said it, I'm not angry anymore. I'll never be angry with her again, but I want to kill the brain cells that will store her words and how she said it. I don't want to be here anymore. I shouldn't have come here. I should've let her be.

I say, "I don't think there's anyone living in our apartment building anymore. There wasn't anyone in our apartment, anyway."

She says, "I don't miss City at all. I have a nice place now. It's a yellow bungalow in the southwest quadrant of Farm, near a brook and a grove of pine trees. Very bright and cheery. I can see the stars at night. I probably shouldn't have told you where I lived."

"Are you happy, Mom?"

"They let me keep my own garden, grow my own food."

"Mom?"

"I have tomatoes, cucumbers, and summer squash. The squash came out the best."

"Are."

"I was thinking about getting a puppy."

"You."

"Then I'd have to pay for a fence to be put up. I still might do it. I haven't decided."

"Happy?"

There's silence, and both my hands are on the mirror. I'm staring into myself. Do I like what I see?

She says, "No. But I think it's close. I think I can be happy eventually."

There needs to be something important said. Damned if I know what it is.

She says, "I am . . ." Then her voice cuts out. Unplugged.

"Mom? You still there?"

No answer. Nothing feels quite as alone as being in a room with a giant mirror. I bang on the mirror and call to her some more, and nothing. I pull out the Batphone and it isn't glowing red anymore. Power button doesn't work. No dial tone, no beeps when I press buttons. I'm getting the Titanic-sinking feeling that the vote is in and I'm no longer City's Mayor.

I have to leave. I hope that she's still there watching and listening. She as the Impotent-Omniscient behind the one-way glass, this time not rendering a decision, this time not expelling me from Eden, this time powerless to help or hurt me. I never realized how much she and my father are alike.

I want to leave her as happy as she can be. I'm going to give her a gift that isn't a puppy. I say, "This book is for you, Mom. Goodbye." I open the book to a special page. It's not at the beginning, or end, or middle. But it's in the book somewhere. That counts for something. I hold the book up to the glass. What I see are jumbled and backwards letters that fit together to make up a word that I know but still don't understand.

Here's the page:

V

L

E

O

The book gets heavy quick, and I put it down on the table, face up, still opened to the special page. I leave the sandwich-pen in the spine to mark the place. As I walk away from the desk, I wonder if she'll come into the room right away and take the book, go after the thing madly, busting through a mirror panel to get in the room because she just has to have it and then tear out the page and clutch it to her bosom, weeping and convulsing. Unlikely.

I leave the conference room and shut the door. If I wait a moment or two and go back in, will I find her there collecting the book? I really don't know and I won't know, because I jog down the hallway to the elevator, taking care not to stop and chat with the people calling to the Mayor, even taking care not to make eye contact. The elevator is full so I run down the emergency stairwell.

Is Mom not allowed into the room by supervisors? Is she sending someone to get the book for her and then devastated when they won't give it to her?

The stairs dump me outside and, bless that Chicken 2.0, he did leave the tram for me. I get in and start the engine, and here's what I think:

Mom is still behind the glass. She hasn't moved from her position. She hasn't called or talked to anyone. She's replaying our conversation and replaying our lives, finding what fits and what doesn't. She'll get the book eventually, but for now, she'll just sit and watch from behind the glass, safe for now because the book can't look back. And I'm okay with this.

67

I'M JVST GONNA GET YOV AGAIN, MOMMA'S BOY

I drive the tour tram back to my old Barn. Back to my stall. The tram must've tripped some a-tour-is-a'-comin' switch somewhere, because . . .

Animal noises fill the air, and they make me tense up, like something is going to happen to me. The noises: You've got your moos, whinnies, snorts, squeals, oinks, grunts, growls, ruts, barks, meows, mewls, bahs, brays, clucks, cock-a-doodle-dos, and quacks. Yes, the Muzack-quacks, and it's the same as it ever was.

So I pick up a shovel and, well, I shovel. I'm going to do some work. It'll be easy, and a comfort. I'm going to do what I know, even if it's only for five minutes before the Farm storm troopers pick me up. Just five more minutes of what I used to be. Five more minutes of letting the faceless Farm conglomerate make all my decisions. Five more minutes of life without thought. It's just so easy.

Still in my tieless Mayor-suit, you'd think I'd look

as misplaced as a yellow penguin in Barn. Apparently, I'm not. A Duck rolls by on an empty tourist tram, stops next to my stall, and she says, "Told you I'd get you. And I'm just gonna get you again, Momma's boy." She hops out and gives my groin a squeeze, then jumps back in the tram.

Over there is BM. Bowtie, handlebar mustache and a smile as fake as silicon breasts. He waves from his office window, and gives me a thumbs-up with no thought given to Duck's sexual harassment or my current status as impeached-Mayor and reinstated terrorist. Would you think I'm crazy if I say this place feels like home?

The animal sounds fade out. I don't miss them. I'm tiring of the shovelling faster than I thought I would. Maybe I don't need those five minutes after all. So much for home. I drop the shovel and walk out of the stall. Another Chicken jumps into the tram before I do and takes it away, and here come ATVs with sirens echoing in the Barn and flashing their important blue lights. The animals don't like the commotion and stir in their stalls.

The ATVs form a wagon train around me, and one jackass in his blue security overalls, straw hat with the mini-blue sirens on the brim, yells into a megaphone even though he's only ten feet away. There's too much amplification to his voice and I don't understand him.

But I understand guns being drawn. I understand guns pointed at me. There's a good chance I'll be shot. Because I'm not going with them.

The ATVs screech to a synchronized halt, filling the air with dust, hay, and exhaust. Jackass still screams at me through a megaphone. His mouth is a wide funnel of white plastic. I look beyond security to see BM close the shades on his office window. Duck leans against the rickety staircase up to BM's office. Duck sees that I'm looking and gyrates into some over-sexed celebration dance, rubbing Duck ass up against the railing and wings pawing the Duck chest.

That wide funnel of white plastic mouth details my crimes in a wash of static. The men and guns shrink their circle.

I say, "No need to see me out. Me and the bomb strapped to my chest were just leaving." I pull my suit jacket closed and the reaction to my bomb-bluff is appropriate given my re-documented terrorist history. Someone yells, *Jesus Christ!* and the rest of the men-and-guns circle breaks apart, losing its regimented set of points.

I say, "Tell the Ass-May they can have City and they'll never hear from me again."

There is a regulated and trained grumble through the security ranks. There is two-way radio chatter and there is listening to invisible earpieces. There are instantaneous high-level, government and military discussions. There are decisions. There are orders to be taken. I won't let any of it affect me.

I walk and they don't stop me. I walk past Duck, still dancing the Duck dance, humping the railing now, faux-masturbating with one hand and giving me the finger with the other. I think I'll miss Duck most of all.

I walk out of Barn. No one seems to be following, which doesn't mean anything. They could still shoot me, especially once me and the imaginary bomb are safely beyond the perimeter of Farm and on the access road.

If they shoot me, twice in the chest and once in the head it means I'll end up in that lost place among the lost, in my father's personal library. I'll become words. I'll be a story in one of my father's books. The title will be "Swallowing a Donkey's Eye." It'll be perfect. The ultimate final gesture. Fantasy becoming reality. I'll be part of all those books, part of all those stories, the stories of nobody, but somehow the stories of everybody, everybody but him, everybody but my father. He should have a story too, so I'll give him one now, a story for Father-my-father: he is a god, one who knows what is going to happen but doesn't like it, a god who means well but who actively works to forget his creations, a god who only collects stories, an archivist god, a librarian god doomed to know these fantasies replacing realities, these stories of the forgotten that will one day be forgotten as well. He'll be another impotent-omniscient god, another god who only sits and stares at his own burning bush; they're everywhere if you look hard enough.

That won't happen, though. Here's my true Kreskinesque reading of the future. They aren't going to shoot me. Well, I'm pretty sure they won't shoot me. My newly flexed ESP muscle, my psychic vibes tell me it's 80-20 I don't get shot. Umm, maybe 70-30.

They're not going to shoot me. I'll leave Farm. I'll leave my mother and her bungalow and her garden and her one-way glass and her impotent-omniscience. I'll leave my mother, again, because I don't need to be here anymore. I know she'll be okay. She'll get used to it.

Me and my imaginary bomb will just keep walking, a one-man exodus, a one-man walk across the desert. I'm going to do like Melissa did and try and help the person in front of me. If they don't shoot me, me and the imaginary bomb are still going back, not to him, but to Home.

So listen. Like father like son, I am going to tell you all about the future.

ACKNOWLEDGEMENTS

This weird little book was a long time coming. Aren't you glad you waited? I know I am. *Always* thanks to Lisa, Cole, Emma, and the rest of my family and friends who put up with and support donkey-me. I know it ain't easy.

Special thanks to everyone who pitched in and bailed some considerable hay for this one: Susanne Apgar, Shawn Bagley, Stephen Barbara, Allison Carroll, Kurt Dinan, Steve Eller, Jeffrey Ford, Jack Haringa, John Harvey, Sandra Kasturi, Louis Maistros, Helen Marshall, Laura Marshall, Paul McMahon, Erik Mohr, Stewart O'Nan, Brett Savory, and Lucius Shepard.

ABOVT THE AVTHOR

Paul Tremblay is also the author of the novels *The Little Sleep*, *No Sleep Till Wonderland*, and the short story collection *In The Mean Time*. His essays and short fiction have appeared in *The Los Angeles Times*, *Five Chapters.com*, and *Best American Fantasy 3*. He is the co-editor of four anthologies including *Creatures: Thirty Years of Monster Stories* (with John Langan). Paul is currently on the board of directors for the Shirley Jackson Awards. He fears many things, including the return of his banished uvula.

www.paultremblay.net
www.thelittlesleep.com

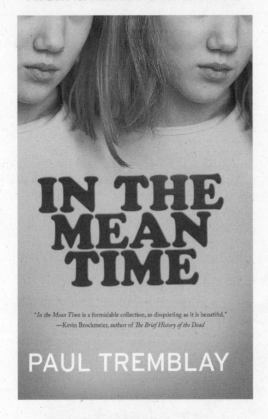

EMB
RACE
THE
ODD

BULLETTIME
NICK MAMATAS

AVAILABLE AUGUST 2O12
FROM CHIZINE PUBLICATIONS

978-1-926851-71-6

ALSO AVAILABLE FROM CHIZINE PUBLICATIONS

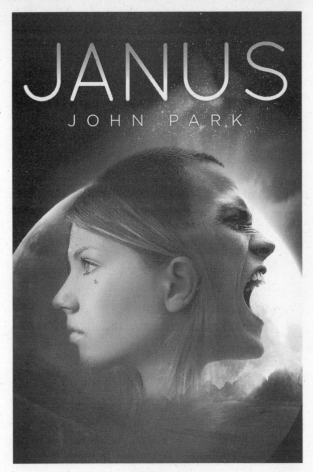

JANUS
JOHN PARK

AVAILABLE SEPTEMBER 2012
FROM CHIZINE PUBLICATIONS

978-1-927469-10-1

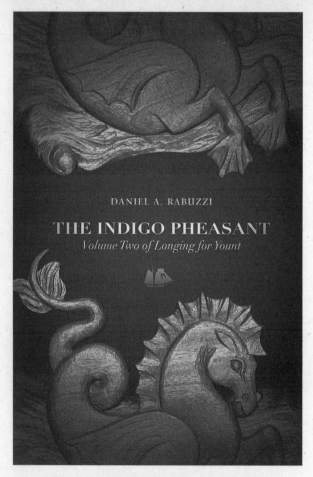

THE INDIGO PHEASANT
VOLUME TWO OF LONGING FOR YOUNT
DANIEL A. RABUZZI

AVAILABLE SEPTEMBER 2012
FROM CHIZINE PUBLICATIONS

978-0-927469-09-5

"Ian Rogers' stories are old-fashioned in the very best sense: classic chillers in the spirit of Shirley Jackson and Richard Matheson. *Every House Is Haunted* is full of well-crafted, satisfying twists, a fine companion for any reader of literate horror."
—Andrew Pyper, author of *Lost Girls*, *The Killing Circle*, and *The Guardians*

EVERY HOUSE IS HAUNTED
IAN ROGERS

AVAILABLE OCTOBER 2012
FROM CHIZINE PUBLICATIONS

978-1-927469-16-3

CHIZINEPUB.COM **CZP**

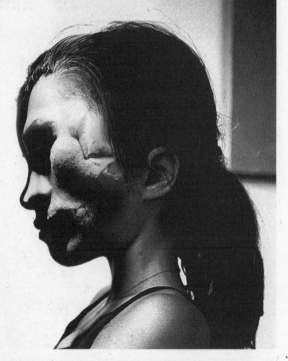

WORLD FANTASY AWARD-WINNING AUTHOR

THE BEST DARK FICTION OF ROBERT SHEARMAN

REMEMBER WHY YOU FEAR ME

REMEMBER WHY YOU FEAR ME
THE BEST DARK FICTION OF ROBERT SHEARMAN

AVAILABLE OCTOBER 2012
FROM CHIZINE PUBLICATIONS

978-0-927469-21-7